FREE BASE

WMU
BOOK 1

S.J. CRAWFORD

EVERNORTH BOOKS

Free Base

Copyright © 2026 by S.J. Crawford

All rights reserved.

ISBN: 978-1-0691196-4-3

First Edition: February 2026

Cover Illustration by Caravelle Creates

Editing by Clara Abigail

Published by Evernorth Books in Canada

AUTHOR'S NOTE

Free Base is a **romance novel** between two adults that contains mature themes. Reader discretion is advised.

This is a work of fiction, and creative liberties have been taken for the sake of the narrative. Free Base is a college sports romance, with greater emphasis on the college aspect, given the time of year in which the novel takes place. The depiction of certain aspects of the game may not always reflect the exact rules or nuances of college and professional baseball. Readers are advised to consider this information in the context of their individual preferences.

If further information is required, specific themes and subject details are provided on my website. These details may reveal elements of the plot. **Please be aware that the novel references firearms; no shots are fired.**

https://www.sjcrawfordauthor.ca/

CHAPTER ONE
IAN

White Mountain University
Graniton, New Hampshire
JANUARY

"Dude, hurry up!"

Nick needs to get his ass in gear, so I knock on his door for a third time. After an excruciating thirty-second wait, the lock clicks, and he lets me in with a yawn. He's still in sweatpants and a loose tank top, which tells me he only woke up because I'm persistent.

Typical.

I check my phone for the time, and when my attention goes back to Nick, he's lying on his couch, stretching his arms up like nothing in life matters.

"Not to be a douche or anything, but are you gonna get ready?" I ask. "You're the one who asked me to walk to class with you in the first place."

He groans, reaching for a hoodie and slipping it over his head. "Didn't your first three semesters teach you that first classes don't matter? It's called syllabus week for a reason."

"Yeah, but I want to get back into a good routine."

"Whatever. I need coffee," he mumbles, and I place a thermos on his dining table.

"Here. Remember our deal? I make you coffee, and you don't make me late. Let's go."

"Okay, okay. I'm ready now."

I point at his bare feet. "Are you?"

He looks down, grits his teeth, and proceeds to wrangle a pair of jeans, fresh underwear, and some socks from the laundry pile next to the dining table.

And then the shameless, not-so-little fucker gets changed right in front of me.

"Jeez, put your dick away—you know what? I don't care. Just hurry up. I don't want to miss the stupid surprise clicker question if the prof springs one on us."

Nick finishes putting his socks on, slips into boots, and grabs the flask of coffee. "Course registration ends next week. Again, the first class doesn't matter. Let's roll."

I follow him out of the apartment and onto the sidewalk. Nick is the kind of person who's smart without even trying. As for me? While I've never come close to missing the GPA cutoff to stay on the baseball team here, it's because I stay on top of myself.

But I'm only human, which is why I agree to sit in the back of the lecture hall when we arrive five minutes early for Human Movement II. The half-empty room fills up as we get closer to eleven, and it's the usual group of familiar faces. Kinesiology is a tiny program here at WMU, and we all know each other, or at least know *of* each other. New people stand out.

And the new guy who walks into the lecture hall stands out for a lot of other reasons.

Hot fucking damn.

He's *tall,* too.

Jesus. It's like the energy in the room shifts with every sexy step he takes.

And besides his chiseled features, he's built like an athlete, which isn't uncommon given what we're studying. Powerful legs clad in light-wash jeans bring the mystery man a few rows ahead of us where he sheds his faded parka, revealing a wide, flannel-clad back.

Whew. If the shirt he was wearing didn't fit so well, I'd say it was one size too small, but with his broad shoulders sticking out the way they are, the whole outfit *works.* I'm not complaining, not with how the fabric clings to his muscles just right—revealing but not obnoxious.

Ugh, I need to focus on the lecture today, and the poor, unsuspecting stud muffin in my field of vision isn't gonna make it easy.

Nick elbows me, and I turn to face him. "Stop staring," he says, his mouth curving up into a knowing smirk.

"At what?"

"At him." Nick nods at the new guy. "I didn't even notice the dude until I saw you making heart eyes. Try some subtlety for once."

"Why are you blaming *me*? He looks like he rolled out of bed and straight into an L.L. Bean catalog."

"And that's supposed to be appealing?"

"Yes, it is." I sigh, admiring the way the new guy's body twitches as he scribbles in his notebook. When he pats down his short brown hair, his back flexes, and I have to look away.

Nick flicks my forehead. "Dude, you need to get laid, like, yesterday. Unless you're still too much of a softie to hook up."

Rolling my eyes, I knock him on the head and force my grimace into a smile. "Hookups are overrated, man. You might understand if you weren't so picky."

Nick snorts, and the lecture gets started. I dragged my ass all the way here, so I might as well try to pay attention. I steal a few peeks at the new guy here and there—yeah, Nick isn't the only one who's shameless.

Maybe I'll call him Mr. Flannel since I don't know his name, and his shirt is what catches my eye every time I glance in his direction.

Mr. Flannel is very straight-looking. I know that's not a *thing*, but jumping to that conclusion will make it easier to avoid a stupid crush. It's a tactic that dates to high school—one that kept me out of trouble back then, and one that keeps me focused on this hour-long lecture today.

After Dr. Kumar wraps up with an overview of the group

project, I stand up and head for the exit, but Nick grabs my shoulder to stop me.

"Hey, why don't you talk to the new guy?" he asks. "You might stop staring at him if you get to know him as a person."

I blink at him a couple of times. "Nah. I'm not trying to get all flustered this early in the day."

Nick jabs my shoulder. "Hey, I think I'll put you out of your misery and go introduce us."

"Dude, don't do that to me."

"Watch me."

Oh, come on.

Nick doesn't say anything else, and I can only follow him for the short, awkward walk to the front.

"Hey, what's up, man!" Nick waves, and Mr. Flannel jerks his head up, shoving his phone into his pocket. "I'm Nick. Are you new here?"

"Hi, yeah. I'm Callum." His face tenses as his blue eyes flick between us with some kind of guarded caution.

Okay. Yeah. I need to introduce myself and do something other than stare at—

Sheesh. Callum's eyes are so blue. I didn't even know that color existed in nature.

Nope. Gotta stay focused.

"And hi, I'm Ian. Nice to meet you." I stick my hand out like the business major I'm not, and Callum gives me a shake that's firm yet warm.

How is it possible for someone's hands to feel rugged and soft?

"So, uh, how are you new here?" I ask, both because I'm curious, and also to make it known that I do indeed have a voice. Even if said voice conjures up the strangest phrasing my poor, scattered brain can think of.

"I transferred in from a community college in Wisconsin."

"Nice, nice." I fall silent, and Nick elbows me.

Yeah, no. I don't want to know what he's up to.

"Welcome to WMU, man," Nick says. "Now that we've got

you here, do you want to join us for that group project? Ian and I are down a guy."

For some reason or other, Callum is backing himself into the wall, and I'm not sure if he realizes. I fight the urge to close the growing distance between us so that I don't encroach on him.

But then Callum nods. "Sure, that sounds good. Thanks for the offer."

Nick gives him a fist bump, I do the same, and yeah, I should probably say something now.

"You play baseball?" I ask Callum.

He furrows his dark eyebrows, which throws me off balance even more than my random comment. "No?"

"You should try out for intramurals next month," I find myself saying. "You have serious guns right there, and I heard the Kinesiology team is down a few strong hitters."

Oh my fucking god.

Why the ever-loving hell did I have to say *that*?

I should have stayed shut up before making a fool of myself. Nick is red in the face, stifling a laugh with a series of bad fake coughs, and I will the earth to swallow me whole.

"Nah, I don't think I'd be any good at sports." Callum's tone is deadpan, but the tiniest hint of a smile materializes around his full lips.

It's weak, but the effect that smile has on me? Outsized. My hands were already sweating when Nick dragged me over, and now they're drenched.

My voice comes out way higher than I'd like. "That's cool, no problem."

Callum shifts from one foot to the other. "Yeah, so, it was great talking to you guys, but I have to get to class," he says before spinning around and marching out of the lecture hall.

Someone slap me now, please.

"That didn't go bad, did it?" Nick says, his eyes watering.

I sigh. "He hates me."

"No, he doesn't. Besides, you gave him a flirty little compliment! How could he hate you after that?"

Heat creeps up my neck, and I resist the urge to smack Nick across the chest. "I'm an idiot," I mutter.

"Nah. You just get flustered around attractive dudes. How are you so smooth with chicks but so inept around the guys you're into? Isn't it supposed to be the other way around?"

"Dudes are intimidating, man." They're intimidating, *and* I lean toward them. Maybe those two things are related.

"Or maybe you have a type."

Tall, attractive, and almost certainly unavailable? It's possible.

"Anyway." Nick breaks the silence. "He's working on the group project with us, so try to avoid jumping him when we meet up for that."

"Because I need the reminder, of course. No. I'm more than capable of behaving myself." Sighing, I leave the lecture hall with Nick in tow.

I *am* capable of behaving myself. My initial interactions with cute guys always play out the same way: I get a little crush on them for a day, and then my mind goes elsewhere. Sure, I give myself more than a day if it's mutual, but that hasn't been the case for a while. I can be a lot, I hate rejection, and avoiding that is what's most comfortable for me.

Callum can have the next twenty-four hours. Then, if everything goes to plan, we might be friends.

CHAPTER TWO
CALLUM

Is it normal for student athletes to proselytize to people who apparently look the part? And then ask you to join them for a group project?

College is turning out to be weird as heck, but at least meeting people isn't as hard as I expected. I just didn't think the first students I'd strike up a conversation with would, one, approach me first, and two, be student athletes with team backpacks and more swagger than I've seen in my life. When I saw the two of them walk up to me, my first thought was to get out of their way.

I mean, at least Nick was confident. Ian, not so much.

Well, I'm one to talk.

Still, I don't think that popular group is *supposed* to mix well with the weird new guy, but here we are. Maybe being popular isn't a thing once you're out of high school.

Shoot. I'm making a lot of assumptions—it isn't like I have a frame of reference for any of that, given that I stopped going to public school when I was fourteen.

And the comment from Ian about my arms? What was that? Totally random, although he had great arms himself underneath that long-sleeve shirt. He could have been trying to be relatable, even though his arms are so much nicer than mine.

I shouldn't focus on that. Or his smile, or the way his blond hair fell in front of those bright eyes that lie somewhere between brown and green—

Nope. Absolutely not.

I cut my wandering, inappropriate thoughts off and make my way to my next class, which is my Introductory French elective.

The hour passes, and no student athletes approach me afterward. Or anyone else, for that matter.

I guess that makes sense. After all, I'm still the guy who showed up on campus halfway through sophomore year. That's not doing me any favors for blending in, and then there's the fact that my sparse, ragged wardrobe makes me stick out, too.

It is what it is.

I'm done for the day, so I trudge through the falling snow to my dorm for a long stretch of doing nothing. It's peaceful, knowing I can exist here without anyone springing a random check on me.

Locking my door still seems subversive, though. The click makes my heart twinge, and I power through it, taking a breath and stepping out of my work boots.

I roll onto the hard bed pressed against the wall, which is only long enough for my unwieldy legs by a couple of inches, and shuffle under the thick down comforter that had absolutely no business being given away for free. Bless rich graduating students who are too cheap to pay twenty-five dollars at the dump, seriously. Not that I particularly *want* to be a charity case at the college with the highest average household income in the country, but hey, free stuff is free stuff.

My thoughts are interrupted by my phone beeping, and I stretch over to pull it out of my jeans.

It's an email. From Ian.

From: Scott, Ian
To: Russell, Nicholas; Cross, Callum
Subject: [KIN207] Group Project 1 - Task Breakdown

Sup Dudes,

Okay, even I know you aren't supposed to open an email like that, and I've sent a grand total of ten in my entire life so far.

I've taken all the deliverables for the first group project and divided them amongst ourselves in what I think is a fair split, but you can bring up suggestions or improvements during our meeting before class tomorrow.

Ian (me): Research and written report preparation.
Nick: Compilation of presentation slides and video script
Callum: Video narration and model for limb movement demonstration

Huh.

So he's assigned me...reading a script and moving my arm. For a project that's worth twenty-five percent of our final grade.

That isn't fair, but not in the way I expected. My parts are going to take all of half an hour to finish.

Does he think I'm stupid or something?

But if he did, then he would have given Nick more to do.

Maybe he thinks me *and* Nick are stupid.

Maybe he thinks he's the only guy smart enough to be here and he's only teaming up with me because each group needs at least three people.

Come on, Callum. Be normal and stop judging.

I shake my head and read the rest of the email.

We still have time before this is due, so we should probably meet to go over our parts before the lecture tomorrow in case we have any questions for the prof. Here's my number so we can coordinate that and anything else we need going forward. Feel free to hit me up.

I copy Ian's number and enter it into my contacts app. Hovering my finger over his name, I debate messaging him first, so he has my number, too.

That's a normal thing to do, right?

After tapping out a message, I shut my eyes and hit send.

Hi, this is Callum.

His typing indicator pops up almost instantly.

IAN SCOTT

Hey man!

Noticed the 603 area code. You get a new
number after coming here?

Yes.

IAN SCOTT IS TYPING...

And he stays typing for a while.

Oof. Touchy subject?

Not really. Just got a new one.

Oh lmao those periods at the end made me
think I said something wrong

What? I switch to my browser and go to the search engine.

Are periods rude in text messages

They *are*. Darn it. I can't do anything right.

Sorry

dw man it's chill

I gotta head to practice. See you tmr

I don't text back, and instead, I spend the next two minutes
searching up what his texting abbreviations mean.

And then look up *how* to text and not accidentally insult the person on the other end. The fact that I know how to work my new fifty-dollar phone is nothing short of a miracle, given that my old one still had a freaking keypad.

When I roll over, it's dark outside, and I realize I spent the better part of an hour researching how to be a normal nineteen-year-old.

God, that's bleak. I wish I was actually normal.

But I'm here now, so I sure as hell can try my best to learn, even if that means going against every gut feeling I have.

———

It's snowing when I wake up, the kind that's annoying and wet and slippery. Perfect.

I stand in front of my makeshift closet, which is just my small pile of clothes hung over the back of the desk chair, and assess my options. While I didn't bring much with me, dressing to impress seems like the right thing to do, although I don't know who exactly I'm impressing with my choices: the flannel I wore yesterday, a slightly different button-up that's indistinguishable from the first when you stand farther than ten feet away, two T-shirts that don't fit too well, and a hooded sweater.

I choose to layer the sweater over a T-shirt. Those are the only things I own that don't cling to me, and the last thing I want is to look like I'm wearing the same stuff I've owned since I was seventeen and still growing.

Hopefully Ian and Nick won't notice I'm in the same jeans as yesterday. My other ones are fraying and still have mud on them from the thirty-hour trip over here.

At the sink, I dampen my fingers and rake them through my hair, hoping to tame the strands that are already growing longer than I'm used to. Longer than a man "should" keep his hair.

I won't lie—the length doesn't exactly bother me, as long as I can make it neat. I suppose I could slick it back if I had gel or something, but I don't, so I make a mental note to buy some when

I have the cash, and settle for looking barely groomed. Not like it matters, anyway, since it's snowing outside.

The Kinesiology building is next door to my dorm, but the snow still manages to soak through my clothes and saturate my hair. At least it isn't too cold—that'd suck.

As I push the heavy doors open, I check my phone and confirm the meeting location, hoping I'm the first one there so I have time to dry off and look at least half-presentable. When I round the corner, those hopes are dashed at the sight of Ian. Despite the nerves that creep up, and the preemptive thinking of an explanation for why I resemble a soaked rat, my body warms from seeing him.

That's not good. Still, I take a breath and march forward, drawing as little attention to myself as I can.

He's wearing a plaid shirt, the kind that you know is thick only from looking at it, and I swear the color is custom-made for him. The earthy green stands out against his light tan, which makes me wonder *how* he's tanned in *January*.

Probably some vacation house in Florida or something.

Yeah, he looks so good, and it's not like he even has to try. Hell, his hair is a total mess, likely from wearing a beanie, but it's almost as if it's curated. His whole vibe is so casual and effortless, and I couldn't even hope to pull something like that off.

Ian's frowning at his phone, tapping away and not noticing me walk up. As soon as I sit down in the chair across from him, he places his phone away and tilts his head up.

"Hey, what's up, Callum?"

God, I can't remember the last time someone smiled at me the way Ian is now.

"Uh, I'm good," I reply, before wondering if that made any sense. *What's up? I'm good...*

He doesn't seem to care. "Man, it's fucking snowing like shit out there."

"Yeah, it's, uh, yeah."

Why am I so bad at this? I mean, all that cussing threw me off, but still. Kicking myself, I brace for Ian to laugh at me for being an idiot.

He doesn't laugh at me. He frowns instead, running a hand through his tousled hair as he stares at my—

He's scrutinizing my clothes.

Ugh.

I can practically see the judgment clouding his light eyes as he tilts his head, parting his lips—*I shouldn't stare at his* lips, *for crying out loud*—

"Are you warm enough in that?" he asks, pointing at my hoodie. "Or are you guys just built different out in the Midwest?"

I don't know why, but I bark out a quiet chuckle, the sound almost foreign to me, given how long it's been since I had a reason to do that. Maybe it's because I'm surprised at his lack of judgment, or maybe I actually find Ian funny. Either way, my reaction seems to have rubbed off on him because he's clearly amused, too.

"I'm used to it," I finally reply, and his grin grows wider. I thought people in New England were supposed to be reserved. Seems like it's the other way around for us two.

"Lucky you, I'm a total baby when it's cold," Ian says, sticking a thumb at the thick parka that's hanging over the seat next to him. "Low-key jealous of people like you."

That's gotta be a joke. There's no way someone like him could be jealous of me.

"Where the fuck is Nick?" he mutters under his breath, to nobody in particular, at least until he swivels his head up to face me. "Don't get me wrong, he's great, but he can't get anywhere on time to save his life."

"Have you tried messaging him?" I supply, and Ian rolls his eyes.

"His phone's probably dead again. How he manages to keep himself alive is beyond me, but Nick is Nick. You can't help but love the guy."

I sure hope I can help it, especially with how Nick looks. It makes sense that the two most attractive guys I've seen on campus so far are best friends.

Ian fishes out a plastic container from his backpack. "Anyway, you want a cookie while we wait? I made 'em myself this morning."

He—what? Where did that come from?

"Do you...carry cookies around everywhere you go?" I ask, like an idiot.

"I sure do!" He beams at me while shaking the container. "Want one?"

"No thanks," I say out of instinct.

Ian doesn't reply immediately, instead choosing to send me a smirk that sends an inconvenient blush up my neck. "Come on, Cal."

Did he give me a nickname? I realize I'm smiling, so I try to play it off as nervous laughter.

"Not to hype myself up too much, but they're so fucking good." He waves the now-open container at me again, and I oblige, picking out a small cookie. He watches me with palpable expectation, so I take a small bite.

As soon as I do, I wish I grabbed a bigger one. He's right—they're so freaking good.

"This is ninety percent chocolate," I say, and then I stiffen. "That's a good thing. I didn't mean it as a criticism or anything." I restrain myself from squashing the remainder of the cookie in my fingers out of stress, waiting for Ian's response.

"Dude, it's fine. I can tell you like them; it's written allll over your face," he drawls. "It's fuckin' cute as hell."

Relief washes over me at the same time my blush moves up into my cheeks.

Did Ian call me *cute*? He has to be joking. First the comment about my arms, and now this. The most likely explanation is that he says this kind of stuff to everyone.

I stuff the rest of the cookie into my mouth to silence myself.

He snickers again, but almost as quickly as his mood shifts, it swings back. He sits up straight, scratching the back of his neck. "Yeah. I wonder when Nick is gonna get here—"

Nick chooses that moment to appear, smacking the back of Ian's head and ruffling his hair. Ian responds by punching Nick's shoulder.

Is violence affection? If that's what friendship entails, I sure hope that isn't the case.

"Sup, fucknugget," Nick coos at Ian, who sticks his middle finger out as a voiceless reply. "And hey, Callum. What's good?"

"These. These are good," Ian replies for me when I make an uncomfortable pause, shaking the container of cookies at Nick. "You don't get any because you're late."

"Yeah, yeah, what did you expect from me?" Nick quips, flopping into the seat beside Ian. "Anyway, we're here to talk about the massively unfair project plan that Scotty here stacked against himself."

It takes a second for me to connect the nickname with Ian's last name, Scott, and when I do, he's blushing. Not that his cheeks need any more color to look good, but the pink tint makes him glow.

Shoot. Not again. He's a guy who's being nice to me—I can't be rude *and* get all hot for him.

"I can do part of the report," I offer, hoping it serves as a distraction from my own imminent blush.

"Can you still do the voiceover?" Ian asks.

"Why the voiceover?"

"Uh, it's because...uh, you have a great, neutral-accented speaking voice!"

"I believe your exact words after class were 'ideal timbre,'" Nick supplies. He nudges Ian, smirking widely and ruffling his hair.

"Dude, shut the fuck up!" Ian smacks Nick's hand away.

"I'm telling the truth, ass-muncher."

Ian fights back a laugh before wiping any traces of it off his face. "Suck my dick, bro."

Holy swearing. I dart my gaze between the two bickering athletes, not sure how to react. Nick's eyebrows are raised, and he's...biting his lip. That's odd.

Then he strokes Ian's forearm. "Oh, I know you want it. I'm gonna give your poor, deprived cock the best sloppy toppy it'll ever have."

Huh. I was *not* expecting that. Wait, are they...

Ian scoffs. "Sloppy toppy? More like toothy torture, coming from your sorry ass. I don't know about you, but I've kinda grown attached to my epidermis..."

Two pairs of eyes flick over to me, and my breath catches. They definitely forgot I was here.

"Sorry. We have an...interesting friendship," Nick says.

Seemingly agreeing, Ian punches Nick's chest. They do have an interesting friendship, I'll give them that.

"Okay," I say, changing the subject. "I'm fine with doing the voiceover, that video thing, and more of the research."

Ian opens his mouth to speak, but Nick beats him to it. "Yeah, that would be a good idea. I'll send the final split today or tomorrow."

"Sounds good," Ian and I say at the same time.

The three of us stand up and head for the lecture hall, and even though I'm used to silence, the lack of conversation somehow gets to me.

"I can film my part and send it over by next Monday for you to edit," I say, if only to make some kind of noise, and Ian stops walking, turning to face me with a confused expression.

"Dude, this part isn't due for another two weeks. You're chilling."

"I mean, I have time, so..." My phone buzzes, distracting me, and I pull it out. There are two emails in my inbox, and my palms dampen when I skim through the first one.

Inbox: West Wisconsin Community College
From: reginacross

I hit delete and block Mom's contact before I can even read the subject line. It can't be anything good, or anything I want to see. I should block Dad's email address, too, since I still need to look at my old account to finalize my college transfer, and then I skim the next, hopefully better, message.

Inbox: WMUMail
From: WMU Health
Subject: MHW Triage Complete

Callum Cross:

We are pleased to inform you that the triage process for Mental Health and Wellness Counseling is complete. You are scheduled for an initial appointment with Anita Young, MSW at 2:30 p.m. on January 12.

My heart jumps, both from excitement and trepidation, all at once. I power off my phone and shove it back in my pocket, even though I *know* nobody could have peeked.

I'm a mess, and that isn't lost on me, but this is a chance for me to change that. Coming all the way to WMU is only half the battle, and if I want to be a normal member of society again in a reasonable timeframe, I'm going to need a push.

I just wish I didn't need it in the first place.

"Hey, Callum, you okay?" Ian asks.

Oh, shoot. He was waiting for me?

"Yeah. I, uh, got an admin email," I say.

"Cool." He rotates his head, pointing to the lecture hall. "Anyway, you should come sit with us. I promise Nick and I won't be too obnoxious."

That gets a smile out of me, and I follow Ian in. Those two *might* have an unfamiliar dynamic with each other, but they seem like good friends.

And they're both being nice to me. Unexpected, but not unwelcome.

CHAPTER THREE
IAN

"Is there a reason you're smiling into your laptop?" Sabrina asks, waving her hand in front of my screen and snapping me out of my editing.

I force my face into a neutral expression. "No. Why do you ask?"

"Bullshit."

There's no escaping what's about to come next. Sabrina and Nick are two of my best friends on campus, and they're equally good at reading me.

"What's their name?" She walks around to my side of the library table and plants herself next to me, giving me a knowing, side-eyed smirk.

"Callum," I supply. "Group project partner."

I'm in the middle of editing the video for the Human Movement project, which involves a lot of looking at Callum. Mostly the same close-ups of his toned forearm and listening to his deep, sultry voice pouring through my earbuds whenever I refine a section of the video.

And then there's that pretty face of his right at the beginning when he's introducing the project. I go back to that shot a *lot*, because I want to get the color grading right. Not because I need an excuse to look at him, not at all.

He's a tough one—it's taking more than twenty-four hours to be normal about him, but I'll get there eventually. Not seeing him for almost a whole week helped, I think. Or hope.

Sabrina clasps her hands together when Callum reappears in the video. "Ooh, I didn't know you went for the broody type."

"Shut up. He's, like, a hundred percent straight." I keep my voice firm, with the hope of driving the point into my brain. "I'm not going there."

"Yeah, straight until proven otherwise, right?" She pauses, shifting a strand of her light brown hair out of her eyes. "Is he nice, though?"

"Why? Do you want his number or something?" I reach for my phone, and she backhands me across the chest.

"Totally. Laura might have something to say about that."

Laura is Sabrina's girlfriend. Neither of them are into men.

"You didn't answer my question," she says. "Is he nice, or just a pretty face for you to fawn over?"

Oh, yeah. I don't know much about him, but that quiet shyness, coupled with how eagerly he got his part of the project done, speaks volumes. The guy's endearing as hell, I'll give him that.

"I think so," I say. "Cal's pretty quiet, though."

Sabrina snickers. "You're already on a nickname basis with him? That's so cute!"

I shrug, taking a sip of my iced coffee that isn't playing too nicely with my ADHD medication. And what if we've only exchanged a few sentences here and there? He was polite enough to put up with me and Nick's petty bickering during our first official meeting, and he returned the filmed clips way before his self-imposed deadline. All signs point to him being at least a decent person.

"He seems like a good guy," Sabrina says. "He's got kind eyes."

"*Pretty* eyes," I supply. "My god, and those eyelashes—"

She slaps my shoulder. "Ian, stop it. You're gonna get a crush on him if you keep that up."

"Yeah, well, crushes are fun," I mutter.

"Only if you have a chance with the person. You've already written him off as straight."

She's got me there.

"Look, I don't know him, but you said he's nice." Sabrina

pauses, picking at a chip in her blue nail polish. "You could try being friends with him, *normal* friends, and then you can nip that crush in the bud."

"Yeah, I *know* how to stop a straight crush. I'll, uh, bro it up with him."

"Like what you did with Nick?"

"Exactly. Completely foolproof." I cringe internally at how stupid I was for having a little crush on Nick when I was a freshman. Still, I got over him super quickly, and the fact that we're teammates was more than enough to overpower him being tall, dark-haired, and—

Yup, I have a type, that's for sure.

I just need to find someone who fits that type *and* is available for me. I haven't had much success so far.

Whatever. I have time to deal with that.

Callum's video was low-key shot in potato quality, so color grading it and applying filters to make the feed less grainy takes a while. I'm almost done and ready to move on to fine-tuning the audio, when a group, I'm assuming freshmen, annoys the whole library with obnoxious chattering.

I roll my eyes, and I'm about to make a whispered complaint to Sabrina when someone tells them to take their noise elsewhere.

Thank god—

Wait. That's the same voice as the one in my earbuds.

I glance up, and sure enough, it's Callum. The offending group is fleeing the library, and Callum turns around, depositing a stack of books on a cart before heading in our direction.

"Hey, that's him, isn't it?" Sabrina whispers.

I nod.

"Oh damn, he's so fucking tall."

"Yeah, I know." *I'm* not very fucking tall at five-seven, so I stand up and wave at Callum to say hi.

"Hey, man, what's good?" I ask, reaching over to dap him up after he walks over.

He freezes for a second before giving me a stiff kind of sideways high-five. It's gentle, but I still feel how soft those big hands are.

"Are you studying too?" I continue.

He shakes his head. "No, I work here."

Wait, he works in the library? What are they making him do to give him guns like that, move all the shelves across the building by hand?

"Mostly shelving and telling people to be quiet," he adds.

That makes sense. That group of freshmen are nowhere to be seen, and peace has been restored, thanks to Callum's bouncer-like intimidation skills.

"Cool, cool," I say, shifting from one foot to the other. "Well, I'll let you get back to work, but it was nice to see you."

"Yeah, nice seeing you too." He leaves.

"You could have fooled me," Sabrina says, and I turn to face her, raising an eyebrow and prompting her to clarify. "Total bro moment. No crushy vibes at all."

My stomach settles. "Really?"

"Ha, no."

Shit.

"Your voice didn't give anything away, but your eyes?" She makes a dramatic, wistful sigh. "It was like you caught the first glimpse of your husband coming back after a decade at sea."

"It sure feels like a decade since I touched someone else," I mutter.

"Bro, you should think about changing that," she says, causing my face to burn. At least she has the decency to keep her voice low so the whole library doesn't know I'm not getting any action.

"We've been through this," I reply. "That's a terrible idea. All I'm gonna do is catch feelings after making eye contact and then get ghosted."

Sabrina blinks, her expression softening. "Again, Ian, those guys were dicks. That doesn't mean you need to take yourself off the market."

Sighing, I run a hand over my face. "I get that, but I need time to recover." That's the truth—I don't have it in me to get thrown aside again, not so soon.

"Alright. Just take care of yourself, okay?" Sabrina offers me a sympathetic smile before returning to her biology notes, leaving me to keep plugging away at the video.

———

The edits don't take too much longer, and I upload the video to our group drive for Nick and Callum to review, or at least I try to.

The upload fails thanks to the spotty internet in the library.

Whatever. I'll upload it once I'm back home.

It's not even noon yet, so I scarf a protein bar and head to the campus gym for a workout. I scan in through the separate entrance reserved for varsity athletes, get changed into my leg day outfit, including a fun pair of shorts that are a bit too short to wear outside, and stick my headphones in.

Then, after a few warmup sets, I take them out again because Nick is here, too.

Hell yeah, I can make him spot me. I send an upward nod at him, and he lumbers over, clearly hurting somewhere. Probably his legs; he's a sick bastard who does cardio in the middle of leg day. He's sweating like it's a hundred degrees outside, and he daps me up with a tired, boneless swing of his arm.

The dap doesn't crack. No surprise there.

"You got enough energy to spot me?" I ask him.

"Always," he wheezes, lifting his shirt up to wipe his face. For a second, I consider asking Nick to put a towel between us, but that'd be weird. We'll just...share sweat. Not like that's any less weird, but we're teammates and bros. It's whatever.

I line up my shoulders, and Nick takes his position behind me, grabbing my waist.

Wait.

"Oh yeah, take Daddy's big cock," he says, leaning down to get close to my ear.

I scoff, not turning around. "Behave yourself. We're in public."

"Ooh, someone could catch us. That sounds so hot."

Jesus. I bend my knee to kick Nick in the nuts, and he dodges me, chuckling, before taking his *actual* spotter position and letting me get on with my workout.

For someone who's hooked up *maybe* three times in total, he sure is fluent in sex jokes. His ex must have done some heavy lifting in that department, but I can't know for sure, and I'm not gonna ask.

I bang out a few brutal sets before calling it quits on the squats. Nick leaves to shower, and I head for the public area of the gym. The athlete section is well-stocked, but the one thing it doesn't have is a hip thrust machine. That exercise isn't technically in my program—I added them to my leg days because I want to rock a total dump truck of an ass. Sue me for trying to look good in my uniform.

One glance at the public area has me pressing pause on my quest for a callipygian figure. It's *packed*. There's even a line for a broken treadmill. Holy shit, this school needs to build another gym.

Right as I'm about to retreat to the athlete section and hit some split squats instead, something in my peripheral vision makes me pause. I turn, and it's Callum. He's changed, of course, wearing black sweatpants and a faded tee that, like the rest of his clothes, gently hugs his arms. His vibe? Focused, knows his stuff, and... perturbed.

Right. His expression doesn't give anything away, but he's gotta be at least a little grumpy at how little room he has. I wave over, he does a subtle double-take once he sees me, and his head does an adorable little—scratch that, a *relaxed* little tilt as he walks over.

"Sup, dude," I say, stretching my hand out. Remembering our dap that fizzled out earlier, I go in for a fist bump, which he returns.

"Nothing much. It's busy."

I scoff in agreement. "For sure. I'm heading back to the athlete's gym. Wanna join me? It's almost empty."

It seems like Callum is on the cusp of nodding, and I hold my breath for his agreement that doesn't come.

"Am I allowed in there?" he asks. "I don't know if I'm, uh, dressed right to go in, even if I was."

Yes to both. I wouldn't be the first person to sneak a guest in with me, and there's nothing that stands out about his clothes, other than the fact that they've gotten him sneaky, appreciative glances from no fewer than three girls in the one minute we've been talking.

"Dressed right? Dude, look at me." I gesture at my oversized team shirt and leg-day shorts. "You'll fit in, don't worry. Just pretend you're a hockey player who got benched or something, not that anyone is gonna ask."

With any other guy, I'd give him a shove on the back toward the athlete entrance. With Callum, though, that'd seem rude. Instead, I haul the door open and step back to let him through.

"Wow, you weren't kidding about it being empty," he says.

"Yup, no football yet, both hockey teams are on the road, and most of my teammates work out in the morning. All ours, buddy."

Callum thanks me and makes his way to the free weights, and I notice he didn't bring water.

Huh.

I make a quick detour to the merch bin and grab him a team water bottle. The dean's cousin makes them, so we always have a massive surplus—nobody is gonna notice if one goes missing. I give it a quick rinse and dry it off before filling it from the filtered dispenser, and I hand the bottle off to a confused Callum on my way to the leg press.

We don't see much of each other for most of my workout, but Callum starts a set of lat pulldowns as I'm wrapping up my leg curls. He's right in my line of sight, and holy motherfuck, I'd sell my soul twice over to have back muscles like those. I hadn't noticed them as much when I first saw him in the gym, but now his shirt is damp with sweat, clinging to his lower back. He really should think about playing a sport.

Maybe water polo—the other team would be too slack-jawed and jealous at the sight of Callum shirtless to put up any real competition.

Mmm. Shirtless Callum. That's one hell of an image.

Damn it, that's rude. He can't help how he looks, and I'm here ogling him while he's trying to get through a workout.

Snorting to myself, I push the visual of tall, hunky Callum in a skimpy swimsuit out of my head, which is good timing since he chooses that moment to wrap up his set. I give him a nod when he turns around, and he smiles, walking his worked-out self over and wiping his forehead.

"I'm running late for something so I have to go, but thanks again for bringing me here," he says through a breath.

"No problem at all, man. Hit me up if you wanna escape the crowds again. I'm here most days, anyway, so I'm open."

Okay, Ian. Dial it way *down.*

I don't get a chance to because Callum gives me a shy wave and a tiny, endearing smile before speeding out of the door into the general area. Sighing at how my heart is flipping, I go to wipe off the leg curl machine, when I run into Polina. She's one of Sabrina's teammates on the women's softball team, and we've hit some drills together over the past year. We give each other a silent greeting, and she takes an earbud out.

"Hey, not to be weird or anything, but who's your friend?" Polina asks me.

Ugh, I know where this is going. "A guy I met in class. Saw him in the public area and thought I'd sneak him in."

"Well, feel free to sneak him in whenever. He's hot as fuck."

I know. "I'll try."

Polina gives me a friendly grin as she puts her earbud back in. All logic leaves my brain, and a pang of jealousy spikes my stomach. I shake my head and leave for the showers, pushing it aside. Seriously, I thought I was doing so well, only to get jealous over someone making an innocent thirsty comment over my new friend.

Yeah, I'm a mess.

This is why pretty much everyone I've hooked up with since getting here, mostly guys at this point, have backed away from me and shooed me out of their lives.

I get clingy when I shouldn't.

Or even a little possessive, like I am now with poor Callum. I try to keep that part of me under wraps, I really do—I stay chill, light, and casual, rather than letting my emotions go uninhibited, but no matter what, I can't stop myself, and my annoying affection always pokes through somehow. Often through me entering barnacle-cuddle-mode after sex or going a little overboard with the morning-after breakfast spread. Who knew homemade muffins could weird someone out?

Needless to say, my strict sex and rejection diet has to stay.

With Callum, I can keep that first pledge intact for sure since I'm sure he's *straight*, and I have to keep myself calm if I want to maintain the second one.

CHAPTER FOUR
CALLUM

If there's one upside to running a little late, it's, well, *running*. For once, I'm almost too warm in my porous jacket, and I shed it as soon as I step into the chaotic WMU Student Health Center. I bumble around the second floor for a while, searching for the counseling offices before I finally find them on the other side of a glass overpass.

Some signage would have been useful.

Checking my phone for the time, I let my pace slow when I confirm that I've made up for my post-gym, post-shower tardiness on the way over, and I knock on the door to room B207 after a quick check-in on the Health Center app.

Anita Young, my assigned counsellor, opens the door after a few seconds. "Hi, you must be Callum," she says after I enter. "Please, have a seat."

I settle into the green beanbag chair across from her desk and immediately sink way too far into it.

What a way to make a first impression.

With my cheeks burning, I unfold myself and plant my legs on the floor to keep myself vertical.

"Sorry," I mutter, keeping my gaze low.

"No big deal." Anita's voice is soft, and when I tilt my head back up, she's smiling gently at me. "Trust me, you aren't the first person who's done that. I keep asking this place to give me another real chair, but you know how slow admin can be to move things along."

I let out a quiet sigh of relief. Not that I was expecting Anita to be judgy, but it's good to know that she isn't overly clinical.

Besides, she's affirming. The little pride flag decal above her desk certainly isn't lost on me. If I'm going to get any kind of benefit out of coming here, I know I need to open up, which hasn't happened in years.

"Okay, you were triaged rather quickly based on your intake questionnaire," she starts, pushing her long black hair back, "so let's get into it. Have you had any kind of counseling or therapy before?"

I shake my head.

"And do you have any questions about the paperwork you filled out?"

"Nope, I think I'm okay." The intake form was pretty basic, asking me for basic medical information questions, some of which I didn't have clear answers for.

Anita nods once before giving me a quick overview of how all this works. I get two sessions a month with her for six months, before dropping down to one indefinitely. Everything stays in this room, other than if I'm at risk of harming myself or anyone else, and while I'm not sure if that'll make it easier for me to spill my secrets, who knows?

After a pause, Anita looks up from her tablet. "I know you answered this in the intake form, but what are you hoping to get out of our sessions, if you decide this is a good fit for you?"

Where do I even start? Become a functioning person? Erase the first nineteen years of my life and start fresh? Learn how to talk to people without clamming up?

Finally convince myself that I'm not gonna wake up back in Wisconsin tomorrow?

"What I put on the form, basically," I say. Sheesh, that's not helpful at all. "I mean, I'd ideally like to be normal."

Or at least the version of normal that I wasn't raised to be.

"What does normal look like to you?" Anita asks.

My mind goes to Ian, and I remind myself not to make a habit of it. In this case, though, it seems appropriate. He's a normal guy —casual, collected, funny.

Cute.

Really, *really* freaking cute.

Come on, that's rude.

"Sociable, I guess?" I say instead. "I don't really speak up that much."

The scratching of Anita's pen on her tablet is the only sound in the room for a couple of seconds. "Being a quieter person isn't anything to be fixed, Callum. There's nothing abnormal about that."

"I know, but I think I'm more than just quiet. Besides, I'm already so different from everyone else, here and in general."

"In what ways do you think that?"

Again, I'm at a loss for where I can even start with answering that. But I'm in my head pretty much all the time anyway. All I have to do is take my mental voice and put it into my real voice.

"Do you mind if I ramble a bit?" I ask.

"Go right ahead."

I don't ramble; I say the first two words that come to mind.

"I'm gay."

For the first time I've said that out loud, ever, my voice comes out a lot stronger than I would have expected. I do my best to not stare directly at Anita, even though I'm desperate to see how she reacts, so I keep her in my peripheral vision.

And she nods. She does that a lot.

"Thank you for telling me," she says. "Is that the first time you've told anyone?"

"Yes."

"Is that something you're struggling to accept? As part of being 'normal,' that is."

Surprising myself, I manage to smile, even though this isn't a topic I thought I'd be happy to discuss. "No, honestly. It's been six years since I suspected, and I'm at the point where it is what it is." Pausing, I wait for Anita to say something, and when she doesn't, I fill the silence. "I didn't come here because of my sexuality," I clarify, bending the truth a little. "I'm here because I need to..."

Anita still doesn't reply. She probably wants me to finish my sentence. Discomfort brews in my stomach, but I power through it. After all, if I stayed in my comfort zone, I wouldn't leave my room. Ever.

"I need to undo what my parents taught me," I get out.

Anita nods. "And what exactly is it that your parents taught you, that you're trying to reverse?"

"To be quiet," I reply.

Jeez, I'm going in circles.

"Okay." She thinks for a second, clasping her hands together. "That's quite a bit to go over here, especially for a first session, so why don't we focus on your goals. Could you name one or two outcomes that you'd like to work toward as we move through our sessions, should you choose to continue?"

My mind goes back to how I froze up when I met Nick and Ian, and how poorly I handled their joking during our group project meeting. Like, seriously. I could have *tried* to engage.

I sigh. "Maybe...be more confident. And learn how to be friends with people."

"That's a good start, and you're already ahead of most people who seek help. Why is it, do you think, that you need to learn how to be friends with people?"

"I was sheltered," I say. And I leave it at that.

The rest of the session is super logistical. What treatment might look like. Who to call and where to go if I need anything urgent.

If my parents could see me, they'd sneer. Or spit in my face. Or something else I don't particularly want to think about.

Yeah. I don't feel any better after this, but I don't feel *worse,* either. I'll keep coming in case I eventually do. I just want to *breathe.*

Hopefully undoing nineteen years won't take another nineteen.

As I push the door open on my way out of Anita's office, my

palm leaves a streak of stress-induced perspiration behind. God, that's *disgusting*.

As quickly as I can, I wipe the marks off the metal handle with the cuff of my sweater and dart into the nearest bathroom to scrub my hands clean. While drying the wetness off under the weak puff of an ancient hand dryer, my eyes drift to a clear bowl sitting next to the sink. Like every other public bathroom at this college, it's full of condoms, which I figure is a nice touch, but it'll be ages, if ever, before those are of any use to me.

Still, something, possibly the lack of anyone else around me, compels me to make a closer inspection.

Huh. The bowl is split in two.

Condoms in one half, packets of lube in the other.

My breath hitches as ideas intrude my mind. I could use lube on myself. I never have, given the hell that would break loose if anyone found sex supplies in my room at home, but I can guess it'd feel way better than spit or shampoo.

Even the *thought* makes my dick stir.

I'm ridiculous—I can't keep myself in check over something so *basic*. Still, I can't get the thought out of my head. The post-workout buzz I always get isn't helping my self-restraint any more than it never does.

I grit my teeth and pull my sweater down to cover myself. The last thing I need is to broadcast my lack of control to the whole college.

After an unnecessary glance around to make sure I'm alone, I grab a handful of lube packets and stuff them into the depths of my backpack before making a hasty exit, trying not to look like I pulled a heist. My eyes stay fixed to the ground in front of me as I make the short, icy walk back to my room, and I lock the door behind me before unclenching my jaw and releasing a tense breath.

Here, it's just me.

I slip my jeans off and climb into bed, and I can't stop focusing on the fraying cuffs.

Yeah, I catch how other students stare at my stretched-out jeans and the shirts that catch under my arms, but can I blame them? I've got to be the only person on campus who still wears stuff that's over a year old. I'll have to wait until I get my first check from the library before I can get anything new, and even then, I'll only be able to afford some kind of imitation of what people here wear.

Kind of fitting for what I am—an imitation of who belongs.

The voice in my head pipes up. *Shut up. You belong.*

Sometimes I listen, sometimes I don't. I mean, WMU wouldn't have given me a full ride if I *didn't* belong, but the student body isn't responsible for admissions.

My wandering thoughts are politely interrupted with a chime from my phone.

Student Portal Updates:
Ian Scott has uploaded Draft Video 1.mp4 to HM2 Project Drive (Today, 12:37 p.m.)

I click the link I missed and watch the video, which makes me wonder if Ian is minoring in Creative Studies. He made my cheap phone video look almost professional, making the audio sharp, and applying some kind of filter to smooth out the static.

> Just watched the video, looks good, thanks for editing it

Again, I remind myself not to add a period.

IAN SCOTT

> Thanks man!

> You're the best

That line hits me square in the chest, and I grin. Warmth spreads through me, fast and almost overwhelming.

He said I'm *the best.* I mean, he's probably the kind of guy who says that to everyone, but still, I let myself smile wider. Ian is so *nice* to me. He has the kind of smile that lights up the whole room while also looking like it's meant for you.

He's—

Cute.

Oh, god, no. Why did I have to think—

He's so hot. He'd look amazing without a shirt.

I try to shove those thoughts out of my mind, but instead, my brain feeds me replays of all the lewd glances I stole at Ian earlier in the gym. His arms. His bright smile. Him flicking a lock of pretty, sweat-damp hair out of his flushed face.

I shove my phone under my pillow and close my eyes, hoping I calm down.

It doesn't work. I get a close-up, true-to-life memory of his thick quads flexing in those tiny, tiny shorts.

That's what does me in. A twisted shiver bolts down to my dick, hardening me right up. I've been half-reared and ready to go for ages now, and Ian's kind, innocent message poked a hole in my feeble dam of decency.

God, Ian is dangerous. He has to know how attractive he is, given how casual he is about what he wears, and that makes him even hotter to me. I want what I can't have and can't be.

I can't help it, not even when I think back to Ian and that pretty girl in the library. I'm guessing they're together.

And I'm here alone, getting aroused by nothing more than the thought of him.

I need to get a grip. Rubbing the bridge of my nose, I make another weak attempt to banish all visuals of him from my brain and recline into my flat, dorm-issued pillow.

I flit my gaze around the room, scanning to make sure it's safe, and I exhale, letting my hand slip into my boxers while I strain to keep my mind blank, focusing on how good my hand feels.

As pathetic as I am, not thinking about Ian is gonna be way easier after I take care of this immediate problem. Heat zips up my body as I make a fist around my dick, the gentlest contact making me thrust upward. It's been days, and while I know that nobody cares anymore, old habits die hard.

Emphasis on the *hard*.

If I was any less screwed up, I'd take care of myself all the time, but instead, I force myself to wait days, until I'm drowning in hormones and incapable of thinking about anything beyond how badly I need to come. Until I start falling apart, when my body betrays itself, and when every single shift in my boxers makes the situation a hundred times worse.

Because life decided to give me two things that mix like oil and water: a family who told me that pleasure is poison, and the world's most soul-crushing, hyperactive, unignorable sex drive.

I bring my hand back up and suck in a sharp breath as I drag across the sensitive area below the head, feeling myself firm up beneath my fingertips.

Yeah. I'm gonna go for it.

Whatever messed-up beliefs my parents have, I'm sure as heck trying to leave those behind. I'm a thousand miles away now—I can jerk off in bed without getting paranoid.

Maybe. Again, old habits die hard.

I release my grip and glance at the door, making sure it's locked, before sliding my boxers all the way off and grabbing a packet of lube out from my backpack. My fingernails catch on the ridges at the edge as I tear the foil open, and I let the thick, clear liquid fall into my hand.

I squeeze the rest of the packet onto my hard-on, and then I spread it.

My god, that's so good.

Sick pleasure zings through me as soon as I close around the head, the bliss thickening my dick even more and putting me at risk of making noise. Keeping my breaths quiet and level, I slide down my shaft in a slow, gentle drag. The light touch still makes my thighs clench, and the silky lube makes this feel ten times better than anything I've tried before.

I tighten my grip, a breath escaping my lungs, and I stroke once, then twice.

Then my hands move on autopilot. My left goes down to squeeze my balls as my right speeds up, working its way up and down, making my core twist and unravel while sending spikes of need through my length to crest at the tip.

There's no way I could resist this. I tried, I really did before, but stronger heads prevail, and the one lower down won out. It's messed up how I have to fight back the sounds stuck in my throat, almost as if my weakness is being punished with another test of strength.

At least I have enough of that strength left in me to stay dead silent.

It doesn't take long for the first signs of an orgasm to prickle in my balls; it never does, but even for me, this is fast. A couple of slick, devastating pumps later, I come hard, biting my lip to hold back a stubborn moan as my body tenses. I unclench my core as I fall back to reality, dropping my softening cock onto my stomach and letting my arms slump against the mattress.

Jesus, this is so addictive.

That, apparently, is precisely why I had to hold out and fight against my own body.

Because "shooting heroin is also supposed to feel great, but that doesn't make it right."

What a bunch of bunk.

A dopey smile plays out on my face, and out of instinct, I force it away. I grab my shirt and wipe myself down with hurried movements, scraping off every trace of what I just did.

Then I pause, slowly flipping the shirt inside-out before placing it into my laundry hamper. After washing my hands in the sink and slipping into sweatpants, I lie back on my bed, sighing.

Even though I got what I craved, as always, the short burst of relief darkens into filthy, gnawing shame.

I try to power through it, and the twisting lingers deep in my stomach. So much for being normal—I can't even jerk off like other guys without being weird about it.

Still, I *know* that nobody's coming for me. I'm alone in my room with a bag full of free lube and the same sex drive I've always had, only now, it's less of a betrayal and more of an annoyance.

One day, it might be something I can appreciate.

That day is not today. Words that I heard out loud almost every day until two weeks ago echo in my head.

You're corrupted. Unworthy. Spineless. Disgusting.

Abnormal.

Deviant.

I kept every part of myself hidden from my parents. They didn't know about my solitary sexual escapades, or at least I *hope* they didn't, but I still got thinly veiled warnings about rotting away if I succumbed to temptation. Always theoretical, of course —I don't even want to think about the wrath I'd face if they knew how I kept constantly giving in to myself.

Sighing, I pull the blankets over me to hide from nobody and turn onto my stomach, hoping sleep comes for me.

Now, like how it was back at home, sleep is the only reprieve I can get.

CHAPTER FIVE
IAN

Oh, man. The rush of relief and satisfaction that comes with turning something in on time hits *different*. I lean back in the library chair and crack my knuckles while shaking stiffness out of my body. The first part of this awful self-inflicted report was the last thing standing between me and a full week of assignment-less freedom, and man, I can't wait.

Nick wants to get wild and wasted tonight, and he's having me, Sabrina, and Laura over at his place to do just that, before going to The Barrel, a bar in town with lax ID checks, to get wilder and wasted-er. More wasted. Whatever.

I text Nick my go-to order of vodka and transfer him the cash on my way out.

Great. One of the exit turnstiles is broken, and there's a bottle-neck. I take a breath, waiting, and because I'm shameless, my eyes roam around and catch on a tall, hunky guy. Hot damn—

Oh. It's Callum. Oops.

He's wearing a flannel again today, and holy hell, blue is his color, hands down. He shouldn't be allowed to wear anything else.

Okay, I should stop before I get carried away. I'm not *supposed* to check him out, but this is only harmless, friendly admiration.

I mean, I can still look, right?

We haven't seen each other in a while, since Nick always makes me late to our shared lecture. Sure, Cal and I have shared a few nods of acknowledgement here and there, but nothing more.

I should invite Callum to hang out sometime.

Hold up. Nick said that tonight is an open invite. I'll bring Callum along if I can. Chilling with him outside of class would be sick.

"Yo, Callum!" I give him a quick upward nod, which he returns after a pause. He's still outside the turnstiles, but I want to talk to him.

I leave the line and approach.

"What's up?" he asks.

"Nick's having a party at his place tonight. Wanna come?"

His eyes widen, and I can't tell if he's shocked, confused, or offended. I hope he's none of those and is receptive instead.

"Oh, I can't, sorry. I'm about to start a shift here."

Right, he has his job shushing freshmen with his nightclub-bouncer vibes. It's in the biceps.

Damn it, I'm staring at his arms again.

"The libraries all close at eleven, right? We'll all be out pretty late," I say, silently begging him to say yes.

"I'm good, but I appreciate the invite. Thanks." Callum offers me a tiny smile which manages to undo the knot of rejection in my core.

"Shoot, okay. Next time?" I scratch the back of my neck. "Guess I'll see you around?"

I *know* him saying no means nothing. Even so, getting turned down for anything still stings like nothing else. At least I'm good at keeping a straight face now that I have almost twenty years of practice under my belt.

"Sure." He opens the staff gate and lets me out. "I, uh, have to get to work, but it was so nice to see you."

Aw, Callum is so *sweet*. God, this man is precious, not to mention affirming as hell.

I offer a wave, and he smiles back before heading into the library. My head follows him, and I steal a glance at his jean-clad legs as they walk him away.

Sheesh, those are some nice jeans. Faded just right, a little scuffed at the bottom cuffs, and fitting him like a glove.

And when I lift my gaze, I lock eyes with a cute blonde chick across the foyer who apparently had the same idea I did, only with a bit more intention since her head tilts right back to Callum's... quads.

Yeah, we're totally admiring his *legs*. Not his ass. Not at all. Nope. Even if his ass is super nice and super hard to miss.

I chuckle, raising a friendly eyebrow at her, and she smiles back with a shrug before walking up the stairs to her left.

I linger on her departing figure for a few impolite seconds. Holy hell, she's hot. Callum could *get it*. Good for him.

But I don't have time to stand around thinking about Cal.

The walk home only takes me a few minutes, and as soon as I kick my shoes off, I grab a beer and head for the shower.

As I wait for the water to warm up, I strip and grab my dick out of pure instinct. For a quick, fleeting second, I contemplate whether I'm gonna find a hookup when we head out tonight, before letting out a breath and deciding against it.

While I might be in a lengthy dry spell, that beats being called a level-five clinger for wanting some post-coital cuddles.

Fuck that.

Instead, I step into the warm water and crank my hormones away while imagining that I'm being stroked off by someone else. I won't lie, even though spilling into my own hand isn't the same, at least *I* won't scoff at myself and say I'm a creep for cooking breakfast.

Oh well—tonight, I'll get messy drunk with Sabrina and Laura, try to wingman Nick, and maybe run into some of my teammates so we can all be idiots together. That's my kind of fun.

Then comes the ever-present question of what I'm gonna wear. It should be simple, especially since I'm a dude who wouldn't give too many shits anywhere else, but WMU sure has preppy vibes running through most of the student body. Nobody, outside of a few tryhards in the business school, wears suits to class, but there's a definite pressure to dress up.

I roll my eyes as I rifle past a quarter-zip in my closet. Isn't college supposed to be more relaxed than this?

Leafing through my closet, my fingers land on the flannel I wore when I saw Callum for the second time. I smile to myself while pulling it out, deciding that yes, I'm gonna wear it again. Honestly, I have to give it to Callum for breaking that mold for me. He clearly doesn't care about weird groupthink, and he looks real good in the process.

Great, I'm thinking about him again. It's the age-old dilemma: do I want to *be* him, or do I want to be *with* him?

Like, we're friends. It's fine if I admire that part of him. It's totally natural to take pages out of a cute guy's book. Besides, it isn't like I went out and bought a bunch of clothes to match his wardrobe. I've owned flannel and jeans and hoodies and a few pairs of boots since I can remember, anyway.

A whiskey and a quick bite later, I bundle up and head over to Nick's apartment. I knock on the door, and it swings open almost instantly, a buzzed Nick leaning on the frame with a drink in his hand.

"Yo, what's upppppp," he drawls, dapping me up before wrapping me in a friendly bear-hug. "Are you ready to get blitzed tonight?"

I grin, pulling a beer out of my backpack. "Oh yeah."

Nick snatches it out of my hand. "None of that weak shit. I'm making you a real drink." He heads straight for the kitchen and pulls out a bottle of vodka—his own, not the one he helped me buy earlier. "I'm kinda short on mixers, so I hope you aren't allergic to peach juice."

"Sounds good to me."

Nick nods before unscrewing the bottle of vodka, and then he tilts it, depositing what's probably half its contents into a highball glass.

I scoff. "Bro, are you trying to kill me?"

"Nah, I'm only helping you catch up," Nick says, adding an

extra little splash of vodka for good measure. He fills the rest of the glass with juice, tosses in some ice, and hands the drink to me.

I take a sip, and it isn't half-bad.

After a gulp, it tastes even better. I might have another.

The two of us are half-drunk by the time Sabrina and Laura knock on Nick's door half an hour later, and I stumble over to let them in, making sure not to spill my drink on Nick's carpet.

"Is it cowboy night at The Barrel or something?" Sabrina asks as she walks in, clapping my shoulder. "If it is, you're missing a hat."

I chuckle and wave her off. "Nah, I thought I'd try something different tonight." After a pause, I decide to make a Nick-level joke. "But I wouldn't say no if I found someone to save a horse with me later."

Laura groans, smoothing her dark, snow-dampened hair down. "Ugh, that's awful. Why'd you have to say that?"

Nick coughs. "Our guy here is in love with a flannel-wearing country boy."

Jesus fuck. I give Nick the finger and deflect by helping Laura and Sabrina bring their drinks to his fridge.

Sabrina unscrews a bottle of white wine. "Is anyone else coming with us?" she asks me and Nick, who shakes his head.

"Nah, I invited Callum, *who's my friend and nothing more*, but he's working," I say.

"Aw, that's too bad." She takes a large drink from the bottle before passing it to Laura, who does the same. "Anyway, shots?"

Again, I won't turn those down.

———

"I love you guys so much," I slur, wrapping an arm around Sabrina and leaning into Nick.

He rolls his gray eyes and snorts, flicking my forehead and draining the rest of his beer. Laura comes back from the bathroom and snickers, passing a glass of water to Sabrina and opting out of our chaotic jumble of limbs by sitting at the far end of the couch.

"Yo, loverboy," Nick says, scruffing up my hair, "are you ready to head out?"

"Oh, yeah." I sit upright and unhook myself from Sabrina. "We should check how long the line is."

"I'm on it," Sabrina says, pulling her phone out and checking The Barrel's social media. After a few seconds, she frowns. "Guys, The Barrel got their license revoked for a month."

"Fuck, what happened?" Nick yells. "That's the only place in town that doesn't ask for ID."

Sabrina furrows her eyebrows. "That's...probably why they got shut down. Fuckin' sucks. I was so looking forward to going out tonight."

My response comes automatically. "You guys all have fakes, so you can—"

"No, Ian." Sabrina cuts me off. "We aren't gonna ditch you."

I wave her off. "Don't worry about me. I'm good."

Three heads turn toward me, intensifying the unease that's settling in my stomach. They're my friends. They should be able to do what they want without me holding them back.

"Ian, come on. We aren't going to leave you out," Laura says, narrowing her brown eyes.

"No, it's fine. I really don't mind," I lie, hoping I'm convincing enough.

Sabrina shifts between her feet. "It's not a huge deal. We'd just end up going to that Turbo club to pay through the nose for watery shots."

"Oh, Turbo? Some guys from the team are gonna be there," I say, and Nick's head perks up.

"That might be nice," he starts, before faltering. "We'd only go if you're *actually* okay with it."

I offer a smile that's stronger than my drink. "I am, alright? I'll go as far as *telling* you guys to go."

"Alright. Get home safe, okay?" Nick says, sighing. He turns to Laura and Sabrina, who shrug and nod.

What is it about me and signing off on my own exclusion?

Well, not everything is about me, and I shouldn't be the one to keep my friends in.

Leaning over, Sabrina wraps me in a hug. "We're still on for hangover brunch though?"

I reply with a grin, "Definitely."

Hangover brunch started when those three crashed in my dorm after a wild night around a year ago. I brought back a massive spread for their hungover asses, and a tradition was born. I bring the food, Sabrina brings mimosa ingredients, and Laura brings Sabrina, who might not ever leave the bed if it wasn't for her girlfriend.

"Nick, are you coming tomorrow?" I ask.

He lets out a snort. "Man, I love you, but I'm not dragging my ass out of the house before noon." He's only made it to two brunches, and nobody blames him. He's a tired boy whose internal clock is constantly set to China time.

Nick slams another shot while Sabrina and Laura put their jackets on, and we head downstairs. Turbo is in the other direction from my house, so I say bye again before we part ways.

And then I'm alone. Campus is almost deserted, and the faint sounds from ongoing frat parties float through the air. As far as Friday nights go, it's an early one for me, given that it's barely past eleven.

Maybe I should bite the bullet and get a fake ID.

While I would have liked to hang out a bit longer, at least I won't be hungover tomorrow. Even if that defeats the point of hangover brunch with Sabrina and Laura. Then again, I'll be conscious enough to make pancakes instead of throwing in the towel and ordering in. Pancakes are always a hit with those two.

The already-quiet sounds coming from campus fade even further with every step I take, and by the time I get to the West Library, I'm accompanied by my footsteps.

I stop, leaning against a tree. The alcohol from earlier is wearing off. It's still keeping me toasty, and I have a pleasant buzz going—

"Hey, Ian?"

I spin around, recognizing that voice. It's Callum, and I can't stop a grin from materializing. Catching myself, I mold my expression into something more socially acceptable.

"Yo, what's up?" I ask.

"Nothing. I just finished my shift. Didn't think I'd run into you, but I thought I'd say hi or something."

My chest warms as I give him a fist bump. "Awesome. I'm glad you did. It's always nice to see you, man."

"Are you calling it a night?" he asks. "It's only eleven."

"Yeah," I reply, pausing to take in a cold breath. "Unless you wanna chill with me for a bit? I live right around the corner, and I have drinks at my place if you're down."

His eyebrows rise slightly, and I brace myself for him to decline.

But Callum surprises me.

"For sure, I'd like that," he says.

I break into another smile, which probably gives away how much I've already had tonight, but I don't care. "Awesome! I'll lead the way."

CHAPTER SIX
CALLUM

"Wow, you've got a nice place," I say as we step into Ian's apartment.

He shrugs like it's nothing, but it's *not* nothing. We're both sophomores, but Ian is an *adult*, at least based on where he lives.

For how excitable Ian is, the place is neater than I would have thought, but that's me making assumptions again. Sure, there's stuff lying around, but that's what happens when you have more than five outfits and college supplies. He has a dining table. And a couch. *And* lights that aren't harsh white—they're almost candle-like.

It's comfortable here. I imagine this house is what people would call "homey." Ian's place is as warm as he is, which I guess makes sense.

"Yo, Cal," he calls out from the kitchen. "Beer?"

"Yeah, sure." I have no idea what to expect, given that the only alcohol I've ever had before was an accidental sip of the diluted communion wine at church.

Yeah. That got me a whack to the head from Mom when she saw me "going astray." Still, that didn't stop her and Dad from drinking for fun.

Hypocrites.

Right as I settle down at the dining table, my darkening thoughts are halted by Ian, who's carrying the promised beer.

I do a double-take. He's carrying the biggest glass mug I think I've ever seen, and he sets it down in front of me with a sweet smile.

"If you'd like, I can add a shot to that," he offers, walking to a cart stacked with various bottles. "I'm making myself another drink anyway."

"Uh, I'm good, but thanks. Also, weren't you at a party fifteen minutes ago?"

Ian chuckles as I take a long sip of beer, and I can't tell what warms me up. "Hey, I'm not about to make you drink alone," he says, uncapping a small brown bottle.

I linger on his long, solid fingers as they shake a couple of drops from the bottle into a short glass. With a smooth movement, he adds something clear from a different bottle, a generous pour of what I'm guessing is whiskey, and then he stirs before placing one single giant ice cube in the glass. Everything about that is so precise and graceful, and it takes Ian turning toward me to make me snap out of it. I can't get caught staring at him.

"What's that?" I ask him, hoping to deflect any suspicion.

"An old fashioned." He takes a sip. "You want one?"

I let out a quiet laugh, nodding to my almost-full mug of beer. "Not much of a drinker," I say, stretching the truth before deciding to be completely honest anyway. "Haven't drunk before, actually."

Ian stops mid-drink and widens his eyes. "Oh, shit, sorry. I didn't know when I poured you all that beer. No pressure to finish it."

Smiling, I wave him off. "It's okay. I'm good to try. I'm not twenty-one yet, so I have no way of getting any."

"Nothing in high school, even? At least one person always has a fake ID."

"I was sheltered," I say simply. Avoiding the full story is the best option right now.

He nods. "Well, you're free now," he says, raising his glass. "Allow me to be a bad influence."

My stomach gets even warmer, and I'm almost certain that it's because of his warm, kind expression, and not the beer.

No. Nope. I cut my thoughts off with a sip of beer that becomes a chug.

"Woah, go easy there." Ian grins. "Don't go too hard."

I'm about to say I'm fine again, but he claps a hand on top of mine after I put the glass down, presumably to stop me from taking another drink too soon.

If my core is warm, my hand is *burning* in the best way. Ian fixes me with a naughty, joking expression that makes my stomach flip, and I chuckle to release some of the nerves that are coiling in my gut.

He's trying to be your friend. Get a grip and let him.

The weight of his hold shifts from my hand to my wrist, and he leans in. The alcohol clouding my mind stops me from recoiling how I usually would, and I smile instead.

"Dude, your shirt is so fucking soft," he mumbles, rubbing the cuff of my shirt between his fingers. "Where did you get this?"

He makes contact with the underside of my wrist, and it's electric. Shifting uncomfortably, I try to make the annoying, inconvenient sparks of affection in my tailbone disappear.

"I don't know," I reply. "It might have been my dad's?"

"I don't know your dad, but you wear it better, that's for sure."

Where is Ian going with this?

"Looks great on you," he continues.

Humor, apparently.

I let myself laugh at my own expense, the self-deprecation gnawing a little less than usual, before realizing that Ian isn't laughing. Confused, I open my mouth to speak, and he narrows his eyes at me.

"I wasn't kidding. It's warm and rugged..." He trails off, almost like he's on the cusp of saying something else.

And depending on what comes next, it might clue me in as to whether he's actually being sincere about my lack of options.

"I'm fucking starving," is what he says, reclaiming my attention with what seems to be his favorite word, *fucking*.

"Oh, okay." There aren't too many other ways for me to respond to that, are there?

"Do you want anything?"

My reply is automatic. "No thanks. I'm not hungry."

Right on cue, my stomach grumbles, betraying me.

Ian grins. "Doesn't sound like it. What's your favorite food?"

I shrug. "Don't know. Italian? Or the kind of Italian you get in a small town."

"So, like chicken parm, pizza, that kind of stuff?"

I nod, and Ian taps around on his phone before setting it down. "Okay, I got you chicken parm and breadsticks from the place downstairs. Hope you're okay with that."

What? I jerk the almost-empty mug of beer away from my lips and freeze. "How much... How much do I owe you?" I ask, trying to play it cool while reconstructing my growing but precarious bank balance from memory.

"Nothing." Ian ignores my confusion. "You're my buddy, and I invited you over."

"That's..." *That's so nice of you, Ian. Thank you.* "That's a lot. Are you sure?"

Ian backhands my shoulder. "You bet. Think of me like your college grandma who feeds you, whether you want me to or not. We're eating Italian, so call me Nonna. Nobody leaves Nonna's house with an empty stomach."

That manages to get a quiet snicker out of me. "Okay, thanks, Nonna."

The way his face lights up at me playing into the joke makes my chest tighten, and I shove the inconvenient feeling aside. Or at least I try.

"So what's your story?" He asks, putting his phone down. "A cool, mysterious stranger like you showing up halfway through the year doesn't happen a lot."

I let out a noncommittal huff, a little taken aback at being called cool by someone who actually is. "Yeah," I start, buying myself time. "I needed to get out of my small town. I transferred here for some room to breathe."

He nods, taking another sip of his drink, and my eyes catch on his defined throat jumping as he swallows. All I can do is try to disguise my leering as polite eye contact.

"Makes sense," Ian says. "No better time to make a change than when we're young."

Sighing, I raise the emptying mug of beer to my lips. "For sure. I'll have to wait and see if that was a good choice, though."

"Why's that?"

"I don't know. I'm not sure if I'm making the most of it here," I admit. "I don't need to tell you how quiet I am, and honestly? You're the only person who's talked to me outside of class since I got here."

"That's gotta mean I'm smarter than everyone else," Ian says, grinning. "But in all seriousness, that's New England for you. Don't take it personally."

"I'm not." If that was supposed to be convincing, I failed.

His face softens. "Aw, shit, you are, aren't you? I'm sorry, man. It's not you. It really, *really* isn't."

Was that a compliment? And is that why my heart is flipping out of control?

Oh, god.

He's buzzed. Buzzed and therefore passionate about everything, including me, for some reason.

"No, it's fine," I reply, hoping to steer us toward a safer, less intimate conversation. "I like my space."

Ian tilts his head, and it's clear he isn't completely buying it, but before he can say anything, his phone beeps.

"That'll be the food." He stands up and pushes his chair back hard, and he has to fumble around to catch it before it falls over and onto the floor. Ian shrugs and offers me a sheepish grin before heading out, leaving me alone in his cozy, welcoming apartment.

I lean back in the padded dining chair, allowing myself to relax.

Ian's so sweet.

Gah, no. I can't think that. He's sweet, and it's not for me. It's for everyone, and I have to live with the fact that I will never, not in a million years, have a chance with him.

Even if he was single *and* also liked guys, there's no way he'd go for the likes of me and my emotional baggage. Besides, he's so much better-looking than I am.

At least that stuff doesn't matter as much for being friends.

Shaking my head, I push my swirling thoughts away. I'll get better. In fact, I'm already in a better place than when I got here, and even though there's still a long way for me to go, progress is progress. If anything, Ian can be something for me to aspire to, even though his brand of charm is probably something you have to be born with.

The front door clicks, and Ian returns, snowflakes melting on top of his messy hair.

"Sheesh, it's wild out there," he says.

"Is it?" I ask, and he nods while putting the bag of food down. I swivel my head to peer out of the window, and sure enough, it's snowing. Again.

Ugh.

My face must give me away because he tilts his head and narrows his eyes. "You good?"

I shrug. "Yeah. The waterproofing on my coat is wearing out. I'll be fine, though."

He hands me a wooden disposable fork. "You can crash here. No big deal," he says, even though it's a huge freaking deal. "I don't mind."

What? "That's okay. I don't want to impose."

"That's not imposing, Callum. I'm offering."

"Oh, I prefer sleeping in a bed." I hope that excuse is polite enough.

Ian waves me off. "No problem. You can take my bed if you want."

"That's imposing even *more*," I protest, which gets me a

relaxed chuckle in reply. "Seriously, I'm okay with heading home." My mind lags for a second before I remember my manners. "But thank you. I appreciate it."

"Okay," he replies, digging into his box of pasta. "The offer still stands if you change your mind."

We're both drunk-ish and ravenous, so we don't talk as we inhale our food. Ian finishes before me, grabbing me water and a napkin without me asking, and I try to finish my pasta faster so he doesn't feel a need to do even more for me.

"Well, I should head home," I say, standing up once I'm done. "Thanks again for having me over. And for the food. I really liked it."

Ian leans back and smiles, sending a surge of comfort through my body. "Yeah, it's getting late. I'd offer to drive you in this weather, but..." He trails off and nods to his empty glass.

"Right." I grab my jacket from the coat rack, and I've barely gotten an arm into a sleeve when I notice him eyeing me, his head tilted.

"Jesus Christ, man," he mutters. "You're gonna freeze to death."

I shrug. "I'm from Wisconsin. I'll be fine."

That's a lie if I ever told one. It's well below freezing, and I'm not looking forward to the walk back to my dorm. At least it won't take too long.

Ian jumps up and rushes into his room before returning with something wrapped in plastic. "Here," he says, tearing the package open. "I ordered a parka for my dad, but I found out he bought the exact same one for himself. I think it'll fit so you can ha— use it."

Am I imagining things? Who does this?

"You can't just give me a coat. That's money," I say.

He thinks for a few seconds, the silence swirling around us like the snow outside. "I can still return it, even if it's open," he finally says, stretching his hand out to offer me the jacket.

I don't take it.

"Come on." Another one of those disarming smiles spreads across Ian's face. "I know you want it."

Oh, even *I* can tell that's suggestive as heck, and unwelcome desire pools deep in my gut as soon as his words stroke my eardrums. He's joking. I *know* he is, but my slightly drunk, very hyper dick doesn't get the memo.

My mouth moves before I can stop myself. "Uh, am I supposed to flirt with you now? Like you did with Nick when he said that?"

Woah, way to be direct.

Ian parts his lips, and I brace for him to tell me I'm being weird.

He laughs instead. Loudly. Doubling over and gripping the wall to stay balanced, too. "Oh my god," he wheezes. "That's funny as fuck. Not if you don't want to. It's just how the two of us bond. Pretty common dude behavior."

A tentative smile manages to creep across my face. "I'm also a dude."

"That's true." He pauses, exhaling stiffly. "In that case, you're more than welcome to flirt with me however you want."

"What, like now?"

Ian chuckles and rolls his eyes. "Yeah, no takebacks. Besides, it wouldn't mean anything."

Everything I've seen says that he's straight. I *know* joking wouldn't mean anything, but hearing it still puts another pit in my stomach.

Deciding against overthinking, I say the first words that come to mind: "You're sexy as heck in that shirt."

Oh, Jesus, that was *awful*.

"Nah, man, not quite," Ian says, smirking. "That was too polite. The trick is to go *way* overboard so I know you aren't serious. A rude pickup line that'd get a drink thrown at you if you actually used it on someone."

"Yeah, like what?" I ask.

"Watch and learn, buddy." He steps closer, and I swallow a

lump of nervous anticipation. "Aw, you're leaving already?" He bats his light eyelashes at me and runs a firm hand down my left arm.

I know he's joking, but my heart jumps anyway.

"Are you sure I can't tempt you to stay?" Ian purrs. He leans in, biting his lip and frying my defenseless brain even more. "I can get on my knees for you to sweeten the deal."

That's certainly a visual. An *appealing* visual. Why'd he have to say—

He licks his lips, too.

Why'd he have to *do* that? Now I can't get that image out of my mind. My breath catches as a depraved image of Ian on his knees for me materializes in my head, and I struggle to force it out before I can make poor imaginary Ian do anything worse.

Thankfully, he snorts and brings me back to reality, a place where he isn't into me. "That's how it's done. Make it *absurd*."

I clear my throat. "Got it."

"Anyway, you flirt, you're taking the coat." He thrusts said coat into my unsuspecting arms, and I unfold it, slipping the thick fabric around my shoulders.

This is the nicest thing I've ever worn, hands down. I was already warm from the alcohol and Ian being sweet, but this is a whole other level. The lining is soft, the shell is sturdy, and there's a hood, too.

Ian grins at me. "Does it fit?"

It does, and I nod.

"Thought so," he says. "It looks great on you, too. You sure you don't want to keep it?"

"I'm sure, but thanks." I pick up my empty takeout bowl so I can throw it out, and Ian takes it from me.

"Don't worry about this. I got you," he says. "Get home safe, buddy."

Buddy. My stomach squeezes at the endearing nickname, but I can't get all emotional in front of Ian. I settle for giving him a quick thanks and head out into the snow, pulling the fleece-lined hood over my head, and I make it back to the dorm, dry and warm.

He's so nice, it's almost uncanny, and I'll be damned if I take advantage of him, even though he's actively proving my parents wrong—other people *can* care about me.

Tomorrow is supposed to be warmer. I'm giving the coat back as soon as I can. It's the nice thing to do.

CHAPTER SEVEN
IAN

Deadlines suck ass, which is why their absence gives me a serious case of the fuzzies. The extra drink I had with Callum put me in a great mood last night, while not being nearly enough to make me hungover.

The fact that I finally, *finally* got to hang out with him still puts a silly grin on my face. Last night was so chill, and hell, I fucking loved it.

Callum is way too hot for my own good, but the fact that he's almost certainly straight is more than enough to stop any kind of crush from snowballing. If anything, maybe last night was what I needed to get over him in that way. He's a great guy, if a little quiet, and he sure isn't used to accepting anything from other people.

But we're friends, so he needs to get used to me offering random stuff. My giving streak isn't going to change.

Which is why I haul myself out of bed, take another shower, and start making pancakes for hangover brunch with Sabrina and Laura.

Can I call it hangover brunch if I'm not hungover?

Eh, it doesn't matter. *They're* probably hungover.

My suspicions are confirmed when they rock up fifteen minutes later with electrolyte drinks, tired expressions, and mimosa ingredients that none of us are gonna touch.

"Oh, he's alive!" Sabrina says, wrapping me in a hug.

"Are *you*?" I ask. "It looks like you guys had a fun night."

"Nick and one of your teammates got on the stripper pole at Turbo and earned us two racks of shots," Laura says. "So yeah, it was pretty fun."

I choke back a chuckle. "Oh my god, you're kidding."

Sabrina shakes her head before wincing, and I toss her a bottle of ibuprofen for the headache I think she has. "Nope. Nick gave Steve a super sensual lap dance before getting one back." She pauses to take a pill out of the bottle and swallow it while I scoff at the visual.

Steve is simultaneously the official team grump and the official team hype man. Which one he is depends on his alcohol intake and whether or not he's trying to get laid.

"Our Nicky-boy got a ton of attention, but he ended up leaving alone with us at two," Laura adds.

"Glad you all got home safe." I ease a few pancakes out of the pan and pour a new batch. Nick going home alone isn't much of a surprise. He says he's super picky, and it isn't my place to speculate beyond that. "On a different note, do either of you want pancakes?"

Sabrina and Laura say yes simultaneously, and I serve up a short stack for each of them.

"Damn," Sabrina says after a bite, "how did you get wild blueberries? It's *January*."

"They're frozen—"

A quiet series of knocks cuts me off, and the three of us exchange confused glances.

"Someone flip the pancakes if they start to burn," I say absent-mindedly, heading for the front door.

It's Callum. His hair's a mess, and it's clear from the thin layer of stubble on his face that he hasn't shaved since yesterday.

In other words, he's fucking *divine*.

A cold blast of air from the hallway focuses me, and I step aside, shivering. "Wanna come in, man? It's freezing."

He shakes his head. "I'm good, thanks. Just, uh... I'm here to return your jacket."

Huh?

I don't have time to think of a reply before Callum starts

taking it off, and I clasp a hand around his solid forearm to stop him. "Dude, don't. I gave that to you."

He blinks. "You *lent* it to me."

"Well, I'm giving it to you now. I want you to have it."

"Why?"

Sheesh, he's stubborn. "I'm too lazy to print out a return label, so you're actually helping me out by taking it off my hands."

Everyone has a signature skeptical look, and I'm getting well acquainted with Callum's.

But damn, if seeing him smolder in disbelief means that I have to keep lying to his handsome face, I might as well accept my new job as the second coming of Pinocchio. Purely for aesthetic reasons, of course.

"It doesn't matter," I insist, stepping backward and motioning for Callum to follow me in. "Keep it. The color brings out your pretty eyes."

Did I actually say that?

The surprised pair of eyes I'm staring into are *so* outrageously pretty. Deep, brilliant blue with flecks of gold, framed by the thickest eyelashes I've ever seen. A ton of women would kill to have those eyelashes.

Hell, *I'd* kill to have them.

I should think about getting one of those expensive serums I always see ads for. Or mascara. I'm sure I could make it appear natural.

Callum's dark, straight brows furrow in the center, giving him an almost ethereal ruggedness. "What's that supposed to mean?"

I might as well roll with this. "It means you've got nice eyes. That's it." I weigh my next words, deciding to test the waters a little. "Girls are *so* gonna get lost in them, that's for sure."

He gives me a terse nod in return before slipping into the jacket.

Oh well.

"Anyway," he says. "I'll head back now. Thanks for the coat.

Again." He turns around, and something in my brain compels me to grab his shoulder.

"Do you want to stay for hangover brunch?" I ask. "Sabrina and Laura are here, *and* I made pancakes."

"They're so good!" Sabrina yells from the dining room.

"Yeah, that's Sabrina and Laura." I point both of them out. "Come and—"

"Oh, I didn't know you had people over," Callum says. "I didn't mean to interrupt."

He flees like he's absconding from a murder scene before I can stop him.

"I didn't even get to dap him goodbye," I say, sullen, as I return to the table.

"That's your takeaway?" Sabrina snickers. "You're really bro-ing it up with him, aren't you?"

"Oh, yeah," I reply. "As I said, we're friends, and he pretty much confirmed he's straight."

That little nod after I said *girls* would get lost in his eyes? Devastating.

"Yeah, that's a shame for you," Laura says. "He seems sweet."

"He is," I reply. "Kinda quiet, but I dig the vibe."

Sabrina raises her eyebrows. "Yeah. Maybe he'll be good for you. Balance your energy out a little."

I scoff. "Oh, excuse me. Are you saying I'm not sweet?" I bat my eyelashes at Sabrina, and she flips me off.

"You know what I mean, you shit." Sabrina rolls her eyes as I return the middle finger she gave me, but we settle down. "He's quiet and you aren't, so that's a good match."

"You sure?" I ask. "He keeps declining things, so I should tone myself down a little."

"Don't tone yourself down," Laura says quickly. "Be tactful, sure, but don't be fake."

Sabrina jumps in. "Yeah, don't change yourself for a *man*, Ian. We've been over this. The jacket was generous, but not weird."

I breathe out a sigh of relief. "Good. The last thing I want is to creep my *friends* out, too."

Sabrina brandishes her fork at me. "Ian, stop. You're letting emotionally stunted hookups get to your head again."

"Right," I mutter. "I won't dwell on it—"

My phone buzzes with a text.

CALLUM CROSS

Thanks again for the coat

No problem man

Callum's typing indicator pops up, and my fingers itch as I fight the urge to invite him to hang out later, maybe for dinner. The way he attacked the chicken parm last night makes me think that his dining hall is ass. It probably is.

Jesus Christ, Ian. Leave the poor guy alone.

Do you want to study for movement class tomorrow?

I break into a grin.

Yes ofc anytime

Sabrina snatches the phone out of my hands and locks it. "Hey, it's hangover brunch. Not 'crushing on straight guys' brunch."

"I'm not crushing on him, oh my god."

"You're smiling," Laura shoots back.

"I'm smiling because I'm excited about being friends with Callum, which will help me to stop having a tiny, unrealistic crush on the concept of him," I assure them. "Give me a week, tops. That's all I'll need."

CHAPTER EIGHT
CALLUM

Je veux une café.

Or is it *un café*?

The internet says it's *un café*.

Whatever. I *need* a coffee, but I don't know how to say that in French yet, so I'm stuck with wanting one, in addition to *wanting* this lecture to finally be over. We're learning about the weather, and while I'm trying my best to pay attention, I'm way too tired.

One thing I found out in the month since I got here is that I could probably stay asleep for five days straight. Now that nobody's policing me, I'm getting a solid nine hours a night, and sometimes, it still isn't enough.

Okay, shoot. I need to focus.

Froid. That means cold, not fraud.

I feel like a fraud in this class. The drop deadline came and went last week, and I only got my first disastrous test back on Monday.

Sure, sixty-seven percent isn't terrible, but it's still worse than what I hoped for.

Oh well.

Class finally ends, I make a mental note to review the content that I didn't absorb, and I head out for a much-needed coffee. I don't know what I'd do without my meal plan. It works across campus, and it's a lifesaver for my rapidly snowballing appreciation for coffee. It tastes so much better when it's made with grounds, not the powder that my parents restricted me to.

First, I stop by the too-short bubbler for some water. I bend over, kicking myself for forgetting the sturdy water bottle Ian gave me the first time we gymmed together.

"Hey, Callum?" a voice calls out behind me.

I cut my sip short and turn around to see one of the girls who was at Ian's place last week, trying not to dwell on the fact that my butt was poking out for everyone, including her, to see.

"Yeah." *What's her name?* "Laura, right?"

"Yup! Good memory." She narrows her eyes a little. "Did you just get out of French 107?"

I nod.

"Nice, I thought I recognized you in there."

"That's cool. What do you think of the class?"

Laura's face sours. "I'm dying, and I regret my choices. Anyway, do you wanna grab a coffee or something? I'm done with classes for today."

"Did you read my mind?" I ask, and I cross my fingers, praying for my joke to land.

"Maybe." She smiles and flicks her eyes to the coffee stand nearby. "Let's go."

We place our orders, and without thinking, I scan my ID at the register to pay for both of our drinks.

"Oh, this one can be on me," I say. "I have a ton of credit on my dining plan, anyway." It's not like I'll ever run out, not with how basic my orders usually are.

Laura's face lights up. "Thanks. That's so sweet of you. No wonder you and Ian are friends."

I tilt my head, and my face must be giving everything away because Laura snickers.

"That means you're nice," she supplies, sitting down at a free table. "Like, Ian-nice. You *have* met him, right?"

"I have." Pausing, I join her at the table. I take a sip of coffee and burn my tongue, but I'm beyond caring. "He gave me this jacket out of nowhere, after all."

"Believe me, that's normal for him," Laura says. "Sabrina even gave me a heads-up before she introduced me to him, and then he gave me a four-hundred-dollar bottle of champagne as a house-warming gift."

Wait. Ian is with Sabrina, Sabrina introduced Laura to him, then he gave *Laura* a four-hundred-dollar gift, while being with *Sabrina...*

"Are you both...friends with Ian?" I ask.

Laura opens a packet of sugar and dumps the contents into her cup. "Yeah. Sabrina more than me—she and Ian were friends before we started dating."

Wait, so are Ian and Sabrina *and* Laura—

"Right, Sabrina and *I* are dating, just in case that wasn't clear," she adds quickly. "Ian is single."

Oh. They're...okay. And all this time, I thought Ian and Sabrina were a thing. Whoops.

"That's cool," I say. "He's a nice guy."

"He *is*. Kinda hard to find one of those, so keep him around..." Laura squints and peers behind me. "Speak of the devil."

I swivel my head and make direct eye contact with none other than Ian, who saunters over with a smile on his face and a pair of flattering light gray jeans on his legs. He lifts his chin in a nod, and I do the same to get those killer thighs out of my over-appreciative vision.

Ian fist-bumps Laura and gives my shoulder a gentle squeeze. My body goes all hot just from that. What isn't helping is Ian standing right next to me, allowing me to feel the warmth radiating off his body and making heated arousal expand from my chest.

"Hey, guys, what's up?" he asks.

My stupid dick. Unfortunately.

"Nothing much. We're chatting and bitching about French class," Laura says.

"Cool, cool." Ian thankfully steps back, giving me room to breathe air that isn't filled with his clean, seductive scent.

But it lingers. My god, it lingers, that fresh, musky bliss that invades my senses and makes my stomach twist with guilty longing.

Jesus. Ian is innocent in all this, and it's *me* who's way out of line.

"And what's good, Cal?" he asks, turning his handsome face to me. Then he frowns. "You're a little red. Is everything okay?"

Crap. "Yeah. I burnt my tongue on coffee."

"Ah, shit. Sorry to hear that." Ian drops it, but when I flick my eyes over to Laura, I can't help but think she doesn't believe me. It's subtle, but her eyes are slightly narrowed, and unless my mind is playing tricks, there's a near-imperceptible smile tugging at her lips.

"Ouch," I add, for effect.

Ian stays quiet for a second. "Anyway, I have to get to my next class, but I saw you guys and thought I'd say hi. See ya!"

As quickly as he got here, he's gone, which leaves a strange, inconvenient vacancy in my stomach.

I *miss* him.

Ian said maybe twenty words to me in two minutes, and I miss him after *that*? I'm worse than I thought.

"You two seem to be on the same wavelength," Laura says. She stays quiet for a second, twisting a strand of her black hair between her fingers. "Ian notices a lot about you. It's cute."

I sputter. "*Cute?*"

Crap, crap, crap. Laura can't think I like him.

"Yeah," she continues. "A lot of guys keep massive walls up and hold themselves back from being proper friends. It's always nice when that isn't the case."

Digging my fingernails into my forearm under the table, I take a deep breath. "Oh. Okay."

"Yeah. You're still quieter, but I can tell. You like him, right? In a bro kind of way."

Oh, god. I'll only spill my forbidden secrets if I stay here.

Grabbing my coffee, I stand up and push my chair in. "He's a good friend. I should, uh, head out too. Got a paper to write."

That isn't a lie.

"Okay, we should study together sometime, though," Laura says. "Let's grab each other's numbers."

Sounds like a plan.

———

Holy hell, this college is *hard*. My fingers hover over the keyboard as I will something to materialize.

Whose idea was it to transfer here?

Oh, right. My own.

I blink a few times and refocus on the essay prompt.

This course explores energy transitions, including those occurring now. Given this context, outline the principal obstacles to overcome, as well as the response of at least two levels of government to these obstacles.

I don't know about the government, but my response to *this* transition of energy, from my body to this paper that isn't going anywhere, is to shut my laptop.

And then I open it again because my scholarship isn't gonna renew itself—I need to maintain the grades that got me the money in the first place.

But seriously, I thought I was studying *kinesiology*. How is it that only two out of my five classes this semester are related to my major? At least I'm doing well in our Human Movement course, thanks to the project that Ian, Nick, and I are acing so far.

Sighing, I open my class notes and flip to the start, scanning the pages and winging some kind of outline as I go.

If I have to give my parents *any* credit at all, it'll be for choosing one of the few extremely religious homeschool providers that also had some kind of academic rigor. Writing essays and papers is one of my strong suits, to the point where I did assignments for cash back in community college.

I can credit a certain young, attractive online Language Arts teacher for those skills. Mr. Crofton made it super easy to pay attention in class, and those sculpted biceps under tight polos were a bright spot in an otherwise dark time of my life.

It isn't long before I lose myself in a decent writing flow. If I keep this up, I'll finish this draft with time to spare...

And then the lights cut out, leaving my room illuminated only by the fading dusky sunlight.

I grumble before increasing the brightness on my laptop and continuing to work on my paper. I get a few hundred words closer to the minimum, feeling good about making the deadline, when a loud knock on my door makes my body jolt and tense up.

After a few deep breaths to calm myself down, I walk over and turn the knob to reveal a firefighter standing in the frigid, humid hallway.

An insanely hot firefighter. There's some truth to stereotypes, I guess.

Jesus, Callum. Get it together.

"Look, I'll make this quick," he says. "A tree fell on the building, and the whole structure might be compromised. You need to evacuate, so grab a jacket and head to the dining hall next door for a briefing."

"A-alright," I say, forcing myself not to get lost in his smoky brown eyes like a total creep. "You said the dining hall?"

"Yeah. Turn left and use the stairwell at that end of the building. We've closed the other one for safety." The firefighter has a voice deeper than my repression, and I have to forcibly haul myself back to reality again.

Then he's gone, off to summon more residents.

Uncertainty floods my brain as I make the quick walk over to the dining hall.

Evacuate the building. For how long?

Damn it, and I was *just* settling in.

The dining hall, which is messy at the best of times, is packed to the brim. People are sitting on tables, discussing the situation in voices that are anything but hushed. I inhale through my nose and breathe out through my mouth, trying to keep myself calm. Flipping my phone around in my hands, I manage to keep my mind from falling into the same chaos that's surrounding me.

"Hey, everyone!" one of the RAs yells, and I jerk my head up. "I have an announcement—"

He cuts off, pressing his phone up to his ear, jerks his head back in annoyance, and jams his finger down to end the call.

And then he yells out for our attention again. "Okay, so I'm gonna give it to you guys straight up: admin has no idea what they're doing."

Wow, way to inspire confidence.

"Anyway, they say they'll have an update in five minutes to four hours. You guys can, uh, stay here if you don't have class, and we'll try to figure something out."

Just like that, I know exactly nothing more than I did three minutes ago.

Then my phone beeps, startling me.

IAN SCOTT

Holy shit I just heard what happened

Are you ok???

How on earth is it possible for someone to be so intuitive? It's like Ian knows exactly how and when to cheer me up.

Then again, my chest goes all achy whenever he *looks* at me.

Yeah I'm fine, thanks for asking. Everything is confusing because they aren't telling me much

The RAs are saying that the school will provide an update at some point today

Yeah that's what I'm seeing online, too. Where are you now?

In the dining hall with everyone else

It's a bit packed

I'm in the kin building

Come hang out w me in the common room

I can't help but smile at that casual offer to spend time with him, and I head next door to the Kinesiology building. Ian is sprawled out on one of the couches in the empty undergrad common room, and he gives me a friendly wave once he sees me.

Nobody's ever been as happy to see me as he has, and guilt courses through me with every step I take on my way over to him. He's the best friend I've ever had, and I choose to repay him by undressing him with my eyes and fantasizing about horizontal hugging whenever we run into each other.

"Hey, man," Ian says, greeting me with one of his handshake-clap things that confuse the heck out of me. "Are you doing okay?"

"Yeah, why wouldn't I be?"

He stares blankly at me, blinking. "Your house got destroyed."

"That's a little dramatic," I counter. "A tree fell on the other end of the building. That's far from being *destroyed*."

He presses his lips together in an expression that's half-smile, half-sympathy. "Still scary, man. I'd be shitting myself if I was in your shoes."

Ian doesn't say anything else but pulls a container of cookies out of his backpack, opening the lid and motioning for me to take one.

With how many cookies he always seems to have on hand, I'm not entirely sure how he's as buff as he is. Maybe they're protein cookies, or he does a lot of cardio.

Aaand now I'm thinking about how attractive he would look after a run.

I shove the image out of my mind, swiping one of the oatmeal raisin cookies and letting the addictive flavor flood my mouth, before I choke on the bite when my phone beeps with an email.

It's either a grade notification or an update on where I'm living tonight.

Dear Residents of Maple Hall,

WMU Residence Life and University Administration is working tirelessly to ensure the safety and security of all displaced students. While a more sustainable solution to the recent event is still in development, we are pleased to announce that WMU is making arrangements for affected residents to stay overnight in the Leblanc Athletic Center. In cooperation with the New Hampshire Emergency Response Department, one cot will be provided for each affected resident.

That doesn't sound like a proper plan.

"What does it say?" Ian asks.

I tilt my phone toward him, and he leans over to read the email, his soft hair brushing against my cheek and filling my brain with unwelcome, attractive thoughts.

"Are you fucking kidding me?" he says, his voice echoing in the vast common room. He furrows his thick, neatly groomed brows and scoffs, shaking his head. "Their solution is to put you on a *cot* in the *gym*?"

I nod. "Yeah, it sounds like"—*shit*—"crap, but what else can I do?"

"You're welcome to stay with me, Cal. Say the word, and we can head to mine."

Woah, that's so *generous*, which means there's no way I can take him up on that. "Thank you, but I shouldn't impose."

He lets out a humored huff and bites his tongue in a way that shouldn't be as endearing as it is. "Again, it's not imposing when someone *offers*, Callum."

"I don't want to accept help."

His face falls a tiny bit, and I don't have time to think about why. Maybe he's lonely.

Probably not—he's got friends.

Shoot, I might have been rude.

"It's up to you," he says after a few seconds. "The offer still stands, though, and let me know if you need anything."

"Sure. And yeah, I appreciate the offer, but I want to take care of myself. It's, I don't know, a me thing."

"Hyper-independence," he says with a dry smile. "Be careful with that."

Yeah, the last thing I want is to rely on anyone else. Hyper-independence, if it is what it sounds like, doesn't seem like the worst thing for me to be.

"Anyway," I say, "I'll check out the sleeping arrangements after dinner. They can't be that bad."

Ian hesitates for a moment. "Sounds good. Hope it's decent there."

———

It isn't decent—it's grim. It's so freaking grim.

Fluorescent white light washes over the basketball court from above. Camp beds are placed into rows from wall to wall, with only a few feet between each of them. And on said camp beds? One scratchy-looking blanket. No pillow.

I try not to think about how long I might have to sleep here.

There's a sleeping assignment diagram stuck to the folded bleachers on the far end of the gym, so I head over, backpack in tow, and weave through the grumbling crowd of displaced students as I wait my turn to check.

As soon as I haul myself over and settle into bed 68F, I groan. There's no mattress and no give, and I'm underneath a stupid light that may as well have been designed to burn my retinas to a crisp. Closing my eyelids doesn't help at all, like how facing the sun with closed eyes still causes damage.

I can only hope that someone turns the lights off at some point, but right as that optimistic idea enters my head, a disgruntled member of the admin staff mumbles into a microphone and clarifies that no, they can't do that because of security risks.

From the way the entire population of the gym yells out in protest, I'm beginning to think that this horde of angry students will pose a greater security risk than a little darkness.

Groaning to myself, I reach for my phone and hover over the messaging app. For a second, I contemplate texting Ian and asking him if I can sleep at his apartment, even if it's just for tonight.

Then I wipe that intrusive thought right out of my brain.

It's almost ten, and he might be asleep. There's no way I'm doing that.

Instead, I grab my jacket, the same one Ian gave me, and wrap it around my head to block the light out.

As for the noise, it doesn't do much. I can't have everything. I'm used to it.

———

The next morning, I wake up with heavy eyelids and a coil of sleep-deprived frustration brewing in my gut. My phone says it's already nine, so I scrub a hand across my face and swing my legs over the side of the cot, untangling my jacket and putting it on. There are a couple of texts on my phone, so I answer them, hoping that using my brain will wake me up.

LAURA PIERRE

Yo

I heard the school made you guys sleep in the gym?

Yeah. Rough night

Damn

You're welcome to crash at me and Sabrina's place

Is this...a thing? Do people here really open their houses to someone they've met twice?

Ian offered for me to stay at his but I didn't
want to intrude

Omg Callum

You're too nice

He says it's hyper independence

And he's right. Are you going to keep living in
the gym?

Admin is gonna announce living arrangements
today

At least that's what they say

That's good at least

Then I switch to Ian.

IAN SCOTT

Hey man how'd you sleep?

Bad

They couldn't turn the lights off

Wtf

Are they at least feeding you?

I glance off to the side and see some tired residence employees unpack a box of sandwich ingredients. And then another box, full of the same thing.

Come on, what's the word? It's so basic.

I know it in French—*pain*, which is fitting.

What the hell? Why can I only remember the word for the toast precursor in French? I can barely string a sentence together in that godforsaken language.

I think they'll give us untoasted toast

Untoasted toast?

Bread?

That's the word.

I'm so tired

Sorry

Omw. Hang tight

Hang tight for what?

I get my answer a few minutes later when Ian strides into the gym holding a metal flask and a paper bag. He scans the room, breaking into a soft smile when he sees me.

His approaching figure is backlit by the sun shining through the door, which catches on his dark blond hair and makes it glow. My god, he's *so* cute, and I'm way too tired to fight it, especially when his athletic physique somehow manages to show through the thick jacket he's wearing.

His steps slow as he gets closer. By the time he reaches my cot, that smile of his has turned into a concerned frown.

"Holy shit, Cal. You look *tired*."

CHAPTER NINE
IAN

The man sitting in front of me looks like that rotten pine tree fell on *him* instead of on Maple Hall. Callum's eyes are bloodshot and ringed with darkness, his eyebrows are pulled into a resigned frown, and his skin lacks its usual glow.

If he was anyone else, I'd say he looks awful, but Callum is Callum, so that would never be a true statement.

I snap out of my thoughts, thrusting the muffin and the flask of coffee into his hands, desperate to help somehow.

Callum stares at his food. "What's this?"

"A better breakfast than untoasted toast," I say, trying to lighten the mood.

He takes a long sip of the coffee, not saying a word, and then bites into the muffin. The noise he makes is halfway between a moan and a whine—it's quiet, but audible enough.

"This is so good," he whispers. "Thank you."

I give him a gentle clap on the shoulder. "No problem, man. I didn't know how you take your coffee, so I just made you my usual latte. I take it you *really* didn't sleep well?"

If he forgot the word for *bread*, I don't necessarily need him to answer me.

"No." He devours the rest of the muffin, and I kick myself for only bringing one. "At least I only have to put up with it for another night."

"Hopefully they find some kind of decent living arrangement for you." As soon as I finish that sentence, the students around me murmur in hushed tones, before rapidly getting louder.

A lot louder.

Some of them are shouting, and the few admin staff who were creeping around the gym perimeter make a break for the exit.

"We got an email," he says, glancing at his phone.

"What does it say?"

He squints, his head dropping toward me a few times, and I instinctively stick my arm around his shoulders to give him support. "I'm too tired to read right now." Callum's voice is weaker than I've ever heard it, and he's not a loud guy to begin with. "Can you help me out?"

Did he—

He asked me for help, and I won't make a big deal out of it.

"Of course." I take his phone and scroll back to the top of the email to read it.

And then I read it again.

Then I scan the main part a third time, in case my reading comprehension flew out the fucking window.

Nope, I'm seeing things right. The university's so-called careful, meticulous planning apparently resulted in the most boneheaded solution that's ever cursed my eyeballs: busing the one hundred and fifty affected students to and from hotels in St. Johnsbury.

Almost forty minutes away from campus.

In another *state*.

And the one hundred and fifty students will be three or four to a room.

"What does it say?" Callum's voice snaps me back to the more pressing issue at hand: the fact that he's about to be completely *shafted* by WMU.

I hand his phone back. "Uh, they're sticking you in a hotel. In Vermont. With two roommates. Or up to three."

Callum seems to wake up upon hearing that, and he groans. "Are you kidding me?" He scans the email before shutting his phone off. "That's... I don't know how to describe it."

"Bullshit?" I supply.

"Yeah, that." He doesn't say anything else, choosing instead to bury his face in his hands and sigh, clenching a fist through his dark brown hair.

Yeah. This man is *spent*.

I hesitate for a moment, hovering awkwardly above him. He turned me down yesterday when I offered for him to live with me. But that was before he had an idea of how incompetent this school's administration is, and how horrific his living prospects are.

I settle next to Callum on the creaky cot. "You know, my offer still stands. I live a lot closer to campus than Vermont. Say the word, and I'll set my couch up for you."

He takes his head out of his hands and blinks his red-streaked eyes at me. He opens his mouth, almost as if there are words *physically* on the tip of his tongue, but it still takes him a second to speak.

"That's so generous of you, but I can't. Thanks though."

I don't know if it's stubbornness or something else. Callum is one tough cookie.

Cookies aren't meant to be tough. Crispy, sure, but the center still needs to have some give.

Maybe I can bake him cookies and tempt him into a better living arrangement. I gave him the last of my most recent batch yesterday.

Fuck no. That'd be too much.

Wait, is he turning me down because *I'm* being too much?

Shit.

I fire off a text to Sabrina.

> Is it a bad idea to invite Callum to live with me bc of the maple hall sitch

SABRINA FOSTER

> No that's super sweet

> Unless you still like him and you're using this as an excuse to creep

I'm ninety-nine percent sure I don't have a crush on him, and the one percent that remains should be manageable given that it's one-sided as hell.

> Omg no I stopped liking him ages ago

> Then why'd you have to ask me?

> He keeps saying no to my offer

> So I thought I might be giving off bad vibes

> One sec

Callum taps me on the shoulder. "I've received instructions." He hands his phone over.

> LAURA PIERRE
>
> Stop being polite and go live with Ian
>
> Pls
>
> Or at least live with me and Sabrina but trust me, Ian's place is way nicer
>
> Just don't live in Vermont
>
> Not that Vermont is bad but WMU ISN'T IN VERMONT

The two of us share a quick chuckle.

"The council has decided for you," I say, and Callum shrugs.

"I'll be quiet, and I'll stay out of the way."

I scoff. "The fuck you will. You're getting the living room to yourself." I hardly even react to him recoiling because I'm already plotting out how I'm gonna rearrange the furniture.

"Don't let me take over your house." his voice somehow gets even quieter, and I sling a friendly arm around his warm shoulders to reassure him.

"Again, I'm *offering*, dude. Besides, do you know how lonely living alone can be? You'd be doing *me* a favor, too."

That gets a weak huff out of Callum, and he gives me a smile that manages to be tiny yet warm at the same time. "I really appreciate it, Ian. Thank you so much."

I return his tiny smile with a huge one of my own. "Don't even mention it." Rising to my feet, I place a hand on his elbow. "Come on, let's get you moved in."

He shakes his head. "Not now. I have class."

What in the—

This guy survived a night in this dumpy fluorescent hell, and he's *still* concerned about going to class?

"Dude, you need to *sleep*, not go to class."

His arm tenses, and I don't know if he's about to hug me or punch me in the face.

He does neither. "I'm fine, but thanks. It's only one class, so I'll live."

"Okay. And that email said you can clear your room today. I can help with that if you'd like."

"I won't need it. I don't have much, but thank you."

"Sounds good," I say. "I'll swing by in a few hours to pick you up?"

Callum nods. "Sure. I'll text you."

Everything in me is telling me to give him a hug, but knowing him, he'd probably try to pay me for it, so I don't, settling for a clap to his shoulder instead. "Awesome. I'll head out and set my place up."

I give him a fist bump before leaving, shivering as I make the short, frigid walk back to my place.

"I'm not being too much, am I?" I wonder out loud to myself. I don't think of an easy reply to my own speculation, so I decide to weigh both sides.

He's my friend. I get along well with him. He's in need, and I'd do this for *any* of my friends.

On the flip side, I've known him for a month, and he's the very definition of walking, talking temptation. I've been able to keep my head on mostly straight, but this is different. He's gonna be living with me, maybe for months.

I let out a deep sigh as I climb the steps to my apartment. Yes, Callum is attractive, but above everything else, he's my friend. I can keep myself in check, and I'm gonna give him the privacy he'll want and need.

That's how I find myself rotating a bookshelf to make a barrier between the dining area and the couch. If I leave the hallway closet door open, the living room is completely blocked off.

I drag the coffee table into the middle of the room and then unfold the couch. I got a fold-out so that friends could crash if needed, and I'm feeling pretty vindicated by that decision right now.

That's a mini-workout by itself, so I take a quick shower before putting the final touches on the makeshift bedroom—sheets, pillow, blankets, and a spare phone charger. No sooner than I've finished, Callum texts me to say that he's finished packing. I guess he wasn't kidding about not having a lot of stuff.

———

Callum has one backpack and a plastic container provided by admin.

That's *it*.

I'm standing on the sidewalk outside his barricaded dorm, trying not to think about how this man survives. Yes, I know my consumption habits verge on maximalism, but the container isn't big enough to hold more than a week's worth of clothes. I wouldn't be surprised if it rattles when he starts walking.

It doesn't, but then again, his clothes could be padding things.

"Here, let me load the car. Make yourself comfortable," I say after a few seconds, gesturing to the passenger door.

He doesn't object, handing me the container and settling into the passenger seat. He must be exhausted.

Yup, I'm right—he's already snoozing when I get in next to him. I flip on electric mode so it's quiet on the short drive back to my place.

Or is it *our* place now?

It's our place. Fuck, living alone can suck ass sometimes.

Hardly anyone else is on the road, so it's smooth sailing. Callum stays dead to the world, at least until my backup camera beeps at me for parking too close to the wall.

He stirs, blinking those willpower-melting eyes. "Did I fall asleep?"

"Yeah."

"Oh, shit. Sorry."

Wait. Did he—

He said *shit*. I don't think I've ever heard him swear before.

I will *not* make a big deal about it.

"Don't apologize. Let's get you moved in." I walk around to the passenger door and open it for Callum before he has a chance to unbuckle himself, and I extend a hand to help his lethargic ass out.

His hands are so warm. Like that voice of his—

No. Bad Ian.

I don't let myself say another word or think another thought as I carry Callum's stuff up to the apartment. He follows right behind me the whole way, and I'm itching to get out of the frigid hallway. For how premium this building is, or claims to be, they sure don't turn the heating on in the common areas.

"You moved the bookshelf."

That's the first thing he says after we step inside.

I shrug, trying to play it cool. "Yeah, it's better for privacy and whatnot. Here, I'll show you around your new digs."

We slip past the bookshelf into the living room, and Callum puts his bag down before sitting on the corner of the pullout couch, taking up so little space that I'm not entirely sure how he's balancing his body.

He's going to sleep here, so I sure hope he gets used to occupying more space.

Wait, what if he doesn't get used to it? What if he sleeps on the floor to keep my couch free?

What if he tries to sleep *outside*?

I should have chained the balcony door shut, just in case.

"You set all this up for me?" he asks, fixating on the pillow at the end of the couch.

"Yeah. You got dealt a bad hand with your dorm getting destroyed, but you're my buddy. Of course I'm going to help out."

Callum purses his lips together and makes a slow slide backward, finally occupying a little more than a solitary square inch of seating space.

I don't think I've ever met someone quite as hesitant as this guy. It's almost like—

It's almost like he isn't used to someone caring about him.

No, it can't be. Not *Callum*. Sure, he's way too polite, like, all the time, but there has to be another reason why me giving him a pillow rendered him speechless—*someone* has to have cared about him before.

"You didn't have to—" He snaps me back to reality, and I scoff.

"Shut up, man," I say with a smirk, giving his shoulders a friendly shove that sends him falling backward onto his new bed. "You're gonna take up space here, *or else*. Got it?"

Callum nods, and I beam back at him.

"Good boy." I pat him on the head, and he blushes, forcing back a strained snort.

Sheesh, I'm odd. Why did I have to do that? Callum isn't Nick.

"I'm, uh—do you want a house tour?" I ask, changing the subject.

He says yes and scrambles up, so I show him the laundry closet, the bathroom where he puts a single bottle of three-in-one, and then I end the tour in the kitchen.

"You have a *really* nice place," he says.

"Yeah, I try to keep it cozy and stuff." I just smile—I'm very aware that he's completely independent, and I don't want to be an ass and humble-brag about how my parents got this apartment as an investment property.

"So, uh, I should have asked earlier, but what's rent gonna be?" He fidgets as he says that, sliding his strong fingers between one another, and it takes me a while to wrap my head around what he means.

Seriously, this guy's dorm got evacuated and—

"You think I'm gonna charge rent for my *couch*?" I ask.

"I mean, it *is* your house," Callum replies.

"Doesn't matter," I say. "Like, if you *need* to make yourself useful or whatever, you can make me coffee if you wake up before I do."

There's a mix of confusion and surprise swirling behind his eyes, and I'm readying up another round of rebuttals before he purses his lips and nods. "Thank you so much. I can do that."

Thank fuck. I've never met anyone who's so reluctant to accept something that's being offered.

"Sounds like a deal. The machine is over there, and it's pretty easy to use," I say, pointing. "But if I wake up before you, how do you take yours?"

"Just black."

"Ooh, tough manly man over here," I tease, lowering my voice.

Callum doesn't laugh. "Yeah, my parents said that's a guy thing, so that's what I had to do."

The words "that's some fucking bullshit" jump to the tip of my tongue, and I purse my lips to hold them back. For all I know, he could *like* his parents despite the fact that they think some weird things.

It's best not to prod. He might even agree with them.

"Anyway, I won't keep you up any longer," I say. "You've had a long-ass day."

Callum lets out a tired breath. "Yeah. I'm gonna shower and sleep, if that's okay." He yawns, managing to appear even sleepier than before. "Oh man, I'm looking forward to having a blanket."

Fuck, this man needs a hug. I'm not gonna force it on him, but I'll extend an offer. Without saying a word, I open my arms, and he moves into them, stiff and a little shaky. He's exuding reluctance, so I don't close around him—there's no way I'm gonna force anything.

Luckily, Callum decides for me. Still stiff as a board, he wraps his arms around my body, and the tension in his muscles is impossible to ignore. I return the hug, keeping my arms a respectable distance above his waist, even though he's a head taller than me.

"Not a hugger, huh?" I ask, preparing to loosen my grip.

"Nah, not really." Instead of pulling away like I expect, he pulls me closer.

Oh. Oh, this is *comfortable*.

That stiffness he had? Gone, like it was never there. And my god, for someone who acted like he's never hugged anyone before...

I mentally retract my initial assessment of Callum not being a hugger. He gives *amazing* hugs, even if this is lasting a little longer than I'd expected.

I don't complain.

"Damn, you needed this, didn't you?" I say.

"You're a great friend, Ian," he replies, not directly answering me. "Thank you so much. Again. I owe you big time." He pulls away, and it might be my annoying brain playing tricks on me, but there's reluctance in his movements.

"Anytime," I reply. "And no, you don't. You don't owe me anything."

CHAPTER TEN
CALLUM

Mmm. Oh man, I'm *warm*. This bed is comfy. It smells so nice here, like cinnamon and some kind of herb and—

And a certain extremely hot man.

Who I now live with.

Who I have a *stupid* crush on.

Shoot. Living with Ian is supposed to save me from sharing a hotel room in Vermont with three other people, but less than a day in, it's already clear that I jumped from the frying pan into the fire. With said fire being lit by Ian with the purest intention of keeping me warm, without him knowing that it's burning me alive.

I let out a frustrated, resigned sigh into the spare pillow he gave me. It's firm and plush and probably costs twice the GDP of my hometown.

What do his not-spare pillows feel like? As soft as his heart?

Oh, god-freaking-damn-it. Why did I have to go there? Especially after yesterday? Hugging Ian the way I did made me feel filthy. Even though he's the most laid-back guy I've ever met, not that I've met very many, I can't stop thinking that I'm taking advantage of him.

He offered to let me stay here, but I'm still taking up his living room. Strike one.

Strike two is the fact that I hugged him with *way* more intention than he did. He initiated, but in a friendly, reassuring way. Feeling his solid body on mine made something in me snap, and I *took*. I wrapped my arms around his muscular shoulders, breathed in the smell of his masculine shampoo, and let myself get all mushy and lusty over a guy who's been nothing but good to me.

Why am I like this? All weak over something that should be normal.

Before I can talk myself down from the scary cliff of inappropriate feelings, I hear some kind of clatter behind the bookshelf, and then Ian muttering a muffled curse. After slipping on my hoodie to cover my rumpled hair, I step into the dining room to find him putting jelly on a piece of bread with slow, cautious movements.

"Oh, hey," he says, focusing on his bread. "Did I wake you up?"

"Nah, I've been awake for a while," I lie. It's almost noon, and I really made up for my night in the gym by staying dead to the world for who knows how long.

Ian nods before putting the jar back in the fridge, and the difference in how he's walking is noticeable. Or rather, it's audible because now, I can hear him.

"Were you trying to be quiet before I came out here?" I ask, caution lining my voice.

"Yeah, didn't want to disturb you, not after your night in the gym."

A pang of guilt slams into my stomach. This is why I didn't want to stay here—I'm making Ian slink around his own apartment.

"You don't have to do that. Don't let me make you feel uncomfortable or anything."

He waves me off with a chuckle, one that's a lot more at ease than I would have expected. "Dude, I'm not uncomfortable."

Then why was he walking around on tiptoes?

"And even if I was," he continues, "there's no way that'd be anywhere near as bad as the alternative. If I have to be a little quiet, it's no big deal, as long as it means you're not hauling yourself to and from Vermont every day."

I know Ian's words should be reassuring, but they don't settle me. "Sure, just let me know if I can make this easier for you."

He sighs, leaning against the dining table. He faces me, and his eyes soften. "Cal, you're *way* too nice. I invited you to stay here. You're allowed to exist, man."

I'm about to agree, if reluctantly, when a yawn cuts me off. I stretch up, and when I bring my arms down and my attention back to Ian, he's looking away.

"I gotta, uh, take a leak," he says, darting down the hallway.

Okay. That was abrupt.

Remembering my responsibility to make coffee in lieu of rent, I amble into the kitchen and take stock of the machine. There's a tube leading into a metal box off to the side. It's a mini-fridge full of milk.

He has a separate fridge for the milk he makes coffee with. Holy crap, we lead totally different lives.

I press the most worn-down button on the machine, and it spits out a drink, and once it's done, I make a normal coffee for myself. Ian comes back right as it's finishing up, so I hand him his mug.

"Did you make me coffee? You know I was kidding about that being your rent, right?" He takes a sip before I can think of a reply to fumble through, and then his eyes widen. "It's a latte. You actually remembered what I drink."

I nod, and before I can tell Ian that the faded latte button on the machine was a convenient reminder, he puts the mug down to launch into a hug.

"Broski, oh my god. Absolutely no homo whatsoever, but I fucking love you."

No homo. If only he knew. He sure wouldn't say he loves me, even as a joke.

"It isn't a huge deal," I mumble. That's all I can muster before something raw and tender crashes into me. It's like hugging Ian saps all the reluctance and tension out of me, replacing it with helpless affection, and I can't do anything but hold him back.

Even when it means a lot more to me than it does to him.

Then, right as the warmth in me risks slipping down to somewhere entirely inappropriate, he jerks back and pulls away, the absence searing my skin and tempting me to grab him back.

"Yeah, uh, anyway, thanks," he mutters, scratching the back of his head. "I gotta head to practice, and I'll be back late tonight." He dumps the coffee into a travel mug and shoves a couple of protein bars into his backpack. "The season's starting pretty soon, so you might not see too much of me. I'll send you my schedule."

And then he's gone, leaving me alone in his apartment where I'm still out of place. It takes a few seconds for me to get my bearings, and once I do, I realize I'm wrapping an arm around my waist where Ian was hugging me only a few minutes ago.

I tense up, shaking my head, and my phone beeps with a text. As promised, it's Ian's schedule.

IAN SCOTT

Hey man, here's my schedule, FYI

Basically I'm gonna be out of the house by 8 AM on Mon/Wed/Fri, and by noon on Tues/Thurs. I won't be back before 7 PM on weekdays but realistically I'll be home closer to 9

That's a long time to spend out of the house. What's he doing?

Fucking baseball practice lmao

Makes sense.

Weekends are a bit of a crapshoot tbh but I'm out doing stuff most days

You don't have to send me your schedule. I'll be gone more than you so you can have the house to yourself

My stomach sinks. Is that why Ian's planning to be gone for so long?

Is he trying to avoid me?

I down my coffee and retreat to the couch, curling up under the thick covers, trying to talk myself out of all this negativity.

Realistically, I haven't done anything wrong. Ian told me to move in with him. So did Laura. It's been one night, and he hasn't said anything.

Then again, he could have been impulsive. Maybe his morning routine includes watching TV on the couch that I've robbed from him. He might have had a realization overnight.

Pinching the bridge of my nose, I let out a slow exhale. There's no use dwelling on something unconfirmed. I drag myself off of the couch and get ready for a day of studying here, and I work through a few assignments that I've been neglecting. Other than grabbing food and bathroom breaks, I don't leave the dining table, and it's almost eight when my phone lights up with another text from Ian.

> Hey bro I'm heading home from practice, I'll be back in 5

I type the last few sentences of my French assignment and run it through a grammar checker, and I upload it right as I hear a key in the lock, turning slowly before the handle jiggles a few times.

Does he know how to unlock his own door? I stand up, walk over, and pull the door open.

Ian tumbles forward, falling face-first into me. He lets out a yelp of surprise, and I stick my arms out to catch him.

And my hands happen to snag on his clothes, slipping underneath them.

Oh, Jesus, I'm touching his bare skin. He's so smooth and warm, and my fingers slip into the wonderful little dips of his back muscles.

I yank him upright and withdraw my pawing hands. "Are you okay?"

"Yeah. Thanks for catching me," he says. He straightens and

smooths his sweater down. It's a baseball team hoodie, partially unzipped and revealing a flash of his green practice uniform. "How was your day?"

"Good, I just...studied." *And tried not to overthink you.*

He gives me a small nod before shedding his sweater, his arms stretching the fabric of his uniform and making my mouth go dry. I choose to straighten my sneakers on the shoe rack to stop myself from staring.

"Sorry, I stink," he says, stepping aside. "Let me go shower."

My eyes follow him down the hallway as he walks away, and instead of averting my gaze like a decent person when he yanks his jersey off, I linger for a few seconds. Holy crap, those are some broad shoulders. And holy crap, that back is something else—

Oh, come on. I can't keep doing this. He's already avoiding me, intentionally or not, and I'm living in his house fixating on the dimples in his back muscles, for Christ's sake.

The same ones I felt underneath my own fingertips not two minutes ago.

Shaking my head, I head for the couch and try to relax.

I'll stay out of his way. I'll give him space, give him my schedule, and pick up some more late shifts in the library to give him some peace and quiet at night. That's the only decent thing to do.

———

The supply room in the library is where I take my breaks at work, and I'm sitting in silence.

The door swings open, and it's Ian. My heart flips, and for the first time, I don't stop myself.

"Hey." None of what he says after that registers because I can't focus. He's wearing a green tank top and shorts, neither of which leave *anything* to the imagination.

Jesus Christ, he's *so fucking hot.* He waves at me, still talking, and his arm flexes in a way that makes my dick firm up. He walks toward me, scratching the back of his head like he always does, but this time, he's in that tank top so I get an eyeful of *everything*, even the divot in his armpit. How is it possible for me to find that irresistible, too?

"I really wanted to see you," Ian says, snapping me back to reality, or what I *think* is reality because I'm not sure what's real anymore, and—

Oh, god, I'm in heaven—he's straddling me! Ian is straddling me, and his tank top is gone and he's pressing his lips to mine and his hands are in my pants, and it feels so good. So fucking good. Way too good. I'm gonna—

I wake up right as I come. *Hard.* I let out a low groan as sparks surge down to my toes, my core tightening as the pleasure courses through me. Holy shit, that's so good.

Disoriented, I blink into the blurry morning light as I get my bearings, and my foggy, blissed-out confusion is replaced with the worst sense of dread I've felt in years.

My chest tightens as I force my way through deep, harsh breaths.

I had a sex dream about Ian.

Ian.

The guy who's been nothing but kind to me and hasn't asked for anything in return. For crying out loud, he *took me into his house* and then my depraved brain had to use him for something awful, and I'm not even a *week* into living with him.

I roll over to jam my face into the pillow, and the movement presses my release into my leg, reminding me, again, that I'm disgusting.

Ian is too good to me. I don't... No. I don't deserve a friend like him. All I'll do is mess this up, like I did just now.

A door opens. *Oh, shoot. He's up.*

"Hey, man, are you awake?" Ian calls out from the other side of the bookshelf, and the fact that he's cheery instead of grossed out manages to make my chest lighter.

Right. He doesn't know I had a wet dream about him, so of course he's still being nice to me.

The weight returns.

"Y-yeah," I manage. "Still in bed though."

"Nice. Anyway, I'm going to work out, and I won't be back until late tonight as usual. There's breakfast in the oven if you want any."

"Awesome, thanks," I reply before realizing that I spoke like Ian does. There's no way I would have said *awesome* a month ago.

The front door clicks shut, and I'm left alone with the renewed realization that all I do is take from him.

His food. His living room. His privacy. I can add his body, consent, and even the way he *talks* to that long, shameful list.

I need to stop whatever it is I'm doing. Ian doesn't need to have a voyeur sleeping on his couch. While I've tried to keep myself under wraps, I have a feeling that I'm not being as subtle as I'd hoped, given his constant absence and meticulous scheduling.

It's like he's sick of me already.

The thought makes my core sink. I don't want to keep thinking this way about him, and I don't want to lose the first friend I've had in years.

I've got to get better. I'm trying, but it needs to happen, and fast.

So I do the only thing I can think of and reach for my phone to schedule another appointment with Anita, and thankfully, thankfully, she has drop-in slots open today.

I was doing so well and crawling out of my own hole until I betrayed myself and started lusting after the guy who least deserves it.

Wincing, I push myself off of the couch and strip the sheets, throwing them into the washing machine on my way to the bathroom. While I wait for the shower to warm up, I scrub my boxers with cold water and hand soap the way I always have. Back at home, I had to hide all evidence of my involuntary, dirty transgressions, and I now know that nothing has changed.

Into the shower I go, and I use a lot more pressure than usual when cleaning myself off. I'm no dirtier than normal, at least above my waist and below my knees, but I *feel* like I am. There's something tenacious settling across my body, so I stop just short of scraping my skin off with my fingernails.

I do the same in my groin, where I really need it.

My dick stiffens, clearly missing the memo.

No. Down. You've done enough for today.

My shaft pulses in protest as I yank my hand away, and I hiss a frustrated breath through my teeth, rinsing the soap off and thinking about all the assignments I haven't done as an ineffective distraction.

Water off, towel dry, get dressed. Then I'm off to my impromptu appointment where I'll hopefully get my bearings, and some advice on how to control myself.

"Hi, Callum," Anita says as I walk into her office. "How are you?"

I offer a noncommittal, "I'm okay, thanks."

"What brings you here last-minute?"

After leaning forward in the armchair and picking at a fingernail, I catch her up on the whole dorm evacuation and moving in with Ian, before pausing to consider how I can explain my crush without looking like a total perverted creep.

While I've mentioned him before, she doesn't know the full extent of how bad I have it for him. Not yet.

"I also have constant, unwelcome, and inappropriate thoughts about him," I say. "It isn't fair to him that I think about him like that."

Anita takes a quiet breath, finishing up a note in my file. "Are you doing anything differently, either in your thinking or your behavior around him?"

"My thinking?" I grit my teeth. "Same as always—I'm telling myself that this isn't right and that I need to fix it. And I'm trying not to be weird around him, but hey, I'm me, so that's easier said than done."

Anita doesn't laugh at my poorly timed levity, and she puts her pen down, fixing me with a softer expression than I've seen her use before. "Intimate thoughts about someone you're attracted to are completely natural."

"Yeah, I *know* that, but it still feels wrong to keep having them. He doesn't know I'm gay, and I just *know* he doesn't want me to be attracted to him." Rubbing the bridge of my nose, I search for the right words. "I guess I'm too weak to properly control myself."

"So let me get things straight," she starts. "You say Ian is kind, friendly, he opened his house to you with no strings attached, and on top of that, you found him attractive as soon as you saw him."

I nod, and heat floods my ears. "Yeah, he's kind of irresistible."

"You aren't weak for liking him," Anita says firmly. "You're allowed to like him. But if it's not reciprocated like you say, it's important to manage that so it doesn't consume you."

"Sounds easy enough," I say. "What would that look like?"

"Do you think it might be helpful to get some distance from time to time?"

"We live together," I remind her.

Anita offers me a warm smile. "Physical distance isn't all that matters. For a start, you could see friends who aren't Ian. That's not to say you two *can't* spend time together, but for a while, you could let him initiate plans instead, if you're the one suggesting them."

My mind replays the start of our most recent hangouts, and pretty much all of them, save for a couple of workouts or study sessions here and there, were because he asked me. So I tell her.

"Right, so he keeps himself busy, but often invites you to spend time together," Anita repeats. It seems like she's thinking or holding back *something*, but I can't tell what. "I can also suggest time, because it hasn't been very long. He sounds like a very good friend, and after a while, it's possible that you accept him in that role, rather than as an unrequited interest."

"It's already been a month," I mutter. "Shouldn't that be long enough?"

It certainly should have been long enough to not have a wet dream about him, and to shut down the wild, dangerous fantasies that creep into my brain every time he does something cute. Which, given who he is, is *everything* he does.

I swear, watching him rub his eyebrow when he's tired shouldn't make me lose my breath.

"Emotions are complicated, Callum. That's one of the reasons why I'm here." She writes a few notes into her tablet before continuing. "For now, you could try making that space, and if you continue feeling bad about having these thoughts, you can always use some of the anxiety exercises we've worked through."

Oh, right. Those. I haven't needed to break those out too often, but I suppose they could work on my ever-increasing spirals about how much I like Ian.

The rest of our session is spent reviewing the various anxiety and grounding exercises we've discussed before, and I leave feeling okay—better than before, but not great. Still, I need time to get over him, and it's only been hours.

Once I'm back at Ian's place, I shake my jacket off and grab my laptop to get some work done. The second I sink into the couch, there's jangling at the door, and my breath catches.

He's back. The sound of keys shaking in the lock continues for a little too long, as usual, followed by the door creaking open.

It's not that heavy, and he's an athlete. He's doing that on purpose. Again, he's tiptoeing around me, and that makes my gut plummet.

Ian comes crashing in, dropping his snow jacket to reveal his baseball uniform. Right. He started outdoor training for the season today, hence his lack of a hoodie.

Why on earth do baseball players have such tight uniforms?

He's facing away from me to hang his jacket and gear up, and my eyes stay glued to those pants. They're so frustratingly form-fitting, especially around his butt. That makes my mouth dry and wakes my dick up.

So much for seeing him as a friend.

I avert my gaze to the safety of my laptop mere milliseconds before Ian turns to me. Deciding to be friendly, I give him the kind of upward nod he always gives to me, and his face lights up.

That tiny little action sends delightful sparks into my tailbone.

"You wake up from a nap?" he asks, walking over.

"No, why?"

Ian's eyes crinkle at the corner as he grins at me. "Your hair is kinda messy."

Crap. I bring a hand to my head and try to smooth the unruly strands.

"Hey, I didn't say that was a bad thing," he says. "I kinda dig the relaxed vibe."

"Yeah?"

"For sure!" He somehow manages to smile even wider, and my stomach manages to flip even more. "Tell you what, you should snag some of my hair paste and make your hair all scruffy."

Make myself look disheveled on purpose? That sounds like the best way to make people stare at me even more than they do already. "You think so?"

He remains undeterred. "Totally. Cute, rugged hair on a guy like you? Chick magnet, guaran-fucking-teed..." He trails off, his face firming up. "Anyway. You got any plans tonight?"

Yeah, following Anita's advice and trying not to fall harder for you.

I shake my head instead. "What about you?"

"Me neither. I thought about having some friends over, but some one-on-one dude time with you sounds better. Other than, like, hitting the gym, we haven't really hung out since you moved in, and I really want to do that tonight if you're down."

Ian wants to hang out. With me. Alone.

That should be the worst thing for me and my lack of self-regulation, but I smile and nod instead because he made my night, simply by wanting to spend time together.

CHAPTER ELEVEN
IAN

Do not fixate on Callum's hair. Do not focus on how fucking hot his bedhead is. Do not stare at his sexy stubble that's contouring his handsome face and framing it like it's the damn Mona Lisa.

Yeah, no. I can't. What's the point of telling myself not to do something as I'm actively doing it? There *isn't* a point, so I ignore my logic and let my eyes roam all over Callum's body. That shirt he's wearing certainly isn't helping me stop—it's a basic, boxy T-shirt, but on him, it might as well be tailored athletic wear, hugging his strong chest and accentuating it in a way I appreciate like hell.

I turn away before I can make a fool of myself. "I'm grabbing a beer. You want one?"

"Yeah, thank you," he calls out, and I head for the kitchen.

My attraction isn't out of hand, but it's still there, no thanks to Callum being gorgeous as heck.

Honestly, I can't blame myself for finding a hot guy hot. I'm only human.

Okay, and he's more than hot, but being a great guy is good for friendship, too.

Besides, am I smiling and kicking my feet over Callum and jerking off to the thought of him? No, absolutely the fuck not. What is happening, though, are intrusive thoughts that are becoming less intrusive and more incessant.

Case in point: my general inability to focus doesn't apply to Callum. His back is turned to me as he works on a paper or something, and I have to snap myself out of staring at those muscles twitching under his shirt.

I think he's straight. My little quip about him being a chick magnet wasn't met with the "I'm gay, actually" that would've made me forever grateful to the universe. He's given off exactly zero indications that he's anything but straight, but I need him to confirm it once and for all.

That can happen in one of three ways.

One, I can ask him directly. *"Hey, man, kinda random question, but are you straight?"*

I don't want to think about how he might react.

Two, I could take him out to a frat party, introduce him to a group of willing women, and observe.

That'd be a total dick move, and then I'd get all jealous over the overwhelming action he'd attract.

Three, I could come out to him myself and see how he reacts.

Not the worst option. I'll go with that.

I'm halfway through pouring Callum a beer when I have to yank my arm against my side.

God, I *reek*.

Okay, it's not that bad, thanks to my regimented hygiene routine, but still. Callum has to put up with my perpetual athlete BO while he smells like the concentrated essence of every hot man on earth.

I hooked up with a guy about a year ago who had the same maddening, intoxicating musk about him, and he kicked me out before I could ask him what cologne he used. Now I know it's an antiperspirant called Ocean Ice, judging from the stick Callum keeps next to his toothbrush. It's the cheapest option in that aisle of the drugstore, and that's enough to stretch my self-control to the absolute limit.

Unavailable men have something about them, I swear. I want what I can't have.

Keeping my arm pinned to my side, I deliver Callum his beer and stand a safe distance back to plan our dude night. "It's kinda chilly, so I was thinking we could stay in and watch a movie or something. I gotta shower first, though. Sorry for the stink."

"Don't worry about it. You're fine. That sounds good."

Smiling, I head for the bathroom. Callum is so chill and agreeable. I wish I could be more like him. It must be nice, not overthinking everything on earth, and not having to tamp down a crush on every attractive person who shows me basic decency.

I rinse off, towel myself dry, and put my own boring, unscented deodorant on before getting dressed and heading back out. When I round the corner, I find that Callum has changed out of his jeans and into sweats and a soft-looking gray hoodie that clings to him. The hood is up, covering his eyes, and the mere sight of Callum, asleep and adorable, slams me with a tidal wave of unwelcome arousal.

God, or whatever's up there, please fucking help me.

He's minding his own business, nothing more. He's wearing *multiple* layers, yet my stupid body reacts as though he's buck naked and bending me over the dining table, holding me in place with those big hands and screwing my brains out—

Holy shit, he's the worst kind of trouble, and he isn't doing anything to warrant that label.

I have half a mind to nip into my room so I can take care of this awful spike of testosterone, but Callum chooses that moment to wake up, removing the hood and blinking his tired, lethally beautiful eyes at me.

With all the finesse I can muster, I plonk down into the armchair across from him and bring a pillow into my lap. I can blame the heat in my cheeks on the shower I just took, but I don't want to explain why I have a semi from watching Callum scratch his sharp, stubbled jaw.

Yeah, I need to open that door so he can slam it shut for good.

"Did you have a good nap?" I ask.

He yawns, flopping back against the couch. "Kinda. I'm still super tired, so I might not be a lot of fun tonight."

"No worries. We don't have to do anything too wild."

"Are you sure you don't want to hang out with your friends instead?"

I'm about to shut that self-criticism down before I pause, unease stabbing into my stomach and making me sweat.

Does Callum think he's not one of my friends?

Does Callum think *I'm* not one of *his* friends?

I swallow the lump in my throat. "You *are* one of my friends, at least I *think* so. Do you...not want to be?"

The familiar twist of rejection is already squeezing my chest, and keeping my breathing normal is proving to be a lot harder than it needs to be. If Callum says no, I don't know how I'll react.

His eyebrows shoot up. "I do. I want to be friends with you."

Oh, thank fuck. Just like that, almost all the pressure in my body flies out in a heavy exhale. "Then what's the problem? Let's hang out tonight."

"Yeah, let's do that." He pinches the bridge of his nose between his hands. "Sorry for being weird. I hate, you know, imposing and stuff."

I kinda got that, which is why I'm giving him as much privacy as I can manage. If he won't ask for things, it's on me to meet his needs however I can.

"Alright, no imposing tonight because I'll give you whatever you need. Nick bought me some messed-up liquor the other day. It's like 120-proof. Wanna try?"

Callum offers me a strained smile. "Sounds like a plan. Thanks for suggesting it."

"Awesome. Let's get drunk."

CHAPTER TWELVE
CALLUM

Apparently, I'm a tired drunk. That's what Ian calls me, at least. We're both sitting on the couch that's my bed, and I'm hugging a pillow, trying to keep my eyes open.

"You've had four drinks, Cal. You can't fall asleep on me," he says, slinging an arm around my shoulder.

I break into a stupid smile. Cal. God, that nickname is so silly, but it's affectionate. Ian calling me that adds to the warm feeling that's sloshing around inside of me, and I don't know where it came from or what to do with it.

It could be the alcohol.

Who am I kidding? No, it's not. The alcohol is making me tired and smiley. Ian being nice and side-hugging me is making me fuzzy.

Wait, why is he being nice all of a sudden? He was avoiding me until a couple of hours ago.

"Bro, why do you think I'm avoiding you?" His voice cuts through my alcohol-fueled fog, and I jolt upright.

"Shit, did I say that out loud?"

"Yeah, you did. And I'm not avoiding you."

"But...the schedule, and the knocking, and the texting that you're coming back?"

Ian tilts his head, running his tongue along his teeth. "Yeah, I'm doing that to give you privacy, not because I'm uncomfortable."

What? "Why? This is *your* house."

"I know, but you still need alone time. Besides, don't you need space for, like, dude needs?"

"Dude needs?"

He hesitates but regains his confident expression almost immediately. "Yeah, like, jerking off and hooking up."

I choke on my sip of beer and sputter into my almost-empty glass. "Sorry, what?"

Ian doesn't seem to register my confusion. "I mean this in the least homo way possible, but someone who looks the way you do has gotta be balls-deep in...options."

My body is frozen, except for my blindsided, blinking eyes.

Does he seriously *think I'd hook up with someone in his living room?* Is that something other guys would do? Is he confused that I'm not doing that?

"I don't hook up," I clarify. "And I'm not gonna disrespect your space by jerking off in your house," I say, lying through my teeth and purging the quick flashback to yesterday afternoon's shower out of my mind. Sure, I might have been a little weirded out about taking care of myself when I first moved in here, but he's gone a lot. Besides, I have "dude needs," as Ian calls them, and I'm a lot less weird about those now. At least when I manage to keep thoughts of him separate, not like what happened in my sleep this morning.

He sucks in a tight breath, bringing my attention back to him. "Okay, man, I never thought I'd say this, but you're a dude. You have my full permission to jerk off and bring someone home while you're living here. Like, discreetly and whatever." He lets out a weak chuckle. "Jesus, why'd you think I'd have a problem with that?"

"I thought that'd be impolite." I take a swig from my water bottle, hoping the switch away from alcohol brings my brain back to earth. I might be buzzed, but I could stop and change the subject if I wanted to.

Then again, I'm supposed to open up like I said I would. I just never imagined it'd be about *this.*

"Stop me if I say too much, but my parents believed in some messed up things. It was almost like they had their own brand of religion, and even their church didn't go as far." The alcohol's helping me loosen up, that's for sure. "But hey, they started reading some extreme stuff online about living purely and saving your kids, and then there was no stopping them. "

Ian's lips are pressed together, his expression unplaceable and his eyes soft. Even with my limited experience, I can tell there's an absence of judgment in his gaze, a lack of the kind of pity I'm trying to avoid.

There's nothing but sympathy. Care, the kind I've never seen before, deep in the warm hazel.

That's all I need to keep talking. Or rambling. "It was as if I wasn't allowed to feel good, like positivity was a temptation I had to fight." I grab the beer from the coffee table and take a sip, before remembering that it's Ian's, but he simply shrugs and gestures for me to keep it. "Like, it was mostly my mom who went all gung-ho with the weird stuff. My dad didn't seem to be as extreme."

He sucks in a hiss through his gritted teeth. "But he still went along with it, right?"

"He did." I pause, debating whether to allow childhood memories to enter my consciousness, or to shut them out like usual.

I let them in.

"Still, he tried to get me out of the house and stuff, even when my mom took me out of school to 'preserve' me after they committed the unforgivable sin of having sex ed classes," I continue. "My dad was the one who convinced my mom to let me go to community college in the first place, saying it'd help me provide for a future wife and whatnot. He didn't say anything about what my mom did, but at least he was nicer to me, and the only fun I ever had was going hunting with him once in a while."

"The *only* fun you had?"

"I mean, my parents encouraged me to work out, probably because it's a 'guy' thing or whatever, and I'd sometimes go shooting with my dad. But everything else I could have liked was demonized. Books, TV, games, imagining shit in my head that let me escape for a second, and yeah, sex too. *That* was a huge no-no."

"Yet somehow, you came to be," he mutters. "I wonder how that happened."

I scoff, a smile somehow finding its way onto my face. "Tell me about it. There were always exceptions for them and never for me, hence my hang-ups about everything to do with sex."

"Jesus, that fucking sucks. So you just didn't? At all? Even with yourself?"

"Nah, I'm an outlaw," I joke, letting out a breathy chuckle. "Not that it was easy, or pleasant, but I kept my, uh, solo activities under wraps. My mom would have flipped if she knew, and I didn't dare try to find anyone else. Not like I had options in that tiny town."

Ian's face is scrunched into a concerned frown, his eyebrows raised at their inner corners. I expect him to say something, but he shakes his head instead, staying silent.

Not that I necessarily *want* him to keep this topic active—he's gotta be at least a bit uncomfortable with talking about sex.

Pressing his hands together, Ian sighs. "Look, I'm just gonna say it out loud: your parents are pretty messed up for that. I'm glad you got out."

I chuckle. "Ha, yeah. It only took running away from home to change things."

Oh. I went there. Oops.

His head jerks, and he shuffles upright to face me, sitting cross-legged and wide-eyed. "You ran away from home? Like as a kid?"

The truth hangs on my tongue for a moment before rolling off it with way more ease than I thought was possible. "No, in January. I transferred colleges in secret and climbed out of my window at one in the morning to catch a bus."

A slow twist of unease circles my gut as Ian's mouth hangs open, intensifying with every second of sustained silence that passes. *Is he judging me? Is he going to make fun of me? Is he going to kick me out because he doesn't want to host a fugitive?*

Oh, god, he's—

Hugging me.

Ian is hugging me again. The gnawing in my stomach dissolves. He's almost a foot shorter than me, yet he's the one wrapped around my shoulders like I'm small.

"Fuck, Callum," he mutters. His grip tightens, grounding me to the point where I almost don't care about the pity that's about to follow. "It's so fucked that you had to go through all that. It sounds awful."

There it is.

"But that was so brave. I'm glad you made it here."

Like an idiot, I melt into Ian. I don't even care about how weird it is for me to feel as safe as I do when I'm with him like this. He said I needed a hug when I first moved in; I did back then, and my god, I still do now. I'm getting everything I never had and always missed.

He pulls away after a while, and I have to fight the urge to keep my arms around him. His mouth is pressed shut, we're staring into each other's eyes, and this is nothing other than intimate. Too intimate. His face, his *lips*, are so close to mine, and something primal is begging me to lean forward.

And kiss him.

I want that so bad, but Ian surely doesn't, and I can't let myself get carried away.

"So yeah," I say to break the silence, "I'm here now, and I'm loving it. Freedom and all that."

We're both quiet again, and nerves prickle in my core—Ian wanted to hang out with me tonight, not listen to my sad origin story.

"Anyway, that's how I got here. Should we talk about something else?"

"Sounds good, man," Ian says, grabbing two seltzers from the mini fridge and handing me one. "On a *much* lighter note, how are you liking college so far?"

"It's freaking awesome," I reply. "Like, academically, it's hard, but it's so different from back home. It's exactly what I needed."

Ian taps the edge of his can against mine and takes a sip. "That's what I like to hear."

"Yeah. It's eye-opening, like how the flashy application pamphlet said it would be, since it's diverse and whatever."

He snickers. "Ooh, sounds scary."

"Shut up," I reply, laughing back at him. "It's not *scary*. I like it. I mean, look at Sabrina and Laura—it's so cool that they can be, you know, open."

"Yeah?"

I nod. "Uh-huh. I love it. Not just for them, but everyone."

Ian digs his fingers into the side of his can, leaving a dent. "So, you're cool with...that stuff?"

"Uh-huh. Of course. I mean, I've found that everything my parents hate is actually completely normal," I joke, even though it's true.

I was avoiding eye contact purely out of instinct, and when I return my gaze to him, he's smiling gently.

"On that topic," he starts, "I don't remember if it ever came up, but I'm bi."

Wait.

Wait.

I don't know if Ian kept talking after dropping that on me, and I can't claw my attention back.

Ian is bisexual.

Ian likes guys too.

Ian and his kind eyes and fluffy hair and charming smile and bulging arms and his everything...likes guys too.

Ian, who's been hugging and comforting me for the past five minutes like I'm his best friend, likes guys too.

And now he's shuffling backward, the absence of his touch almost painful. But necessary. Under any other circumstances, he would be safe. He'd be fine with me.

But not when he's a *friend* who *I'm living with.* Not when he's him and I'm me.

Sure, he likes guys, but there are a lot of guys. I'm one, and I'm a basket case.

"That's not a problem, is it?" he asks, crossing his arms and resting against the opposite arm of the couch, twisting his fingers in a throw blanket. "Sorry, I probably should have told you before you moved in—"

I shake my head faster than I need to. "No! Not at all. Absolutely not a problem whatsoever. That's cool. I'm cool with that. So cool."

What's not cool right now is *me,* and it's not like I can help myself.

"I don't think I've met a gay guy before," I continue.

Other than myself.

"Bi," he corrects, and I mentally kick myself. "I mean, I lean toward men for the most part, I'm still way too into chicks for my own good."

He probably means that as a joke, so I laugh, trying not to show that I'm still hung up on the fact that Ian's into men, too.

That fact changes everything and nothing.

Everything, because we have something else in common.

Nothing, because I *want* to do something with that fact, but I absolutely, one hundred percent can't.

"Sorry. I'm not good with all the terms and such," I say. "Small town, remember?"

"No problem. I get it." Ian pauses, pursing his lips. "Did you ever, like, contemplate not being straight? I can't imagine it was even presented as an option for you."

My mouth hangs open. That's an invitation. He wants to know if I'm not straight.

"You don't have to answer if you don't want to," he rushes to say. "No big deal."

It's a huge deal. I want to tell him. I want him to know, but unlike him revealing it to me, everything between us actually *will* change if I do so as well.

It'd be so much harder to hide my inappropriate, one-sided crush.

My heart is in my throat as I gulp down the rest of the beer in front of me. "No. I never thought about it."

That's not a complete lie—I didn't have to *think* about liking guys; it simply *was.* There was a crap ton of denial on my part, so that *could* count as thinking, but getting lost in the underwear aisle at the supermarket when I was twelve served as all the confirmation I needed, even if I didn't acknowledge it for years.

That, and Mr. Crofton's tight polos.

I shove the thought aside, not wanting to go back to that dark time in my life.

"Nice, nice," Ian says. "Even though you're *straight*, I'm glad you're cool with me and the rest of us."

God, he even put emphasis on *straight*. It's like he's taunting me without knowing, goading me to come out and correct him. Ian should be safe—he's never *not* been—but I can't bring myself to tell him.

I know I don't owe my identity to anyone, especially if I'm not comfortable, and right now, I'm *really* not.

So I shrug, offering a weak smile as he yawns and stretches. We're silent for a while, sitting there in the dim light of the ambient lamps, and I'm about to ask if we're getting more drinks or heading to bed when Ian slumps over and rests his head on my shoulder.

"Man, what are you—" I freeze mid-sentence once my eyes catch up.

Ian is asleep on me, nuzzling his face into my shoulder like a blond-haired fawn.

My chest tightens and blooms with heat at the same time.

He's comfortable around me. At least enough to use me as some kind of undeserving pillow.

I hold my breath, not wanting to disturb him, but the way my heart is racing might wake him up anyway. Slowly, I shuffle away and let his head fall onto the couch cushioning, cramming myself into the corner.

If I let his head rest in my lap, he'd get a rude awakening in every sense of the term.

What should I do?

My evil brain flashes a tempting, forbidden image of me and Ian curled up together on the couch, waking up together with his strong arms wrapped around me and my hands in his soft hair.

No. He doesn't deserve that. I'll let him be.

For someone his size, he sure takes up a lot of space. He's still on his back, and he's stretching out across the couch, his arms sprawled open, almost like he's inviting me into them.

But he only does that when he's awake and upright. The last thing he needs is for me to crush him with my cumbersome body.

Still, that sprawl is way too enticing, especially how it stretches the fabric of his old shirt across his chest and makes the hem ride up, giving me a teasing glimpse of his trim stomach. I shut my eyes and let out a long, painful exhale.

If he's taking my bed, I suppose I could crash in his, and try to play it off as a joke tomorrow.

No. That'd blur lines, and I don't trust myself not to have another lecherous dream under blankets that smell like the man I can't stop craving. The idea of cleaning a mess out of Ian's sheets is more than enough for me to drop the ludicrous, selfish idea.

That leaves me with my next option, which is moving him to his bedroom.

Bracing myself, I stand up and slip my left arm under that strong, wide back, and I come close to giving up when he mumbles the cutest sleepy complaint.

"Come on, work with me," I murmur, crossing my fingers that he doesn't do something like try to snuggle me in his sleep.

I scoop my other arm under his knees, making sure not to be a creep and touch his butt, and I lift him with the gentlest, slowest force I can manage. His body slides, lifting his shirt even more and pressing the bare skin of his back into my forearm. Ian runs hot, sure, but god, this feels like he's singing my hair off.

And then his head slumps onto my chest.

My arms burn with his weight, but I can't stop myself from pausing and taking him in. His hair tickles my chin, and I tilt downward instinctively to stop the itch.

Oh, great! I'm kissing Ian's head. That's so weird, and it's also the hottest thing I've ever done with someone else.

Jesus. I'm using him again. He doesn't want this. He *can't* want this with someone like me.

I jerk my head up and lumber around the bookshelf, nudging the door to his bedroom open. I've never seen inside it before, and I'm hoping his bed isn't too far away because my arms are on fire.

Holy hell, Ian sure packs a lot into his frame. And maybe he's packing—

Screw off, Callum. Stop being a pervert.

I manage to avoid dropping him, and I deposit him into the crumpled sheets of the unmade bed. Seconds later, I've pulled the thin comforter over his body, deriving far too much undeserved satisfaction from the simple act of tucking him in.

Ian does so much for me, and he cares more about me than anyone ever has. It's about time I return the favor, even if it's with something as basic and deceivingly intimate as covering him up.

I step backward out of the room, watching the rise and fall of his body to make sure he stays asleep. I fill up a glass in the kitchen and place it on his nightstand, and as I'm about to leave, I notice another blanket draped over his desk chair. It's frigid out tonight, and he could use another one, especially since he's always so cold. I shake it out and place it on top of his comforter, careful not to wake him up, but I'm not careful enough to avoid accidentally hitting him in the face with a corner.

Luckily, he only mumbles something unintelligible before curling into the newly added weight and—

Oh no, he smiles.

I think my stomach sinks, or maybe it jumps or rises, but it doesn't matter. My heart reacts to him again.

He's cute. He's so damn cute, and I'm so damn weak, so much so that I steal another lingering look at his beautiful face before I leave for the couch.

Ian is so peaceful.

Peaceful and oblivious to how hard I'm falling for him.

For a fleeting second, I let myself entertain the thought that in another life, I might have the stones to flirt with him for real. But the only life I have is the one I'm living—I'm a mess, Ian's amazing, and we're friends. That's more than I could have possibly dreamed of when I first came here, and there's no way I'm gonna mess that up.

I settle in for the night and pull the covers over me, hoping they block out the fact that this is Ian's house and his presence is everywhere, and all I get is a lungful of his cologne lingering on the blanket. This time, it's my stomach that lurches with some kind of achy longing that's so strong I almost growl through my gritted teeth.

Why does he have to smell so good? Why did he have to pick a fragrance that wires my nostrils to my dick and makes my heart go all stupid?

Above all, why does he have to be so freaking perfect?

CHAPTER THIRTEEN
IAN

Holy shit, did I know what relaxation was before today? I check my watch to make sure I didn't accidentally sleep for three days straight, and nope, I didn't. I just slept like a damn rock. Or a boulder.

Hell, I don't even remember coming back in last night.

Hold up. The last thing I remember before passing out was chilling with Callum on the couch, and now I'm here.

I'm here in bed, it's past noon, and I'm tangled up in my comforter and my desk blanket. There's no way I would have thought to carry that to bed, which means...

Did Callum tuck me in?

Oh my god, he totally did.

And oh my god, my stomach flips like heck. It isn't every day that I let someone take care of me, and I would never ask, but I was asleep. He did it anyway.

I think I'm in love. In a platonic way, of course, especially after he all but confirmed, again, that he isn't into men. Not that it was any surprise, but hey, that confirmation is stabilizing, and now I can go back to doing what I was before I met him.

Which is essentially condemning myself to celibacy until my sensitive, battered nerves recover from the last few guys who objectively didn't do anything *that* terrible.

Ugh.

I roll over to check my phone, and then I feel it in my pocket. Figures. I pull it out to plug it in, and—

There's a glass of water on the nightstand.

Callum gave me water.

Oh my fuck, he gave me water! He thought about me!

Okay, calm down. It's just water.

But he cared enough to get a glass, fill it up, and put it on my nightstand, all after *physically carrying me to bed* when I passed out.

Like, I know it's only a glass of water. It means nothing serious. Other than that he cares. About me. And he did something for me.

Why am I getting so worked up about this?

I down the glass of water as a distraction. I'm not hungover, only super thirsty, and I heave my heavy body out of bed for a refill. It's already past noon, so I should get moving, anyway. As usual, I don't smell so great, so I strip my shirt off and head into the hallway.

The shower was running when I woke up, so I'll grab water in the kitchen—

I walk face-first into Callum.

"Shoot, sorry, man, I wasn't..." I trail off as I take a step back, contending with the sight in front of me.

Paying attention. What I didn't manage to say is what I'm doing now, because Callum is shirtless, too.

He's shirtless and fucking *breathtaking*.

While it's obvious to anyone who so much as looks in his general direction that he's built like a tank, seeing his brawny frame without a shirt over top is something else.

Why is he allowed to be tall *and* stocky? And have chest hair when he's nineteen? Wait, no, I think he already turned twenty. I don't even know anymore.

Life is not fair. Life is not fair because it's testing me. Constantly. With hot straight men, or rather, one singular, smoking hot straight man who fits my type for guys *to a damn T*.

Still, I haven't failed a single test since ninth grade, and I won't fail this one. In my mind, AP Calculus II is harder than not crushing on someone I literally can't make a move on, so I scrounge up some willpower and snap my eyes up to the space between Callum's eyebrows.

His eyes are too distracting for me to stare into them for real.

He's just another one of my friends who happens to be hot. Nick is athletic, funny, and attractive, but wanting him to fuck me would be like wanting my nonexistent brother to fuck me. Gross.

And yeah, I was kinda into Sabrina for a day before I knew she was lesbian, and now there's nothing but friendship between us.

Callum is like a tall, hairy Sabrina with a quieter sense of humor.

He has to be.

"Sorry, I forgot a shirt," he mumbles. His cheeks are pink, probably from the shower, and he isn't meeting my gaze.

That's for the best—that way he can't catch me staring at his plush, parted lips.

I shrug. "Don't worry about it. You're good."

You're good to never, ever wear a shirt in this house again. Burn them all.

Jesus, that's so sleazy. Poor Callum.

"No bruises or anything?" I ask jokingly. "I crashed into you pretty hard."

"Nah," he says. "All good. I thought you were asleep."

"I was until a minute ago." I hold up my empty water glass. "But I needed some water."

Silence falls between us, and it drags out into uncomfortable, awkward territory, amplified by the fact that we're both half-naked.

"So, about last night," I start, but Callum interjects before I can finish my sentence.

"Yeah. I don't want things to change between us because of what you told me."

I furrow my eyebrows. "Oh, that's not what I was trying to get at."

"It wasn't?"

"Nah," I reply, waving him off. "I just wanted to say thanks for carrying my dumb ass to bed."

His eyes widen, and a little smile materializes at one corner of his mouth.

Is he trying to be sexy? There's no way he *knows* that I go weak for an uneven grin.

He's not trying to be sexy. He simply *is*, and that's ten times worse for me.

"No problem," he says. "It was the least I could do."

"Right, yeah. I still appreciate it, though." Shoot, I'm rambling. "And about the other thing you mentioned, uh, so we're clear, just because I'm bi doesn't mean I'm gonna be all thirsty for you. We're still bros."

I might not be *thirsty* over him, but there's no way I can deny finding him attractive.

"Oh, yeah. Of course," Callum says.

"I'll drink to that." I raise my glass, and what do I do next? I press it straight into his sternum. Like, that physique deserves a toast, but I'm out of line to be the one to give it.

He blinks, and his face flushes even more. So do his neck and chest. Holy, that's as close to crimson as I've ever seen anyone, and a pit drops in my stomach. Despite what we both said, I need to be more careful about how I act around him.

I can salvage this. But how?

By bro-ing it up. That's how.

"Yup, gotta toast those gains, man," I say, forcing nerves away from my throat and back into my stomach. "I'm an athlete, and you're seriously giving me a run for my money."

"Oh. Well, you have nice abs," he blurts out.

Huh, he's joining in, too. Fun!

My brain goes right to locker room talk. "I guess I do, man," I say, smiling and running my palm over said abs. "But why'd you say that? Wanna cop a feel or something?"

Gritting my teeth, I hold my breath. He's finally getting

comfortable enough around me, and that dude-flirting might have set us back—

Callum's hand is on my stomach. Callum's hand is on my fucking stomach. His fingers are heavy, his touch is so light, and the tingles that combo sends throughout my body are unparalleled. Prickly, tense, amazing heat floods my synapses and makes my heart fucking race.

Do not make this weirder than it already is.

And don't get hard.

"Bro, are you gonna go any lower?" It comes out as a joke, even though an annoying part of me still hopes that he'll actually surprise me and go ahead.

Instead, he snorts and gives me a gentle punch on the stomach. "I wouldn't dream of it. *Bro.*"

Oh, shit! Callum called me *bro*. I'm a bro to him, and I break into a stupid smile.

We're bros. I mean, we already were, but *he* called me that!

"Alright, buddy. Put a shirt on and stop tempting me," I joke, returning his shoulder slap.

He shuffles away without another word, and I grab the water I originally came out here for. Callum's closed the makeshift living room door when I'm done, so I go back to bed and scroll social media for a while.

I know how to live with straight-man disappointment. Looking on the bright side, Callum and I are still friends, and we both don't want anything to change. He's cool with me being bi, and that, in the grand scheme of things, is ideal.

Ideal isn't perfect, but I can't change reality to fit my own selfish wants. That's just the way things are.

CHAPTER FOURTEEN
CALLUM

I am the most cowardly, scummy, opportunistic lowlife to walk the face of this earth.

And that cowardly, scummy, opportunistic lowlife is currently touching his stomach while lying in bed, trying to remember the feeling of Ian's chiseled abs beneath his fingertips.

I keep going back to the surprised jump his throat made when I followed through on his joking invitation to "cop a feel." He didn't break eye contact, which would usually be nerve-racking, but in the moment, it was great because he didn't see how my dick firmed up at the slightest brush of his hard muscles against my fingers.

Will I ever get to feel something like that again? The hard ridges of another guy's muscles, all warm and sensual under my hand?

Oh, shit—I'm allowing myself to get all depraved over Ian. While I know there's no inherent problem with attraction, and Anita said the same thing, this kind of thinking crosses the line into inappropriate territory.

Groaning to myself, I turn over and bury my face in the pillow. Nothing is going to change about my wandering thoughts if I don't do anything. Ian's still going to be very bi and very hot, I'm still going to be weird and closeted, and things could implode like a pressure cooker.

I could get drunk and make a stupid move on him, and then I'd lose him as a friend.

The mere thought of that makes my stomach churn. Something has to give before I get to that point. I need to take some kind of action; it's not on Ian to do everything.

Maybe he needs to know about me.

The thought sends terror into my guts. The only other person who knows I'm gay is Anita, and being cool with that is part of her job. As for the rest of the world, it's up in the air.

If I come out now, Ian might go cold on me. It's one thing for him to joke with me the way he does with his other friends, but I'm different. I'm capable of—no, I'm actively liking him.

He was comfortable enough to come out to *me*, but that's only because he thought, and still thinks, that I'm straight.

But he deserves to know. He deserves to know I'm gay so at least he's informed. So he can decide whether or not sharing his home with the likes of me is something that he's still comfortable with.

It's a tough choice—keep myself hidden and hope I don't do something stupid, or be upfront and risk things getting awkward.

I unlock my phone as a distraction, and I find a text from Laura waiting.

LAURA PIERRE

Sabrina is watching some awful TV show and as much as I love her I simply cannot cope with any more

Wanna hang out if you're free?

Maybe I could talk to Laura about this.

Getting a compulsion to unload my issues on others isn't ideal at all, and I make a note to discuss more coping mechanisms with Anita when we meet next. Still, that doesn't help me now, and Laura's been nice to me, and she might be able to put some things into perspective.

I'm free, do you want to study French too?

Absolutely the fuck not

Let's just hang out lmao

Sounds good

Yay! Meet me at the student center in 15 and we can do anything EXCEPT studying French

Right. Okay. I have to get ready; I'm showered, but I'm still only wearing a shirt and my old sweats.

I get dressed for real and grab a stack of cookies on the way out, and as soon as I take a bite out of the first one, my mouth waters, begging me to scarf down the rest of them. These are *addictive*. I'll have to ask Ian if he's putting drugs in everything he bakes.

Despite everything that went down this morning, I still arrive at the student center with a content smile on my face.

Because of Ian's magic cookies.

Why does he have to make this so hard by being bi *and* irresistible? It's like he's trying to keep me wrapped around his finger, but he *isn't*, and he doesn't know that he is—I'm just a massive freaking loser who falls for the first attractive guy he meets after leaving home.

I spot Laura sitting at a table in the student center, and I settle down in the seat across from her.

"Something's up," she says. "What's going on?"

Huh? I go through everything that could be wrong—clothes, hair, face, shoes. Did I accidentally steal Ian's shoes or something?

"Callum. It's chill. I can practically see the gears turning in your head."

I relax, if only a bit.

"You seem a little disturbed. Is everything okay?" she continues.

"I guess, yeah." I shove my hands into the pockets of my coat, the same one Ian gave me last month.

Laura narrows her eyes at me, clearly not believing a word of what I said.

Shifting uncomfortably, I suck in a dry breath through my teeth. "It's about Ian. He told me he's bi yesterday."

"Okay." Laura clasps her hands together, resting her chin on them. "Is that what has you all knotted up?"

"No. Not exactly."

"Not exactly?" She tilts her head. "I don't mean to prod or whatever, but you brought it up—you don't have a problem with living with him because of that, do you?"

"Absolutely not." I take another breath. "I'm gay."

Hoo boy. Saying that faster doesn't make it any easier.

"Oop." Laura... I can't imagine why she'd *smile* at that, so it's probably a wince. "Have you told him?"

"No."

"Anyone else?"

"Yeah," I reply, not going into details. I don't know if Laura wants to know I go to therapy, so I don't bring up Anita.

"Okay. But not Ian. Is there any reason why, or are you not ready?"

I glance off to the side, pursing my lips together. Part of me is desperate to tell Laura; she might have some kind of advice, but again, I don't want to use her as a dumping ground for my chaos.

"I'm not ready," I reply simply. "Besides, he might be weirded out or something."

Laura jerks her head up, making quiet, disbelieving sputters. "Callum, he's bi. Why would he be weirded out about you being gay?"

Staying silent, I try to think of a good response, but I'm caught off guard when Laura grins.

"Wait." She blinks her dark brown eyes at me. "You like him."

My face *burns*. Am I that obvious about how much I like Ian?

There's no denying it now, so I nod. Unless my eyes are deceiving me, the corners of Laura's mouth twitch upward even more.

Wait, is she trying not to laugh at me?

"That's so cute," she says. "You've gotta be the fastest person to admit something like that."

"Well, it's true," I mutter. "God help me. He's treating me like Nick, and he doesn't know that I read way too much into that flirty dynamic."

"Oh boy, what happened?"

Sucking in a breath to stall for time, I debate telling Laura the full story. Do I fully out myself as a guy who totally misreads social cues and takes advantage of everything he can?

Screw it. "We bumped into each other shirtless this morning, I commented that he has abs like an absolute idiot, he asked me if I wanted a feel, and then I...felt them."

Laura barks out a chuckle and claps a hand over her mouth. "Oh my god, Callum! You're a menace."

"Don't remind me. Straight guys don't go around feeling each other's abs."

"You're right. They go around feeling up each other's dicks. You know straight men act gayer than actual queer men sometimes, right?"

I kind of suspected, based on how I've seen some guys around campus act, and what I've read online so far.

"Anyway, Ian is Ian," Laura continues. "Best case, he thinks it's a funny bro moment. Other best case, he..."

He *what*? I fiddle with my fingers, hoping it compels Laura to finish her sentence.

"Uh, I shouldn't say anything else." She rests her chin in her hands, hiding a growing smirk.

I groan. "Okay, you can't say that and leave me hanging. I'm dying here."

"Look, it isn't my place to speculate or anything, but he *does* like guys," Laura says. "It's not *impossible* for him to like you back."

I scoff. Yeah, right.

"Callum. If, for whatever reason, he reacts badly, you can

always live with me and Sabrina. But he *won't* react badly. Trust me on this."

"I'll try. It's just hard."

"Okay." Laura holds up her hand and sighs. "You're his friend, and he cares a lot about you. He isn't the kind of guy to throw that away over something like this, because he hates it when people do the same to him."

"Alright," I say, still not entirely convinced. "I'll tell him soon. And yeah, sorry for dumping all this on you."

"All good, buddy. I don't mind at all." Laura is still wearing that amused half-smile, and I try not to read too much into it. "Anyway, speaking of Ian, I haven't seen him or Nick in *ages*. Why don't we all do something tonight?"

"That sounds fun. What were you thinking?"

Laura already has her phone out. "Let's invade Nick's place since his roommate is out of town again. Here, I added you to a group chat."

> **LAURA PIERRE**
>
> Yo Nick, the four of us are coming over later.
> Will bring drinks
>
> **SABRINA FOSTER**
>
> You tell him what's up
>
> **NICK RUSSELL**
>
> ok
>
> **IAN SCOTT**
>
> Awesome
>
> **NICK RUSSELL**
>
> I'm still in bed though so wait an hour before
> coming over
>
> But don't wait too long bc I'm gonna get bored

"Is it that easy?" I ask, and Laura snickers.

"Yup. Nick loves being spontaneous like this." Standing up,

she checks her phone. "I know we just got here, but if we're heading to Nick's in an hour, we should get ready."

"Makes sense. This is casual, right? We aren't heading out anywhere?" I'll need to change if we're going somewhere other than Nick's house.

Laura smiles. "Oh yeah. The Barrel isn't open yet, but we should all go once it is."

The Barrel? I make a mental note to ask Ian what that is and why it's important.

"Anyway, see you at Nick's," Laura says.

With that, we part ways, and I head back to Ian's place. He's freshly showered when I arrive, and he thrusts a seltzer into my hand as soon as I step through the door.

"You saw the texts, right? We can head out in a bit," he says.

"I did." While taking my shoes off, I survey his outfit and note that he's changed into jeans and a dark sweater, which are what I'm already wearing.

"Are you copying me or something?" I joke.

Ian takes one glance at me and snickers. "Yup. I'm stealing your vibe." He presses his lips together, thinking. "Tell you what, though. You should change into that blue flannel. You always look so good in that."

I manage not to outwardly flinch at his compliment, even though it still makes my heart skip. "Okay."

I head into the living room and shut the door behind me, slipping out of my sweater and fishing the flannel out of the laundry pile. My fingers skim the fabric as I shake the wrinkles out—this is my nicer button-up, not that it's new or anything, but I agree with Ian. I think I do look good in this shirt.

"Is this okay?" I ask, going back into the dining room. I probably didn't even need to ask, given that I didn't change anything but the shirt, and it's the one he told me to wear in the first place.

Ian narrows his eyes at me, scanning me from top to bottom in a way that I'd interpret as judgmental if it wasn't him doing that.

"Almost." He doesn't elaborate and runs into the bathroom

instead, returning with a blue tub. "I offered before, and you didn't take me up, so I'll have to do this myself. Do you mind if I do your hair?"

"Yeah, sure."

His face melts into a charming smile, making my ears warm up, and I sit down at the dining table to give him easy access. He walks over, rubbing a small amount of paste in his hands, and he plunges his fingers into my hair, raking them through the strands with quick, practiced movements. Ian is so close, enough for me to feel his body heat on my face, and I hold my breath to prevent his signature scent from frazzling my poor, overloaded brain.

I don't even think it's cologne at this point—it's so subtle, it has to just be him.

Pure, debilitating perfection.

Every single brush of his fingertips along the sides of my head sends an amazing, sensual burst of tingles down my spine, no matter how fleeting the contact is. He's being careful, biting his tongue in concentration, which firms up his attractive face.

Finally, he takes a step back, surveying his work.

"Fucking perfect," he says, smirking at me.

I head to the hallway mirror, and while I don't concur with his assessment of perfection, how nice my hair is absolutely isn't lost on me. Ian mussed up the top, grouping locks together and dragging them to the front in a way that looks deliberate.

"Any thoughts?" he asks.

I turn to face him "Yeah, I like the style. It's decent."

He raises his eyebrows, scoffing. "Decent? Give yourself some credit, man. Hell, if I didn't know you so well, you'd be my first straight crush in five years."

I—oh. Crap. He definitely wouldn't be making those jokes if he knew.

I really have to tell him.

———

As usual, Ian plies me with alcohol. The two of us shared a six pack of some kind of beer while the group shot the shit, and eventually, the other four decided to start some game called King's Cup.

In short, it's a card game where every card carries a different alcohol-related action. I'm not gonna complain, at least until Questionmaster Sabrina trips me up and has me downing my drink as some kind of sick punishment.

But hey, that gets Ian laughing. God, he sounds so cute and graceful and confident and—

Oh, awesome. Nick draws an ace.

Laura turns to her girlfriend. "You better not get me messed up."

Nick scoffs. "Yo, chill. You're drinking wine."

"Bro, this is fucking port!" Laura replies, thrusting the bottle into Nick's face.

"Laura, why did you bring port to a house party?" Ian asks. "Don't tell me those pompous business students are influencing you."

Sabrina waves her hands. "Guys, shut up. It's time to waterfall."

The room quiets, and she presses her bottle of regular wine to her lips and tips it perpendicular to the ground, the rest of us dutifully doing the same with our own drinks. One by one, Nick, then Sabrina, then Laura, put their drinks down and tap out, and then it's only me, with Ian to my right.

I don't know what it is, but something compels me to have a little fun with him. It seems like a friendly thing to do.

So, with my lips still pressed to my seltzer, I continue taking the shallowest, slowest sips I can muster. Ian's screwing his face into an exasperated expression, and when I don't let up, he gives me the finger.

That does it for me, and I pull the can away, smiling.

"Jesus fuck, man, are you trying to kill me?" Ian groans, punching my shoulder and snickering.

I punch him back and smile, my three-ish drinks warming my

core and lowering my walls. "Nah, I'm kind of used to someone baking for me all the time."

Ian gasps, placing a hand on his chest. "Is that all I am to you?"

No, you're my deep-seated crush, too.

"Anyway, Cal, it's your turn," says my deep-seated crush.

Ooh, distraction. I need one of those.

I draw a card, and I release a snort as soon as I see what it is.

Nick stretches across the table to peek at the card. "Oh, shit, did Callum get the last king?"

I sure did. I reach for the cup at the center of the card pile and inspect its contents, trying to remember what exactly went into it. With four pairs of eyes focused expectantly on me, I take a sip.

It's *vile*.

"Holy crap, what the hell is in this?" I ask, sputtering.

"Beer, whiskey, and vodka," Laura supplies.

"And pickle juice." Ian's confession makes me snort.

Still, I'm not one to back down from anything, so I hold my nose and continue to chug. The group cheers when I empty the cup, and Ian hands me a can of pop to wash the taste down.

"Want any more?" Ian teases, shaking the almost-empty jar of pickles at me.

"Keep your pickle far, far away from me," I warn, shooting him a glare.

That makes the group burst into laughter, and it takes me far too long to realize that I made a sex joke without even trying.

Ian doesn't need reminding to keep his pickle away from me.

Smiling and rolling my eyes to deflect, I finish my pop and go to the kitchen to toss it in recycling, and Ian follows me in.

"Are you tired?" he asks, filling up a glass of water at the faucet. He takes a slow drink, and my eyes catch on his prominent Adam's apple jumping every time he swallows.

Attraction is so weird. Before, I'd notice the obvious on other guys, like their face, smile, body, whatnot. With Ian, I'm drawn to all that *and* the most random things. The hair on his arms. His throat. The way he scratches the back of his head when he's nervous.

"Yeah," I say. "I can head home myself if you want to stay."

He waves me off. "Nah, let's leave together. I'm tired, too."

Ian brushes a hand on my shoulder as he walks past me, and I stay in the kitchen for a few seconds.

I'd better savor those friendly touches, because I don't think he would want to keep those up once he knows that I could, or actually do, read into them more than I should.

Sighing, I throw my pop can away, finally, before joining Ian at the door to put my jacket on.

I'll tell him on the walk home. I'll have to. I can dress it up as something casual, if I can bring myself to be nonchalant about the whole being gay thing with the guy I have unreciprocated feelings for.

Oh, yeah, by the way, I'm gay. Just letting you know that all the bro flirting and friendly touching went straight to my hyperactive dick.

I shudder, and Ian makes it worse by guiding me out of the door with a hand on my back. Unlike my spiraling thought from a second ago, that touch doesn't travel down. It lingers in my core and makes my chest bloom.

I grit my teeth. It'd be one thing if it was simply physical—I could maintain my old repression and keep my feelings under wraps. I like Ian for Ian, though, and that makes my situation messier, if a little less depraved.

"Holy fucking asscracking shitballs, it's cold!" he yelps as soon as we step out of Nick's building. It's a little windy, but it's well above freezing. Ian, as usual, is bundled up, but his scarf is all twisted, exposing his neck.

"Maybe it'll help if you wear your clothes properly," I tease, reaching over to straighten out the fabric. My fingers brush the back of his neck, so I pull them away before I make things weird. "Sorry if I made us leave early."

He steps toward me and bumps his shoulder against my arm.

"Dude, don't worry about it. We stayed for hours, and besides, we can keep the night alive back at ours."

"Yeah?" What do I even say to that?

"For sure. I fucking love hanging out with you."

I think my heart stops, but Ian straightens up and keeps talking before I can process that.

"And I can assure you, it's *not* like that—"

Ian stressing that point over and over again would be reassuring if I was actually straight. Since I'm very much not, all it does is reaffirm the fact that my inconvenient feelings can never be reciprocated beyond us being friends.

"—but I feel like you and I really click. Like, as friends."

Yeah, okay. Just twist the knife even more, why don't you?

I shouldn't complain. Hell, not even two months ago, I was nervous, shy, and alone. Now I have Ian and his friends—I would have been happy with anyone even talking to me, let alone wanting to spend time with me.

"I feel that too," I reply. "I appreciate you."

Ian tilts his head, stopping short of resting it on my shoulder. "Aww, you're the best."

That line. Again. Holy crap, it digs into my eardrums and spreads like warm honey under my skin. My heart skips a beat, and when it makes up for that skipped beat by racing in double-speed, I stop walking.

No matter what, Ian, for whatever reason, likes me as a friend. As complicated as my attraction to him has gotten, I can still credit myself for not acting on it. He can't fault me for being who I am. He's bi himself, so maybe, *maybe*, he'll understand me.

And even though he won't like me back, it'll be good to have a friend who understands me like that, and what it's like to like guys.

He could help me with the whole being gay thing. With guys. Eventually.

I try to ignore the sharp pang of pain that slices through my chest when I contemplate liking a guy who *isn't* Ian. A guy who wouldn't care about me half as much as he does, because I can't imagine anyone else being capable of such pure goodness.

It only takes a few steps for Ian to realize I'm no longer next to him, and he turns around.

"What's up?" he asks, walking back to me.

My pulse is still elevated, pounding in my chest and through my ears, down to my fingertips. It's the same as what I felt when I got on the first bus to Chicago two months ago, when I bolted from home. It's what I felt when I stepped off the fourth bus here in Graniton after thirty hours.

Not trepidation, as I'd initially thought. Just nerves, mixed with excitement.

A bit of hope, too.

"Do you mind if we stay here for a bit?" I ask. "I have to tell you something."

"Of course." Ian looks up at me, his light, messy hair poking out of his beanie. "I'm all ears."

The wind isn't as biting as it was earlier in the year, but it still braces against us and makes his face pinken. He's so endearing and sweet, and I can't help but feel safe when I'm near him.

No matter what happens, I'll be fine.

Here goes nothing. I suck in a breath.

"I'm gay."

CHAPTER FIFTEEN
IAN

I'm not an asshole, and I don't want to be one, so I have to stay calm.

But holy *shit*, Callum is *gay*.

Just like that, the last major reason for me to suppress my stubborn feelings for him dissolves. The flimsy little dam splinters, allowing a steady stream of affection to pour through. Knowing me, that stream is gonna turn into a flood at any second.

The street is almost silent, the air punctuated by wind in the trees and Callum's heavy, nervous breathing. He's gripping his left arm with his right hand, his knuckles pale, and he's pressed his lips together, not saying a word.

Jesus. I can't even imagine what it must have been like for him to grow up gay in the family he had. There's no way his parents would be chill with him being gay, while *also* being weird about sex.

I can't even imagine how hard it must have been for him to say those two words to me. Has he even told anyone else? I might be the first.

I need to handle this right, and I can't get excited about him possibly, potentially, *hopefully* having the ability to also like me.

"That's cool, man," I say. "Thank you for trusting me with that."

Could I have come up with an even more generic coming-out response? Probably not. Generic is fine for now—anything more personal or creative might end up with me losing every last scrap of my self-control and asking Callum to please, *please* feel me up again, because the first time was unforgettable.

Again, I'm trying not to be an asshole.

"Are you feeling okay?" I ask, and Callum gives me a stiff nod. "Was that the first time you told someone?"

"Nah. I told my therapist and Laura."

Offering a smile, I let out a silent breath in relief—he's getting professional help. That doesn't happen often enough.

"That's great," I say. "I'm glad you're comfortable enough to open up to me."

Platitudes, genuine as they might be, are all I have. And now I'm out of those, too. We've fallen back into silence, the street's deserted, and we're simply...standing here.

Oh, god, I want to kiss him. He's got such pretty, tempting lips.

Fuck, I can't. That'd be such a dick move. He *just* came out to me.

He's right there. He likes guys. I don't know if he likes me. We're so different. He's calm and quiet, and I'm an overly intense ball of unwelcome affection. We can't—

"We can't stay here for much longer," I murmur. "It's a little cold." Breaking the unspoken intensity between us is an act of protection. Letting myself fall into liking Callum, when he lives with me out of necessity, would be plain wrong. "Can we head back home?"

He peers off into the distance, twisting his mouth up in a way that says he's clearly conflicted about something, and I can't imagine what that might be.

"There's something else," he says, cutting my thoughts off. "I need to tell you before I can go back."

Ominous, much? I shove my hands into my pockets. "For sure. I'm here for you."

He shuts his eyes, drawing in a shaky breath. "Please don't hate me."

His voice is barely audible, but those words still hit me. How could I ever hate someone like him?

"Callum, I won't be mad. There's no way you could do anything that would make me angry, I promise."

Okay, if he secretly peeked through the bathroom keyhole and watched me take a dump or something, I'd be a little disturbed, but I'm almost certain he hasn't done that.

That's weird. Why did I think that?

Stupid intrusive thoughts.

He purses his lips and lets out a long sigh, which makes my nerves ratchet up a little more. "I..." He sighs again. "I started liking you."

What—

My heart stops.

Callum likes me back.

Callum.

He's sweet and hot and amazing and *he likes me back.*

And he was afraid I'd hate him because of that?

"Hey." I reach up and put a hand on his shoulder to reassure him and to steady myself. "Buddy. Do you know how hard it was to avoid crushing on you?"

He manages to be even more silent than before. He stands there, head tilted, lips parted, and seemingly dumbfounded.

"Do you have anything to say about that?" I prod.

"You'd have a crush on me?"

I bark out a dry laugh, unease sinking in my gut as I fight the fading voice of self-preservation in my head. "Dude, I'm way past the point of 'would.' Now that I know you're also into guys, there's nothing stopping me."

He furrows his eyebrows. "But you're...you."

I scoff. "And you're *you.*" Okay, I *think* he's genuinely confused, but I can't wrap my head around how Callum has the self-esteem of a pinecone. "Like, are you fishing for compliments or something? If you are, then you can drop the act because I compliment people I'm into so much that it's weird."

"I'm not." He nudges a rock with his boot, stopping short of kicking it. "I've only been here for two months, and I'm still so far from fitting in. I'm still the weird transfer kid from the Midwest who doesn't know how to talk."

Jesus fuck. He was so nervous about this before, and to hear that he's still feeling down about being new? I think my heart splinters for him. No, scratch that. It *shatters*.

"You aren't weird. Seriously, you're the furthest thing from it."

"Then why does everyone else on this campus give me weird looks all the time?"

Wait. "What kind of weird looks?"

Callum shuts his eyes and sucks in a breath. "I don't know, like, I walk to class, and I catch people judging me."

"What makes you think they're judging? Everyone's probably—"

"Sometimes they'll laugh with their friends after I notice them."

No. Oh my god. This poor, sweet man thinks people are judging when they're actually *eye-fucking him.*

"Callum, nobody is judging you," I say, giving his shoulder a firm grip. "They're checking you out because you're hot as sin."

His head jerks up, and he furrows his eyebrows.

Okay, maybe telling a guy with probable religious trauma that he's "hot as sin" isn't the best idea, even if it's true. Still, I shouldn't be annoyed, and I'm not annoyed *at* Callum, rather, the thought of him feeling less than stellar about himself makes me want to beat up whoever made him think that.

His voice catches in his throat. "I'm...what?"

Really? Time to ramp it up.

"You're hot, Callum. You're so *fucking* hot. You're the kind of guy who makes people lose focus in class and walk into lampposts."

He stays silent, those full lips slightly parted, so I continue.

"And it's not just how you look. You're the gentlest, sweetest guy I've ever met. You listen. You care. You don't judge me for being chaotic and loud and stupid. You're so kind, almost to a fault, and—"

He makes some kind of groaning noise, covering his face with his gloved hands, and I immediately reach up to spread them apart.

"Hey, nope. Nope, nope, not having it. None of that hiding, Cal," I tease. "You gotta take it in. You need to hear how awesome of a person you are—"

"Stop," he says, a strained smile playing across his lips. Callum tilts his head up, maybe to hide his expression, but all that does is make the blush creeping up his neck all the more obvious.

"Why? Is it because you aren't used to hearing people say nice things about you?"

No response.

"Come on," I drawl. "What's the harm in getting a few compliments from a guy who's really into you?"

That manages to make him relax, and he returns his gaze to me. "It's, I don't know, almost too good to be true."

I bark out a chuckle that's part surprise, part disbelief. "That's not a reason for me to stop, is it?"

He shakes his head. It's so subtle, it's barely perceptible. "I guess not."

"So believe me when I say I like you back. And if you can't, I'll make you." I press my hands together. "How much did you have to drink tonight?"

Callum raises his eyebrows, probably a little confused at the subject change. "Uh, like four? And my last one was that awful concoction."

I grin, thinking back to Callum forcing down the King's Cup. He's had more than me, though not by much, and he's bigger.

"I'm not drunk or anything, if that's what you're asking," he adds.

Awesome. I can spill my feelings for his sake, and he won't do something drunken that he ends up regretting.

"Look, I'll spell it out for you," I continue, gazing into his confused eyes. "I want you. You're the whole package of everything I fucking *crave*. Fuck, I want to kiss you so goddamn bad, and if you want it too, just come and take it. I want to feel your hands on my face"—*and your cock in my mouth*—"and your tongue in my mouth, and—"

Callum cuts me off with a strangled noise from his throat. He parts his lips in the silence, sucking in a breath.

Then he swoops down and crashes his lips onto mine.

Callum is kissing me.

Holy *shit*, Callum is kissing me.

My watch beeps with an elevated heartbeat alert, and I don't give a flying fuck. Callum is kissing me.

He tastes like orange soda and man. It's gentle. My god, it's so tender and tentative, but he may as well be shoving his tongue down my throat because my body reacts all the same, sending desire shooting south and making my dick stiffen. My synapses fire as I groan into his soft mouth, and when we pull back, I already want to dive back in for more.

He's blinking, almost like he can't believe what we did. His tongue darts out, wetting his lower lip, and I swear it's the most sensual thing I've ever seen.

"Any thoughts?" I prod.

"Holy shit," he says. "That was amazing."

A cute smile spread across his face, making my heart go all soft.

Callum twists his hands together. "Can we please do that again? Only if you want to, though. I probably sucked."

My mouth falls open. "You didn't suck." I scoff. "You were *awesome*. Kiss me whenever the hell you want—"

He cuts me off by doing exactly that, and the pleasant, burning surprise makes me gasp. He's still being restrained, but there's a heated desperation behind every swipe of his tongue along mine and in every heavy sigh that he breathes out.

And that's when it hits me. He's shedding years of hiding, secrets, and repression, and he trusts me enough to do all that in front of me, and with me.

I deepen the kiss, and something in Callum unlocks as he places a firm hand in the small of my back. A heady groan spills out of his mouth and into mine, followed by his tongue. Warmth blooms in my gut and travels down, and we can't keep ramping up like this in public, not if we don't want to end up on some kind of list.

Even if I *really* wouldn't mind his hand going a tiny bit lower. He can squeeze my ass if that's what he wants.

He doesn't, and my hands travel along his body, slipping under his jacket and pressing against the fuzzy fabric of his shirt. I'm tempted to slide underneath and roam across his soft skin, but that'd be going a little too far.

"You're not kidding about whenever, right?" Callum mumbles, pulling back. His pupils are blown, his lids are drooping, and I don't think I've seen a more kissable face than his.

I shake my head. "No way. Kiss me whenever and wherever you want."

He freezes.

Wait, was that too much?

"Wherever?" Callum runs his tongue along his upper teeth in a move that fries even more of my self-control. "Are you sure?"

I huff. "Dude, I'm so sure. You take the lead."

"Can we go back to yours and do that?"

Holy shit, yes.

Heat flashes in his eyes, and it's unmistakable.

It's want.

Callum got his first kiss out of the way. If he also wants to punch his V-card in the same night, I'd be honored to help. The mere thought of stripping him down, nestling myself between those thick, thick thighs, and getting my mouth on him is firing me the hell up.

"For sure," I say, tamping down my inner horndog. Feeling bold, I stick my hand out, and he places his fingers over mine.

Everything tonight has been so tender—kissing, touching, and now holding hands, but it's *satisfying*. Like the first tiny sip of a piping-hot bowl of soup you've been craving all day long. I could hold his hand forever.

But someone rounds the corner in front of us, and he drops it like hot coal. The absence, while totally understandable, is devastating.

"Sorry," he whispers. "I'm still not used to other people seeing me like this."

"Don't worry about it. That just means we need to hurry up and get back to our place."

It takes all of three minutes. I'd run if he was game, but I don't want to tire him out. That'll come later.

If I have things my way, Callum is gonna be wrung-out, gasping, and happily delirious by the end of the night. Man, I wanna make him feel so good.

I kick my shoes off and go right up to him, and his mouth lands on mine again. My hands circle his back and pull him into me, and I don't even think as I guide us to the bedroom, discarding our coats and my sweater on the way. Still kissing, I lean against the footboard as I undo a button on his shirt, revealing more of that glorious chest and giving him the next move.

That next move consists of Callum tripping and launching us onto the bed. I land first, my back colliding against the mattress and he follows right after, making me sink into the bed under his amazing heft.

Yes, please.

He tries to push himself up, but I latch onto his firm back muscles and drag him down. My dick presses against my pants, and I make an involuntary thrust up as he lands back on top of me, his face falling next to my head.

Callum lets out a disbelieving snicker. "Do you *want* me to accidentally crush you?"

"Nah. I want you to do that *on purpose*. Let's make out."

The speed with which he lunges at me has to set a world record or something. We're kissing deeper than we were earlier, and Callum is a total natural. He's messy, but that's kind of the point. He slides his tongue against mine so smoothly, I'm moaning like that tongue is working its magic somewhere else. And the noises he's making? They're hot as hell.

Him grinding against me is even hotter, and him reaching for my waist is enough to end me.

"Wanna go further?" I grunt out.

He replies with an abrupt moan. "God, yes." His hands make a pass along the bottom of my T-shirt. "You turn me on so much."

I don't *think* I have a praise kink, but hearing Callum say that might have given me one.

"I need you." Pressing up, I slam my mouth to his, needy and emboldened. "Want me to take this off?" I slide my fingers along his, curling them around the hem of my shirt.

"Yeah, do it." His voice is sharp, clipping at the end of every syllable, and I chuckle. Oh, man, he's as impatient as I am.

As soon as the fabric clears my head, my mouth is on his again, hot and rough. Now he's the one on his back, and I straddle his waist, heaving myself up on top.

I've seen him shirtless exactly once before, and I'm dying for a repeat, except with my hands and mouth added to the mix. As I run my hands down from his neck, my fingernails catch on his shirt, and I slip underneath, sparks shooting through me as I make contact with soft, bare skin and the thin fuzz on his stomach.

Jesus, I need his cock so bad—I bet he tastes like heaven. I wanna hear him moan while I suck him off and listen to his voice break as he unloads down my throat, curling his toes and grabbing my hair.

I reach down to stroke him over the top of his jeans, his breath catching in a gasp as my fingers land. *Fuck me*, he's packing.

I want to lose myself in his body. I want more, so much more.

And Callum...

Shit, he *doesn't*.

My eyes widen. Something is off. He's stiff as a piece of driftwood. Breathless.

Reluctant.

Did I go too far and too fast with him, too?

"Callum, do you want to stop?" I ask. There's no reply, but the hesitation in his wide eyes is clear as day. "Should we keep going?" I shuffle away to give him some space.

He shakes his head. "Sorry." His voice is so quiet, it breaks me.

"You have nothing to apologize for," I say, putting my shirt back on. "I shouldn't have pushed."

"You didn't push me," he says, and the stiffness in my jaw loosens a little. "But you want more."

"If you don't, that's all I need." I place a hand on Callum's thigh to give it a quick rub, and his little smile returns, if a bit weak. And honestly, seeing this man smile might be better than sex. "You can take as long as you need—"

"I really want to, with you," he says. "Just not tonight. I got... I don't know. It was amazing, but I got nervous out of nowhere."

"And that's okay." I don't know what exactly to do, so I keep my arms open in the hopes that he lets me give him a hug. He sure could use one. "I'm ready whenever you are."

That earns me a strained huff, and much to my relief, he falls into my arms. I close around him, and he sighs into my chest.

"Do I..." he starts, and sucks in a ragged breath. "Are you going to make me go back to the couch?"

"No!" I stop myself from tightening my grip, and Callum nudges into me, making my core ache. "If you want to sleep on the couch, you're always free to go, but I want you here. I want you to stay." Even though I loosen my grip, he stays still, so I bend down and plant a soft kiss in his cute hair while rubbing his back. "I've got you. You can stay."

"You're so good to me, Ian," he whispers. "Nobody ever has been."

My heart splits even more, and when he wraps his strong arms around me, sighing into my chest, I have to blink back tears. I almost don't want to believe it—*nobody* has treated him nicely? *Ever*?

"Why wouldn't I be good to you?" I murmur. "You're the best, Callum. You make it so damn easy."

CHAPTER SIXTEEN
CALLUM

Ian is sound asleep next to me when I jolt awake the next morning. A sharp pang of panic rises in my throat, and I rub a hand across my face, trying to force it back down. It...kind of works, but that panic gets replaced with guilt. It crawls across my skin, and I fight the urge to curl up and let it win.

This is Ian's bed. He belongs here, and I'm the jerk who made him stop last night.

I messed it up. He was so *clear* about how much he wanted to have sex, and I should have been ready for him. Hell, I wanted it. I completely lost control of myself and kept taking non-stop, until I started overthinking about what exactly *I'd* be expected to do with Ian, and then I completely shut down.

And now I'm lying in Ian's absurdly comfortable bed, spiraling.

He stopped when I asked, like it was nothing. He does so much for me, and I can't even have sex with him even though I *also* wanted to?

I'm fucking pathetic.

He shifts around, startling me, and I roll away to give him space.

"Morning," he mumbles, his eyes still closed. He stretches out an arm and pats around the sheets where I was lying a few moments ago, scrunching up his face and shuffling toward me. I tense up, holding my breath, as his roaming hand lands on my waist, narrowly missing my traitorous morning wood.

Ian lets out a low hum as soon as he makes contact with me.

"There you are." The way his body softens confuses me and makes my heart flip. "C'mere."

I loosen my clenched jaw ever so slightly, noticing the warmth in his tone, but my nerves stay stuck in my chest. "Why?"

"Callum," he whines, dragging my name out, and his low, husky voice sends tingles into my tailbone. "I'm *so cold.*"

At that, he pulls himself into me, and I give in, letting myself relax. We're in an awkward position—he's shorter, but I'm the one in his arms. Not that I'm complaining, especially since I've never been this comfortable before.

"Did you sleep okay last night?" I ask, trying to break through my own tension.

"Mhm." He sighs and tightens his hold on me. "But waking up next to you is even better."

As soon as those words leave his mouth, the last of my nerves melt away. How can he just drop something like that?

But then he stiffens his body and loosens his grip on me. "Shoot, sorry. That was too much, wasn't it?" He sighs. "I can be a lot."

"Nah, it seemed right to me. Maybe I needed to hear that," I admit. Now I'm the one wrapping around Ian, and I don't miss how solid and warm he feels in my arms.

He huffs and opens his mouth to speak before pausing, seemingly hesitant. "Be careful what you wish for. I wasn't kidding about being a lot."

"That's fine," I say. "Come here."

"Fuck yes." He drops his head to my chest, relaxing into my body.

It's so peaceful like this. Somehow, I'm calm.

Then my stomach grumbles, interrupting the moment.

"Are you hungry? I can make eggs." Ian mumbles.

No, you don't have to. You already do so much for me.

I ignore my annoying inner voice. "Sounds great, thank you."

His face lights up, and I take in how happy he gets when I don't push back or try to stop him from doing things for me.

Then he kisses my forehead on his way out of the bed, and I go all mushy. Ian stretches up and yawns as I'm collecting myself, and the bottom of his shirt lifts to reveal his trim waist, making me fall apart all over again. My greedy eyes linger for so long that he catches me and chuckles.

God, I... Fuck. I'm helpless.

I look away. "Sorry."

"Oh no, I'm getting checked out by a hot guy. Send help," he deadpans, stepping toward me.

The proximity makes my heart race, and when he threads his fingers through my hair and scratches the back of my head, I swear I stop breathing.

"Stare at me all you want," he continues, gesturing at himself. "I'm all yours."

Those words send a bolt of arousal to my balls. He's saying he's mine? That's a bit... I don't know how to feel about that, but I don't have to because Ian sticks a hand under my chin and tilts my head up. I part my lips, he leans down, and—

He's kissing me.

Holy shit, holy *shit*, we're kissing again. It's like something possesses me, and my arms spring out and pull his body closer while my tongue works on autopilot. I have no idea how he isn't complaining because I have no idea what I'm doing, but from the sounds he's making, he seems to like it.

So I spear my tongue deeper into his mouth, and he lets out a moan. Holy... It's so loud and deep, and the sound travels right to my cock.

Ian pulls back, breathless. "Whew. I wasn't planning on getting this hot and heavy."

"Plans can change." I slip one hand under his shirt, grabbing his back muscles, and the other through his hair to drag him back in.

Last night, Ian said I could take the lead, and until he says otherwise, that's what I'm gonna do. And I want to finish what I started. I don't think I've needed something so badly before, and if he lets me...

Aw, no. He's pulling back.

"Do you think we should leave this until later?" he says.

My crotch burns with need. Why does he want to wait? Is Ian scared I'll freak out like I did last night?

Just like that, the sinking feeling from earlier returns to my stomach.

He continues. "Especially since—"

I groan, stopping him mid-sentence. "Don't handle me with kid gloves. Please. I want this."

"So do I." He runs a rough hand through his bedhead. "Fuck, I want you so bad, but don't you have to work on Sundays?"

Oh. Yes, I do.

I palm my erection while checking the clock, and yeah, I have five minutes to spare before I have to leave, if that.

As much as my dick protests, I still feel like my first sexual experience with someone else should be a little more...glamorous than something rushed.

I hope I don't have to focus today—I just *know* my mind is gonna be occupied.

Ian's face is still flushed, and he steps back, adjusting himself in his sweats. "There's no time for eggs, but I can grab you a protein bar or something so you don't get hungry" he says before walking out of his bedroom.

I reluctantly get changed and am about to comb my hair before remembering that Ian likes it a little messy. My hair's growing, and the look is growing on me too, so I settle for running a few damp fingers through the strands.

Ian is making coffee when I emerge into the kitchen, and he freezes once he turns around, staring straight at me.

"Is there something wrong?" I ask, instinctively reaching up to pat my hair back down.

His gaze goes down, then back up to my face. "No," he says, dragging the word out. "You're just so absurdly hot."

A blush floods my cheeks as a smile crawls across his face. He's said it before, but it's still surprising to be reminded that he finds me attractive. I'd be a liar to say I don't like hearing it—the fact that I have this effect on someone like him is nothing short of astounding.

"Do you mind me checking you out?" he asks, snapping out of it. "I can try to keep myself in check if it makes you feel weird."

I shake my head. "Go ahead."

There's a pause as Ian and I regard each other in silence. His eyes leave mine and dart lower again for a few seconds before returning, but my chest blooms in that short moment.

"I... I appreciate knowing that you're interested," I confess.

"Thank fuck. I'm so weak for you," he mutters. "Anyway, here's breakfast. You should get going so you aren't late."

I accept the protein bar he hands me, hesitating before putting it in my backpack.

Then I smile, unfamiliar courage finding its way into my head. "There's one more thing I should do before I leave."

"Yeah?" Ian tilts his head to the side, and I crash my mouth against his. He lets out a breathy moan and pushes up into me, making the kiss go right to my dick.

When he backs me into the wall with one hand cupping my cheek, I get a sudden urge to call in sick. I'll have to ask him to corner me again.

"This was a bad idea," I say, and Ian blinks at me.

"How come?"

I let out a dry laugh. "Because I'll have to figure out a way to survive the next five hours when all I can think about is finishing what we started last night."

Ian flicks his gaze down again, and I move my jacket so it covers my crotch.

"Jesus, you're gonna have me rocking a semi all day," he says. "You're irresistible."

Heat surges up my neck, and I get harder.

"I need to leave," I blurt out, turning around and rushing through the door.

My jacket hangs from my arm, casually draping over the front of my jeans, for the entire walk to the library.

Ian is so flirty, I'm defenseless, and I like that I'm defenseless.

He can get under my skin any day of the week.

Great, now I'm thinking about him again.

God, I'm a mess.

————

Thankfully, I settle down once I leave Ian's place and get through my quiet shift. Sure, my mind drifts to him too many times to count, but I manage to keep my wits about me and avoid drooling in the stacks.

Still, as soon as my shift ends, I waste no time getting back to the apartment. As Ian would say, I "rock a semi" for the entire walk, and like this morning, I make sure to keep myself covered. The elevator ride to the second floor feels a lot longer than it usually does, and my hands shake when it comes to unlocking his door.

I enter holding my breath.

The apartment is warm as usual, with the familiar, comforting smell hitting me as soon as I step in. Ian is lazing on the couch-bed, scrolling through his phone, which he puts down once he spots me.

"Hey, what'd you get up to while I was gone?" I ask.

"Nothing much. I hit a workout, grabbed lunch with Nick, and showered. How was your shift?"

"Decent." I do my best to filter out the impatient edge to my voice. I don't say anything else as I hurry into the living room, settling next to Ian. "Couldn't wait to get back here, though."

He smirks. "Hmm. Someone's eager."

I scoff, but he trails his fingers along my forearm, the touch sending electricity down my spine.

Leaning forward, I return his smile. "You aren't lying."

It isn't clear who moves first. Maybe it's both of us closing the distance at the same time, and we press our lips together.

He tastes like heaven. It's sweet and sharp with the aftertaste of the electrolyte drink he was drinking, and I press my tongue deeper into his mouth because I can't get enough of him.

Keep it calm. Keep it fucking calm. I repeat that to myself as I brush my tongue along his teeth. I'm already giving in, but even I know not every kiss needs to be desperate. Slow can be sensual.

Oh, Jesus, Ian moans.

Why did he have to moan like that? My breath hitches, arousal clinging to the corners of my mouth. Screw being slow. My whole body burns with a kind of need I never knew I'd get to feel, and my instincts take over, compelling me to bring a hand to the back of his head. I twist my fingers through his coarse hair, which gets him to straddle me, and now it's his turn to breach my lips with his tongue. It's like he knows *exactly* how to decimate my self-control.

My breathing picks up as I embark on a greedy exploration of his mouth, noticing the low squeak he makes when I tease the top, and the rumbles from his throat that come whenever I run my tongue along his. My arousal surges, coursing through every vein and concentrating in my groin. So far, Ian has been a total saint, not bringing his hands anywhere close to there, so I make the decision for him and thrust upward.

Between the many layers of fabric, our hard cocks collide, and I can't take any more.

I pull back. "Fuck, I want this so bad."

"Same here. I want you."

"Should I shower first?"

Ian waves me off. "Only if you want."

I get a whiff of Ian, and as usual, his irresistible scent overwhelms me. I sure don't smell as good, so shower it is. Even if it has to be a fast one.

Wasting no time, I dash into the bathroom and strip, not even waiting for the water to heat up before jumping in. The icy jets suck the air out of my lungs while I lather in shampoo, and I'm already halfway through soaping myself up before the shower gets warmer.

Then I'm done. I step out, dry off, put on deodorant, and reach for my change of clothes...that I forgot to bring.

I eye the crumpled clothes on the floor and immediately decide against putting them back on, hooking my towel around my waist before marching out into the living room.

At least this time, I *want* Ian to see me undressed.

He does a double take and drops his jaw when I round the corner. "Jesus fuck, Callum. Get your sexy ass over here."

Something unplaceable gives me the courage to straddle him.

Ian's eyes widen, and he grins up at me. "Someone's eager."

"Yeah, you could say that."

His fingers brush my chest. "Goddamn. You're almost too hot to be real."

My dick stiffens under the towel, even though his hands are still on my torso.

Wait. Do I get turned on from being complimented? I don't—

Okay, he's kissing my chest, so nothing else matters. He's going lower—oh, god, he's going really freaking low.

"Don't stop." My voice cracks. "Please."

"I wouldn't dream of it." Ian chuckles onto my skin and kisses the hair above the towel, flicking his eyes up as he pauses. My vision goes blurry as my cock jumps. I need... Fuck, I need him to do *something*.

That something ends up being a hand to the small of my back.

He pulls me down and angles his face so our lips collide. I grin into the kiss, accommodating his wandering tongue, and I return the favor with some tongue action of my own. Hopefully smiling through the hottest experience of my life will stave off whatever nerves I got last night.

"Woah, you kiss like you're trying to claim a piece of me," he says through a gasp of air. "You're amazing."

That's one way to make me hungry for more. I pull him

toward me, kind of like I actually *am* trying to claim a piece of him. I have no idea what the hell has gotten into me—I want Ian, and maybe him so clearly wanting me back has me feeling like I'm actually allowed.

"Can't get enough of you," I mutter, mindlessly skimming the bottom of his shirt with my fingertips.

Ian groans something unintelligible. It still sounds hot. "Want me to take my shirt off?"

"Yeah, oh my god."

And he does. He sheds his T-shirt, and that body is as amazing as I remember. His proportions are to die for—broad shoulders and chest, tapering down into a tight waist adorned with the same abs that turned my common sense off yesterday. He's by far the hottest guy I've seen on campus. I might be biased, but to me, nobody else comes close.

I grab onto Ian's thick arms, savoring the sweet resistance beneath my fingers, and try to make sense of the fact that this guy, this perfect fucking guy, wants me.

"You know, I like to think my face isn't half-bad, either," he jokes.

My response is to kiss his chest, biting at his skin with depraved desperation. Ian grunts and bucks up, placing a finger under my chin and tilting my head so he can kiss me again.

It burns so good, and I'm on the road to full-blown obsession.

"Need you so bad," I say, barely breaking the kiss.

"You call the shots," he murmurs. "Tell me what you want."

My heart jumps into my throat. Nerves prickle in my stomach again, but Ian's caring gaze and the warmth of his arms help to keep me grounded.

"What *can* I want?" I ask.

I want whatever Ian is willing to give me, nerves be damned.

He runs his hands down my sides. "I can jerk you off, suck your dick, you can bend me over—"

I chuckle, but my gaze falls to his full, parted lips as he darts his tongue out. All I can imagine is how they'd look wrapped around me, and how unreal his hot, wet mouth might feel.

Heat surges down my spine and into my balls.

"Can you use your mouth?" I ask.

He smirks. "What was that? Sorry, I couldn't hear you."

I groan and suck in a breath before letting my words out. "Please, Ian. Please suck my dick."

He reaches down, flashing those poster-worthy teeth at me. "My god, yeah. I wanna find out how fucking good you taste."

With slow, teasing fingers, he palms my aching hard-on through the towel before slipping underneath the fabric and curling around my length. Shivers shoot up my back, and I can't take any more.

"Please take your pants off," I say. "I want to see all of you."

Ian shuffles around underneath my thighs to slip his sweats off. My breath catches as I trace my gaze down along his abs, over the neatly trimmed swath of hair below his waist, and onto his full, uncut dick that's pointing straight up at me.

This man is hotter than I could have ever imagined, and he *wants to suck my dick.*

I push the towel off, freeing my erection, and Ian scoffs, smiling wide while recoiling like he got shot.

"Jesus *fuck*, Callum," he mutters. "What did they feed you out in Wisconsin?"

I try to reply, but I can't—Ian nudges my leg up and plants me on the couch, and he proceeds to get on his knees before licking a firm line up my shaft, which shuts my thinking off. His tongue is warm enough to send shivers into my core, and when he clasps a hand around me, I have to suck a breath in to ground myself.

He slides up my length, pressing his thumb to the tip to spread a drop of wetness around. That alone is enough to make me grit my teeth and press my hips forward into his touch.

"I'm *really* sensitive," I warn him.

That's met with a gentle hum. "Perfect. God, you're so... Fuck,

I need your cock." Ian hovers in front of my crotch, his breath hot on the head. The wait is brutal, but finally, *finally*, he inhales a gulp of air before—

Holy. Fuck.

Sheer, unadulterated bliss slams through my body as soon as he closes his lips around me, and I wrangle back a visceral moan, constraining it into a tight gasp. I grab onto a couch cushion, trying to steady myself, but it's no use.

This is downright unbelievable.

I had no idea I was capable of feeling anything *close* to what I am now. I'm panting, barely holding on, and my throat is tight with the noises I'm pushing down.

Then Ian slides off, leaving me aching for more. "Don't hold back, Cal. I wanna hear you lose it." With that, he slips me into his mouth again, and everything I was keeping down escapes at once in a loud, ragged groan.

Ian slicks me with practiced swipes of his tongue, making my head fall back, and then, oh *fuck*, he does something with his throat that encases my dick in the most delicious, mind-melting sensation I've ever experienced, and I swear I see galaxies.

He does everything on repeat, keeping my dick so freaking wet and twisting his hand around. It's like he's unscrewing my body and dismantling me into a million tiny pieces.

"Ian, how are you doing this?" I grit out, and he doesn't reply. He simply flicks his eyes up to mine and smiles around my shaft, not stopping for even a second. I'm swearing, grunting, and making a complete fool of myself, but I don't care. I'm going to come so fast, I might set a record.

"Fuck," I pant, and Ian makes eye contact again. The sight of his reverent, tear-dampened gaze almost makes me lose it right there. "I'm so close."

He doesn't let up—he's in complete control, I'm giving it to him, and he's rewarding me with goddamn *euphoria*.

The more I let myself go, the more he makes up for it, making my balls tighten with every disarming second that passes.

"Oh, god, I—"

That sentence catches in my throat as he sucks hard, and I spill the most intense, brain-wiping orgasm of my life into his hot mouth. He swallows around me, making my body seize up, the climax blanketing me in total pleasure.

Every single one of my muscles clenches as I ride the high, only relaxing when the short, sharp waves recede. My god, I've been missing out big time.

Ian drags off of me, popping off my softening dick and leaning backward. He wipes his mouth with one hand while stroking himself with the other, and before I can offer to help, he comes onto his abs with a garbled moan.

"Fuck, that was good," he mumbles, wiping himself off with the towel on the floor. "Did you have fun?"

"Holy crap." That's all I can manage.

Ian slips his clothes on and settles next to me. I reach down and pull a pair of my sweatpants out from under the couch, and he nudges my head under his outstretched arm, giving my hair a few gentle scratches as I lie down and relax into his lap. It's comfortable.

At least until it isn't.

That familiar feeling of sick, thorny shame twists in my gut as I close my eyes and try to shut it out. Without thinking, I latch onto Ian even tighter and try to steady my heartbeat while shoving the little voice in my head aside, the one telling me that I'm wrong for liking this.

It isn't even because it was with another guy. At least that's not the biggest part.

It's because I had sex and dared to enjoy myself.

"Hey there." Ian's soothing voice cuts through the fog in my head. "Whatcha thinking about?"

"Nothing." I take a shallow breath. "I never feel great after this kind of stuff. Perks of growing up how I did."

He doesn't reply straight away, but he holds me tighter. The bundle in my stomach is still present, but it shrinks.

"I don't know what to say to make it better, but there's a reason why we get horny and have sex and why it feels so good." He gives my shoulder a gentle squeeze. "It's because it's natural. Some people don't crave it, but if you do? There's nothing wrong with that."

Yeah, the last half hour solidified that I'm firmly in the "craves it" camp.

"I know there's nothing objectively wrong with sex," I reply. "But emotionally, I don't know. It's weird—I had to hide the fact that I even *thought* about sex for so long, and I can't just turn that off now that I'm free from my parents."

"And that's okay. I can't relate to what you're going through, but I'm here for you whenever you need me."

My face flushes as I interpret Ian's overwhelming kindness in a completely different, dirtier way. I'm a mess, but embarrassment beats shame any day of the week.

"Feeling better?" he asks.

"Yeah, actually. I don't think I've recovered this quickly before, after, you know."

"Coming?" Ian supplies.

I snort. "Yeah. After coming. It's getting better over time as I've let myself do more, uh, sexual things."

"Is that so?" He wiggles his eyebrows. "So you're saying lots and *lots* of exposure therapy helps, right?"

Rolling my eyes, I swat him across the chest, even though that little injection of humor was what I needed.

"Too soon?" he asks.

"No, you're fine. I *wasn't* saying that, but I won't say no to more of this."

"Lucky for you, I love giving head." He squeezes my shoulder. "Especially when the guy moans the way you do. It's fucking *hot*."

Heat creeps up my neck, even though Ian's generosity seriously benefits me. I press harder against his body, and he reaches behind the couch to drag the folded covers over us. The sheer warmth seeps right to my core, making me yawn. He simply tightens his arm and gives my back a gentle scratch, saying nothing but communicating pure care. It's impossible not to feel tired when I feel so safe.

"Is it rude to fall asleep after sex?" I ask through a yawn.

Ian snickers. "No, it isn't. Not at all. Snooze away, hot stuff."

CHAPTER SEVENTEEN
IAN

My left forearm is raw and red.

I'm pinching myself just in case I'm dreaming—the last twenty-four hours have set my emotional cravings on fire and hit every single one of my horny buttons a hundred times over.

Making out with Callum. Rolling around in bed with him. Cuddling him. Making out with him some more. Stripping him down to nothing. Getting my hands on his big, strong body. Wrapping my mouth around his cock.

God, that fucking cock.

That pretty, reactive, perfect cock that's well proportioned to Callum's...everything else. I got to suck it exactly *once*, and I already drool like a dog staring at a biscuit whenever I so much as think about it swinging around in his soft black sweatpants. Or how it looks outside those sweatpants as I'm about to blow him.

Aaand I'm hard again.

Not like getting hard is hard when Callum is built for sex and also built for ticking all of my boxes.

He's snoozing next to me on the couch-bed, still shirtless and still sexier than my brain can keep up with. I can't help but reach out and trace my fingers across his pecs, and his mouth twitches into a sleepy grin at the touch, all soft and peaceful.

He's so ridiculously cute all the time, but when he's asleep? Oh, man, he's more adorable than a farm full of puppies, with his tiny smile and twitching eyes and cheekbones and everything else that makes him a total show-stopping dreamboat of a man.

The achy pangs of sweet, sweet affection in my chest won't stop, and I don't want them to.

Then, when I think this can't get any better, he rolls over and wraps himself around me.

Okay, I think this is what being a puddle feels like because I'm *melted* right now. Holy shit, I must have been a *saint* in my past life to deserve this. I might be a natural big spoon, but being all wrapped up in someone scratches a certain kind of intimate itch in my brain for which substitutes don't exist.

Like the total sap I am, I rotate myself and maneuver my head up to kiss his forehead. Callum lets out some kind of half-asleep mumble, and the sound goes to two places: my heart and my dick.

Sheesh. My mind fills with pure filth whenever I so much as remember he exists, and it's not like he's totally innocent either, not with how hot he sounded when I was going down on him an hour ago. If he lets me be as freaky as I want with him, I'm gonna have to start wearing my knee pads at home.

Okay, Ian. Calm down.

On one hand, I know it's a good idea to take things nice and slow with Callum, let him come to me when he's ready, and not go over the top. He hasn't told me *that* much about his past, and the last thing I need to do is feed into unhealthy coping mechanisms.

On the other hand, he's in therapy. That sure counts for a lot.

Oh, and he *likes* me. He said so himself, and as for me? I never knew I could miss something before experiencing it, but after holding Callum in my arms and knowing what the reverse feels like, I don't know how I was ever satisfied before.

Holy hell, I'm so gone for him, and it hasn't even been a full day since we first kissed.

I sink deeper into the couch and let out a massive sigh, a grin spreading across my lips. When I like someone, I *like* someone—I don't know if I've ever wanted someone this much, and I'd be a massive liar if I didn't admit how amazing that makes me feel. Callum is the first guy in way too long who hasn't given me crap for being affectionate. That sure isn't lost on me, and there's no way I'll mess this up, not if I have any say in it.

As soon as I'm about to fall asleep myself, Callum's body jerks, jolting both of us fully awake. His sleepy, captivating eyes open slowly, and once again, I can't notice anything other than his long-ass eyelashes. I'm surprised he doesn't make the wind pick up every time he blinks.

"Did you sleep well?" I ask.

He stretches, yawning and releasing a strained noise from his throat. "Oh yeah," he mumbles, curling back around me. "I napped so hard, I'm all tired out."

I snort, and he devolves into laughter at the sound. For someone who's so quiet most of the time, his loud, carefree laughs are always a sweet surprise.

"Are you too tired for dinner?" I ask. "I can order Italian from the place downstairs again."

My offer is met with a slow, appreciative nod, and I sit down next to him for what I intend to be a quick kiss.

The millisecond my lips brush his, I can't drag myself away. I meet his clear, enchanting eyes for a second before closing my own, and I press harder into his mouth, letting Callum slip his tongue between my teeth.

Screw being quick. I could do this forever.

Yup, I've had ten hits off Callum's lips, and I'm already hooked. He should come with an advisory label the way nicotine does. *Warning: Contains Callum. Callum is a highly addictive man. Consume at risk of being consumed yourself.*

His stomach growling breaks the moment, activating my provider instincts like I'm a sleeper agent, and I pull back a little too quickly. He blinks at me as if I betrayed him, and I use all of my willpower to take my phone out and order pasta instead of choosing to eat a very different kind of noodle for dinner—the kind that's best served extra, extra al dente and is available *now,* not in twenty minutes.

That twenty-minute wait passes in a flash, though, because I spend it making out with Callum while his heavy body pins me to the couch. He gets a little feisty, and his instincts are fucking *primal* because he tries to give me, like, a hundred hickeys, but he's easily distracted by my mouth when I align it with his.

We groan in tandem when my phone beeps, and I'm filled with regret over not paying extra for delivery, even though the restaurant is in my building.

"Don't you dare go anywhere," I say, reluctantly unpeeling myself from Callum when he nudges into me for a peck. "I'll be right back."

Downstairs, I wait for the cashier to find our order, and I stand off to the side and wait with my hands in my pockets. In Callum's absence, the gravity of what went down starts to sink in.

I'm his first...everything. I've been a few peoples' firsts before, but those times were different. There's something else between us beyond late-night hookup feels, or at least I hope there is, given that I'm already down bad for him. That, and the fact that he had a messed-up childhood, leading to him having more nerves than my fingertips.

From one guy-loving-guy to another, it's on me to help him out. It's a responsibility to a baby gay.

A skyscraping baby gay with chest hair.

Still, he's in a fragile place. I can only imagine what's going through his head, so I do the unthinkable and apply *logic*.

We hooked up, he liked it, and he might like other things.

I could take him on a date.

Has he ever been on a date? Not likely, given what he's told me.

And for the first time since the summer, I let my heart race over the prospect of taking someone out. He's a blank slate, so I need to make it good. Way to put pressure on myself, but hey, it's for a good cause.

Callum is waiting at the dining table when I get back, and I find that he's set it. Holy crap, he's so thoughtful.

We eat in silence, our hunger getting the best of us, and I clear our dishes once we're both done. The two of us retreat to the couch, which I hope will stop being Callum's bed, and I gesture for him to lie down.

He places his head in my lap, which sends an affectionate jolt of heat to my chest.

I'm gonna ask him now. There's no reason not to.

"Hey, I was thinking," I start, and he perks his head up, smiling. "Do you want to maybe go out sometime?" My heart is so far up my throat, it may as well be replacing my Adam's apple.

"Yeah," he says, his voice soft. "You mean like a date?"

"Yes, Callum, I want to take you on a date," I confirm. He has his hands clasped together on his chest, and I reach down to run my thumb along his knuckles.

"I'd like that a lot," he says.

There's no way for me to suppress the grin that breaks through my lips, so I don't even try. If this ends up being a dream, I'm gonna wake up so mad.

He continues. "I've never been on a date."

I guessed so, but there's still that pressure to make it good. Even so, he said yes, and he trusts me to be the first guy to take him out. The brewing warmth in my core more than makes up for the nerves.

Tightening my arms around Callum's shoulders, I kiss his head as he nudges it deeper into my lap. He might as well be corkscrewing up into my heart with how he's being so cuddly.

"So," I say, "do you still want to sleep on this lumpy, cold couch tonight, or do you want to join me in bed and use me as your personal space heater?"

He huffs. "You're really selling it. Let's share the bed, if you're okay with it."

Thank fuck. For my own selfish reasons, I'm kind of glad to have the couch back, but I'm happier about him wanting to share the bed. I need morning hugs or I get grouchy, and I've been grouchy for as long as I can remember.

"Let's go, then." I lead him back into the bedroom when he gives me a firm nod. Callum settling into the sheets next to me feels so natural, and I shut my eyes, resolving to do things right.

My god, it's happening again, but this time, the target of my affection doesn't seem to mind that much, not even when I roll over to spoon him. Again.

"You like this?" I ask.

"Yeah, s'okay," he mumbles. The way he snuggles backward into me says that it's more than okay, and him sighing when I tighten my arms around him confirms it.

"Sorry my bed isn't any bigger."

Callum snorts. "I went from a dorm single to your couch, and now to this. It's a major step up."

"Yeah. If I knew I'd share with a giant, I would've sprung for something bigger than a double."

"Come on, I'm not a *giant*," he mumbles. "I'm like, six-five."

I haul him closer to me. "Yeah, that's giant," I fire back. "It doesn't matter because I'm still gonna be the big spoon."

With that, I roll on top of Callum, pressing him into the mattress. He flails around, laughing and pushing me off with a weak shove.

Crap. I snap out of it and fall back to my side of the bed.

"Sorry about that," I say.

"What for?"

I sigh. "Again, I can be a lot. Some people have complained about me being too, uh, affectionate before."

Callum nudges his head into my chest. "Nah, I really don't mind. I like knowing that you care."

My heart fucking gives out. "Sweeter words were never spoken, Cal." I curl around his back, savoring his warmth. It's like I'm a jetpack, but it works.

After what feels like only a minute, he slackens under my arms. As much as I joked about him using me as a furnace, he runs hot, so I withdraw to avoid overheating. His presence never leaves my consciousness, though, and I let myself get lost in the rhythm of his breathing.

Tomorrow, we're gonna plan our little date that I hope he'll want to repeat.

Tonight, I have him in my bed for a second time. That's more than I could have ever hoped for even a day ago.

CHAPTER EIGHTEEN

CALLUM

First grocery run in three years. Let's do this.

This morning, I finally put my foot down with Ian and told him that I'm not going to mooch off him anymore, and that I'd buy us some groceries. He tried putting up a fight, he *really* did, but I practiced using my spine and didn't back down. The compromise was that I'm buying, but that I'd drive his car to the store. That seemed fair enough to me, and it sure beats taking the campus bus.

Oh, and tonight is when we have our date. I spent months trying not to fall for Ian, only to end up starting a petty argument the very day we're going out. It was hardly an argument, if I'm being honest, but still. There's no way I'm not stepping it up tonight. I have to look the part. He'll always outshine me, but I can do my best.

That's why I find myself standing in the clothing aisle, contemplating buying the first new piece of clothing since I got here, save for a pack of boxers I got online, which doesn't count.

After years of wearing the same four outfits on repeat, the multicolored choices in front of me are downright overwhelming. I fight the temptation to text anyone for help choosing an outfit; I'm not going to rely on other people for something as simple as buying a shirt.

Cursing myself for not searching up clothing inspiration *before* I left, I run my fingers across a stack of polos. I suppose I could go full prep, and I might finally fit at this school, but the style isn't me. As messy as my past is, I don't want to completely change myself.

Besides, in the week since we got closer, Ian's taken to stealing my T-shirts and wearing them himself, so that tells me he likes my aesthetic for some odd reason.

Or he just likes seeing me shirtless. Both might be true.

The section to the right brings a lot more promise. The shirts have buttons and regular T-shirt collars.

They're called Henley shirts. I think I'll try a few of those. Also, the model in the promotional poster is hot.

Am I really *picking a shirt based on how attractive the model is?*

Yes, I am. It isn't like I have much else to go on.

I have no idea what size I am in this store, so I grab three options and head for the fitting room. Out of habit, I check that the door is locked more times than necessary before stripping my shirt off.

My eyes catch on my reflection in the full-length mirror, and I pause. My workouts are showing a bit more now, thanks to Ian sharing his protein-rich athlete diet, though I'm nowhere near as defined as he is. His job is to be an athlete while mine is to shelve books, so it makes sense that my body's quite a bit softer.

Okay, nope, it's clothes time. I try the first shirt from the pile, and it's an immediate no—I'm not trying to buy a crop top. A size up is slightly better, but it kind of drapes over me. It's a look, that's for sure, but I'll try the last option.

Tall-sizing is the way to go. Not a crop top, not too baggy, and not tight like my old clothes. The shirt is a lighter blue than my flannel that Ian likes, but it's still blue, and that's enough to slip it into my basket.

It doesn't cost that much, either. I have some wiggle room in my budget, especially since I got refunded my dorm fees, so I head to the pharmacy section for some more poking around.

There's a tub of something called "Mess Paste" in the haircare section, and after giving the container a quick inspection, I toss that into my basket as well, since Ian always has his hands in my hair, trying to muss it up.

Is it weird that I'm only doing what Ian thinks is attractive?

Nah.

He's hotter than the depths of hell my parents would say I'm headed for—I trust his opinion on what looks good, and I'm buying all this for myself, after all.

Once I'm back home, it's already five. I have a little under two hours to get ready, so I rip the tags off of my new shirt and throw it into the washing machine with the rest of my dirty laundry. I let the load run on a quick cycle while I take a shower and switch it to the dryer after I'm done. In the bedroom, I put socks and underwear on, and spend way too much time rummaging around in the closet for my good jeans before remembering that I washed those, too. Out of instinct, I reach for my wet towel and am about to wrap it around my waist before I pause.

I'm alone. There's no need for me to cover up. Nobody can see in through the windows, and Ian said he's going straight to the bowling alley from practice. Besides, even if he was here, he wouldn't care.

And that's how I end up sitting around in nothing but my underwear. It's a little weird, given that I've never been *only* in boxers, except for a few seconds at a time while getting dressed or undressed, but it's...freeing? In a mundane kind of way. I could get used to it.

While I wait for my clothes to finish drying, I bang out a couple of quizzes for my Motor Learning course, and my nerves get the better of me when I peek at the clock to find that I only have an hour to get ready.

I don't need to do much beyond getting dressed, but I don't want to be late. Ian deserves better.

Since I'm short on time, I remove everything except for my shirt and jeans from the dryer and turn up the temperature. Thankfully, those don't need much longer, so I slip into them with time to spare, and I grab my new hair product to finish up.

I stand in front of the bathroom mirror and take stock of what I'm working with. Ian asked me out. He likes how I look, and if I'm being honest, I'm starting to see it. He's right about my eyes—

wearing blue makes them stand out, and standing out isn't necessarily a bad thing. I give myself a smile as I keep trying to replicate the hairstyle Ian gave me a week ago, right before I came out to him and changed the trajectory of our friendship. It's a style that would get me admonished back home for being unkempt and corrupt, but here, it's...attractive.

Okay. If there's wind, that'll help me mess it up even more, which is now a good thing. I put on an extra swipe of deodorant for good measure and head out, my heart pounding with excitement as I make my way to my first first date.

For a second, I entertain the fleeting, wandering fantasy that tonight will be the *last* first date I'll ever have to go on. What I feel for Ian is unlike anything I've ever experienced before, and I can't imagine directing these swirling, chest-tightening emotions toward anyone else.

The mere thought makes my stomach twist, and I take a breath to redirect. Now isn't the time to get caught up in speculation—tonight is about having fun and hopefully starting something more.

From what I read online, I need to take things one step at a time with dating, so that's what I'll do.

CHAPTER NINETEEN
IAN

What do you know, the random iron in the baseball locker room is getting its first use tonight, courtesy of me.

Practice is over, and I'm freshly showered, moisturized, and cologned-up. I'm standing in a towel, making meticulous passes over my pants, and when I turn around to grab my shirt, I'm greeted by two pairs of staring eyes: Nick's and my teammate Jeremy's.

"Scotty's got a date tonight," Jeremy says, his arms crossed. He doesn't even bother turning that into a question.

"And what if I do? Jealous it's not with you?" I joke.

"Aww, fuck you." He flips his mop of messy, light blond hair out of his face, which gives me a better view of his cocky grin. "Any other day, I'd toss my water bottle at your head, but I'll hold back today out of respect for your hot date."

"Much appreciated," I reply, humored sarcasm lining my tone. I finish ironing my polo, and I hang it up in my locker to let the steam evaporate.

"Who's your date?" Nick asks. "Guy or girl?"

"Guy," I reply. "Not spilling any more for now. Don't wanna jinx it."

Nick nods. "Nice. Hope it goes well."

I smile into my locker before turning around, a small coil of nerves materializing in my stomach. "Thanks. I want it to go well. I really, really do."

From the way Nick's mouth is tight from suppressing laughter, and how Jeremy is grinning into his fist, I must have let out a wistful sigh or something.

"Uh-oh, someone has a *crush*," Nick sings.

"And what about it? For what it's worth, the guy I'm going out with tonight is super excited, too."

"Good shit." Nick gives me an excited fist bump. "Way to go, man."

That's that, so I slip into my clothes, shut my locker, and head out into the cold. Callum and I are going bowling, and the lanes aren't far from the ballpark. It's pretty stereotypical as first dates go, but it's still a safe, tame option. Besides, we'll be in public, so we'll be forced to keep things wholesome. Not that I mind being sweet with him, not at all—it's just that up until now, Callum and I have chosen to be calm *after* letting off steam.

And he has a *lot* of fucking steam to let off. I don't know if he's making up for lost time or if he's naturally insatiable, but I'm not gonna complain about him giving me his typical cute pleading expression, like, all the time.

When I asked him out a week ago, I mostly wanted to pump the brakes in case he got nervous about hooking up so quickly. Now that I'm here at the bowling alley, I know it's also for me. I like Callum. I want to be with him. Putting us back on the standard path of going out is the safest way to get there. I just need to keep myself calm, avoid jumping the gun, and stop myself from scaring him off.

The bowling alley is blissfully warm, and I shed my coat to thaw faster. Scanning around, I try to spot Callum, and as soon as I do, I find that it's a lot harder to breathe.

Holy motherfucking shit, he's at risk of burning the whole building down with how scorching-hot he is. My god. He's wearing a simple blue Henley that I haven't seen before, a little looser than I'm used to, but it still shows off his powerful frame and gives my ever-hungry eyes a *lot* to feast on.

Callum tilts his head up and locks eyes with me, sending a sweet smile over my way. I pick up the pace, not wanting to wait any longer.

"Hey," he says. "You look good."

I do? "You're one to talk. Is that a new shirt?"

He nods.

I swallow, finding words as I run a sneaky hand down the fabric covering one of his arms. "You look amazing."

"You're such a flirt," he says, smirking at me in a way that melts even more of my testy self-control.

Since when did he smirk? Hell, his usual small smiles already make me go loopy, but *smirking*? It's lethal. Fucking *lethal*.

"I have half a mind to drag you back home and undress you with more than my eyes," I whisper, getting on my toes to reach his ears, which turn red as soon as I finish my sentence. "But I was looking forward to taking you out tonight, so we're both gonna have to wait."

Callum turns his head to me, his eyes narrow and sensual. "I'm used to holding out for that. At least this time the wait will be worth it."

Whew. Okay. I can stay calm, even in the face of Callum managing to be vulnerable and tantalizing at the same time. Shutting my eyes, I smile and repeat a much-needed reminder in my head: *I will not be a horndog, I will not be a horndog, I will not be a horndog.*

"Alright, Cal, enough of that," I announce, slinging an arm around his waist. "We're here to have some nice, wholesome fun together."

———

And we do. Callum is a *beast*, and he smokes the hell out of me. By the end of the night, I've won a single game out of five, and he isn't gloating nearly as much as he should be.

"I'm telling you, you gotta sign up for the Kinesiology rec league at least," I say as we leave the alley. "You have serious skills."

Modest as ever, Callum shrugs me off. "Nah. Beginner's luck."

"Aw, come on, Cal, you can gloat a little." I dig my thumbs

into his shoulder blades, hyping him up. "Repeat after me: I'm a fucking champ and I got five strikes in a row."

He snorts. "Not saying that, sorry."

"Okay, fine," I reply, lying. "But c'mere."

I stop walking, prompting Callum to do the same, and I stare up at him. As if he reads my mind, he leans down for a kiss, and I press up to join him.

And I pull away at the last second. "Sorry, buddy. You gotta gloat before I kiss you."

"You're ridiculous." He rolls his eyes, and I swear I've never seen sexier sass in my life.

I nudge his head with my fingers so he's facing me again. "Hey, I'm serious. You know what you have to do." For added pressure— uh, incentive, I run my thumb along his lower lip.

That's what gets him to snap. "Okay, fine. I'm a fucking champ, I got five strikes in a row, and Ian's a sore loser because he's finding ways to punish me."

Recoiling, I open my mouth and let out a noise that's somewhere between a snicker and a scoff. "Jesus, the mouth on this guy," I say, molding my face into an expression of false offense. "Where did that come from?"

Callum closes the distance between us and hooks an arm around my back. "I don't know. Can I *please* kiss you already?"

Yes, yes, he can.

And he does, making me regret ever holding out on him. It's official: I'm never withholding a kiss ever again. I'll have to find some other way of teasing Callum, a way that doesn't deprive me at the same time.

Every gentle sweep of my tongue in his mouth imparts more and more of his heady, addictive flavor: the pizza he insisted on buying for us after I paid for his shoe rental, the soda I bought him after betting that he wouldn't get five strikes in a row, and then something unplaceable and uniquely him. He tries to pull away, and I only let him take a quick inhale before crashing my mouth back onto his for more.

I want him in every way: physically, romantically... If he wasn't going through post-religious deprogramming, I'd say I want him biblically, too, but he has the past that he does, so I'll want him carnally instead.

"Okay, okay, let me breathe," Callum says with a chuckle as he pulls away and holds me at a distance with his long arms. "That doesn't mean I don't want more. I do. It's just that we're in public and my pants are already tight enough."

"Tight pants crew, let's go," I joke, giving him a fist bump. "You're good at explaining yourself, that's for sure."

He shrugs a shoulder. "Yeah. I mean, you said people in the past gave you crap for being affectionate, and I don't want you to think I'm the same."

That one sentence is all it takes for the world to stop.

Holy shit.

One thing about suddenly feeling full is that you're made aware of how *empty* everything was leading up to the present. I knew the guys in the past were dicks, but I always thought that how they reacted to me was my fault. Callum considering my feelings like it's no big deal to him has me all raw and fuzzy and *numb*.

"Thank you. I... I really appreciate it." I keep walking so I don't start crying tears of elation in the middle of the sidewalk. "Did you have a good time tonight?"

I don't think I needed to ask—he's fucking beaming. When that man is happy, I swear the world becomes a better place because of it.

"Yeah," he says, tilting his head back. "Tonight was the most fun I've had in... Yeah. I had a great time."

What he didn't say makes my stomach clench, and I bring my hand to him, threading my fingers through his.

And not to be dramatic or anything, but when he squeezes not once, but *twice*, I swear my heart gives out.

"Whatcha doin' there?" I ask.

"Nothing. I felt like it'd be nice to do."

Callum Cross: the oblivious romantic.

We're both tired as hell from the date, so we walk home in near silence. Callum's hand doesn't leave mine for a second, though, not even when someone steps out of a dorm across the street.

That's when it sinks in even more. I'm witnessing, no, *experiencing* him grow into his skin in real time, and he's choosing to do that with me.

Someone is choosing me.

Now it's my turn to squeeze Callum's hand, and then I decide to lean my head against his shoulder like the sap I am.

He breathes out, in something that sounds like a huffed laugh. "Holy fuck."

"You good?"

"Uh-huh," he says. "Can we sit for a while? I'm kind of... I need to sit."

I guide him under the archway of Maple Hall. There's scaffolding all over the building, but the construction workers have all left for the night. It's only the two of us there.

"Is everything okay?" I ask, sitting down on a bench in the quad.

Callum joins me. "Yeah." His voice is soft, and some kind of gentle, almost sad smile plays out on his lips. "Tonight was amazing. Thank you again for taking me out." He leans his head on mine, making my heart race.

"You don't need to thank me for taking you on a date, Cal," I say, placing my hand on his and giving him a squeeze. "I wanted to ask you out from the second you told me you're into guys."

"I..." He trails off, sucking in a breath. "I never thought I'd get to experience anything like this. I've never felt like anyone wants me."

"Hey, come here." I open my arms, and Callum nudges into me, the way he always does, and the way I've come to crave. "I want you so bad, Cal. All of you. I'm so fucking gone for you."

"Tha—"

I press a finger to his mouth and cut him off. Rude, but necessary. "You're not gonna thank me for being into you, my god." I ruffle his cute hair and restore some of the charming muss that flattened as the night went on. "My feelings are all because of you. You're a great friend and—" *Hopefully a great boyfriend.*

One week and one date. That's all it took for me to *almost* ask him the boyfriend question. At least I was thinking hard enough to cut myself off before I lost control.

"—and that's why it's so easy for me. You're *awesome*," is what I say instead.

"Can I say something?"

"Of course. Open book."

"Back when I was living with my parents, after I knew I was gay, but whenever I was still feeling like crap about it, I'd imagine... things. Like things with guys." He sucks in a breath before continuing. "Not that I had any frame of reference or anything, but I'd see people being affectionate with each other at the store, or later, on campus at community college, and I'd think about what it might be like for me to have something like that."

Oh, we're getting deep tonight. Not that I mind, not at all.

He huffs. "Never mind. It's stupid."

"Whatever you're thinking, it isn't."

Callum turns to face me, and I give his knee a gentle press, which seems to spur him on.

"I know we've only gone out once, but I—"

My breath catches. I won't *fault* him for dropping the L-word if he does, but we'll probably need to talk about identifying emotions or something—

"You're pretty much exactly the kind of guy I always used to imagine back then."

Holy shit.

He isn't done. "You're so caring, and patient, and everything I didn't think I ever deserved."

My heart. It fucking hurts so good and is full and now *I'm* tempted to say the L-word even though I know it's way too early and—

I drag Callum's head down and kiss him before I spin out of control. There's no way I'm holding my smile back, not a chance.

"You're so sweet," I murmur. "You're so fucking sweet. And I used to think you were intimidating."

He snickers. "Yeah, I wasn't doing myself any favors when I first got here."

"Eh, I knew there was a total softie underneath that sexy smolder."

"I'm a softie?" He huffs and rolls his eyes, so I place a gloved hand on his face and bring him back to me.

"You totally are, and I dig it."

He lets out a quiet chuckle right as I shiver, and I stand, extending an arm to help him up so we can go home and defrost.

Disguising a tired sigh as a cough, I keep pace with Callum and keep myself grounded. I won't rush things with him like I did with other people in the past. Yeah, he reassured me earlier, but that was about a kiss, not the infinitely more intense aspect of *feelings*.

I won't pressure him—I'll keep the door open and let him do what he's comfortable with.

I just hope I don't end up scaring him off.

CHAPTER TWENTY
CALLUM

Anita's office is warm and inviting as always, and I settle into the small armchair for another scheduled session. As much as I'm okay and functional for the most part, I don't want to settle for that—anything could happen to me, and I need a solid, independent emotional foundation.

"So, what's new with you, Callum?"

I let out a dry, humored huff. "Where do I even start?"

"Perhaps from where we left off last time." She checks her notes. "Your dorm was damaged, you moved in with your friend, and you had certain feelings toward him."

Oh, there's so much to catch her up on.

"Yeah," I start. "So long story short, Ian came out to me, I came out to him a day later, then we hooked up, and now we're kind of dating. We went out for the first time last night."

Anita pauses, her fingers hovering over her tablet. She blinks, smiling, and picks up her pen. "That's great!" she says, writing something down with furious speed. "And very fast. How do you feel about all these developments?"

I run a hand through my hair, smiling as I'm reminded of how Ian tousled some of my new styling paste in before he left for the day. "Really good. I feel safe, and there's no pressure to do anything I don't want to."

What I don't reveal is how Ian hasn't asked me to get him off *once*. Sure, it's kind of difficult to start anything when he gets on his knees out of instinct and has me shaking and tongue-tied before I have a chance to offer, but I know I could take the lead in that area, too.

Anita speaks to me, snapping me back to the present. "I'm glad you've been able to get comfortable around him, especially this quickly. You were very concerned during our last session."

I shrug. "He makes it easy. Like, he doesn't hide anything."

"Do you want to explore that a little more? After all, you've mentioned how much you look up to him."

Oh, Jesus, saying anything more out loud won't come naturally, but pushing through is what I'm here for. "Okay, yeah. I keep thinking he's too good for me, but Ian makes it clear that he likes me. That's, I don't know, reassuring, I guess, to see that someone who I consider to be amazing and experienced and confident likes me back the way he does."

Anita thinks for a few seconds, nodding and taking my answer in. "And I'll be direct here, since this is something that comes up in people with similar backgrounds to yourself—do you have concerns with any mismatch in sexual experience?"

Embarrassment creeps up my neck and into my face. Despite having sessions with Anita since January, I've never fully told her the extent of my sexual hang-ups. It didn't seem appropriate, but hey, now she's asked.

"I did," I admit. "Intimacy was demonized when I was growing up. But I don't know, maybe it helps to share that experience with someone who doesn't beat themselves up for having urges."

"Demonized?"

Discomfort threads through my core. I'll keep things brief. I don't want to go back to that part of my life. "Long story short, anything sexual was on par with a drug addiction. Forbidden and repressed."

"But you've said it's getting better?"

"Oh yeah. I'm not saying he's the *only* reason that's the case, but he's definitely helped."

Thankfully for both of us, Anita steers the topic away from my sexual developments and more to healthy attachment, anxiety management, and communication. I came to the session in a decent mood, and I'm leaving with even more of a lighter chest. It's rubbing off on me, this therapy thing. Hopefully I'll get to see some of those long-term effects I'm excited about.

———

The empty apartment is gloomy when I get back, so I flick the heating and a few lamps on. This is Ian's house for sure—it isn't the same when he's gone. It's too quiet, too empty, and I don't get nearly enough hugs.

I check my watch, my heart skipping when I see it's almost six. He'll be back sometime in the next half hour, and I can hardly wait.

Taking a breath to focus myself, I repeat a mental reminder that we're still friends, and we haven't spoken about anything beyond that. What's unspoken is how we're also hooking up—friends aren't exactly known for doing that, but I'm not gonna complain one bit.

Why on earth would I complain about having a ton of sex?

That one little thought opens up the floodgates in my mind, filling my brain with sweet, sweet visuals of Ian working me over, and in mere seconds, I'm hard. Again. What a surprise.

Running a hand across my face, I let out a quiet laugh. Permission and reciprocity make all the difference between me beating myself up for thinking about Ian and daydreaming about his heaven-sent blowjobs.

Oh, hell, I'm out of control. As much as I love how good he makes me feel, it's definitely time for me to give back. The thought makes my heart race; I'd be lying if I said I wasn't nervous about living up to the standard Ian has set, which is why I find myself pulling up my phone searching up exactly how to do that. It seems like taking care of him should come naturally to me since I know what I like, but he's uncut—the equipment might work a little differently. He's never used lube on himself around me, but I haven't seen exactly how he does it.

A quick search confirms that there are a few things to keep in mind. I might not have to use lube, and I'll need to move my hand with his skin instead of sliding on top of it.

Seems simple enough.

Checking the time again, I jolt myself into action so I'm ready to welcome Ian back. I take a quick shower, dry off, and put some clothes on, contemplating my next move.

Ian knows how much I'm into him, and boy, does he take advantage of that. He started strolling around the house in a tank top, then he moved on to nothing but those skimpy gym shorts that show his ass off. All that progressed in, like, a day and a half, and now he makes a point to hang around me with the express purpose of frying the paltry remnants of my self-control.

It isn't like he even has to *try*. He could touch my arm, fully clothed, and I'd still go all weak for him.

Still, it's not right if I'm the one constantly drooling over my hot friend-turned-roommate-turned-hookup. I should give him a surprise, too, and the mere idea sends heat twisting down my shaft.

Huh. Yesterday, I found him reclined on the bed, buck naked with only a blanket covering his crotch, beckoning me over with a shit-eating grin and an irresistible lick of his lips.

That could be something to work toward. I chuckle as I toss my shirt away, before hooking my thumbs in the waistband of my sweats. Going completely naked, entirely unprompted, still makes my gut twist a little.

Ian should be home any second now, and I can't wait to see his face. Then he can take my pants off for me.

Ha, I'm being the kind of wicked temptress my parents told me to avoid at all costs, seducing men with nothing more than bare skin and harlotry.

I don't give a damn what my parents think anymore, but even if I did, they never told me not to *be* a wicked temptress.

Smiling to myself, I discard my sweatpants too, and as I'm deciding whether I should cover up *something*, the lock clicks. Bolting across the room, I make it to the couch to take my position before Ian opens the door, and I lie back with a hand tucked casually behind my head and my shirt on top of my crotch.

"Hey, Cal," he says, tossing his keys into the basket next to the front door. "How was your—"

He stops dead in his tracks the millisecond he rounds the corner.

"Mother*fuck*." He drags his molten eyes over me, greedy and intense. A lopsided smile curls across his lips, and he drops his gear bag on the floor, stepping closer.

"Is anything wrong?" I ask with fake concern. "You're awfully quiet."

"Cocky, are we?" Ian rolls his eyes and plants his palms on my chest, leaning down to kiss me. It's gentle, like all his casual kisses, but there's a certain hunger behind every brisk swipe of his tongue across my teeth, which turns me on to no end.

"My god, you're a fucking dream," he mutters, moving his hands lower. He starts to bend down like he always does, and I hook a hand under his arm to stop him.

"I was thinking we could try something different," I say. "Bedroom?"

"You don't have to ask me twice. I have to shower first, though. There was a line in the locker room after practice, and I stink."

"Mmm, sexy sweaty jock. Gimme." Did I read that line on the internet somewhere? Yeah, I did, but I still play into it.

Ian freezes before pressing his lips together and snickering. He's unable to hold back, and he bends over, laughing his ass off and resting his forehead on mine. "Cal, you're a hidden gem. Never change, buddy."

"You take ages in the shower," I complain. "I don't know if I can wait that long." For effect, I grab his wrist to stop him from walking away. Purely as a joke, of course.

"Hey, let me take a shower," he says, and because I'm already being cheeky, I keep up the act and don't let go.

He snorts, stilling for a moment. "Alright, Cal. You asked for it."

I don't have time to wonder what he means because he twists around, tackling me onto my back, and—

Oh *fuck*. He's pinning my arms above my head, and my only complaint is that he isn't holding tighter.

"That's what bad boys get," he teases, nudging my barely-covered erection with his knee.

Out of instinct, I try to bring my arms down, and as soon as I feel him put more weight on my wrists to stop me from moving, I immediately relax.

Call me weird, but I *don't* want to break free. Ian is super strong, and I can't move an inch.

That predicament sends a tidal wave of arousal straight to my groin. My already-hard dick stiffens even more, which I didn't even think was possible, and it starts to *hurt*.

What the hell?

He pulls off me, chucking gently and swatting my shoulder with the front of his hand. He says something to me, and I don't respond, instead trying to make sense of what just happened.

The shower turning on snaps me out of my unproductive speculating, and I shake my head.

I got real close to Ian, who has ridiculous sex appeal even when he's sweaty. That's why I got aroused. Palming myself, I will him to hurry up and shower faster, because damn, I'm *dying* to get my hands on his cock and make him feel good.

Look at me, getting this comfortable with sex.

I snort. My parents would be fucking pissed, and I consider that a *good* thing. Mom always told me that no woman would ever be good enough for her pure, precious son, but the joke's on her since I'm exploiting the hell out of the gay loophole.

Not that I *need* a loophole in the first place.

I banish all thoughts of my parents from my brain. I'm not trying to kill my boner.

Ian turns the water off after a few minutes, so I make my way to the bedroom and slip under the covers to wait. The bathroom door opens, there are footsteps in the hallway, and then he strides in, his hair damp and a towel fastened above his waist.

There's no way I'll ever get tired of seeing him without a shirt. His compact body with all its sport-toned muscles, covered with smooth, tanned skin, keeps my attention like nothing else. He lets out a quiet snort, and I lift my eyes to his face, taking in his smile and realizing that I'm wearing one myself, too.

"Such a horndog, this one," he teases, and I don't miss the predictable appearance of a firm, growing lump underneath the towel.

"Come here. Let's cuddle for a bit," I say, doing my best to ignore the pressure in my balls.

"Sounds wholesome." Ian drops the towel and joins me in his bed.

This time, I decide to change things up by wrapping my arms around him instead. He nuzzles into me, pressing his firm ass into my crotch and making me hiss out a cuss.

"You're making it a little hard to be wholesome," I mutter.

"That's kind of the point. I've been craving you ever since I left this morning."

We both chuckle, and I draw in a deep breath behind Ian's neck. If not being wholesome is the point, I can get behind that.

I clasp his erection and give it a slow stroke.

"Callum," he says, his voice deep and husky. "What are you—"

"Shh. Let me do this."

Ian pulses in my hand as soon as I shush him, and I squeeze the tip of his dick. I dig my fingers into the underside of his shaft, which is enough to make him squirm. The movement knocks my hand away, so I slide my other arm under his neck and wrap around his chest to hold him in place.

"Try to make this easier for me," I tease.

Ian nods, and I resume my slow strokes, pressing his warm body into mine as his breaths grow deeper.

"Fuck, Callum." He hums a low, satisfied noise. "You're amazing."

I'm already warm from his body heat and the sheer intensity of what I'm doing to him, and his flattery ramps it up even more. My hard-on jumps against his ass, and he lets out a surprised huff.

"Wait, do you have a praise kink?" Ian asks.

I stop stroking. "A what?"

He groans, not answering me. "Keep going, Callum. You're doing so well."

Feeling bolder, I slide my free hand down to tug on his balls, and he yelps out a desperate "fuck yes" when I resume stroking.

"You're so good at this," he pants. "Please don't stop."

As soon as he says that, I get harder, pressing into Ian's leg.

He chuckles. "Oh yeah, you *do* have a thing for compliments."

Heat floods my cheeks. This is a consideration for when I don't have a quivering, horned-up guy in my arms.

I speed up, gliding the skin up and down Ian's dick, relishing the sounds of his breaths getting heavier and raspier. He leaks generously into my hand, and unable to help myself, I bend my head down to sink my teeth into his shoulder blades. The way he moans when I do that is downright addictive, and for a second, I wonder if that by itself is enough to make me come.

He clenches his muscles, snapping my attention back to him, and thrusts up into my hand. "I'm close. Cal, I'm gonna—" His voice breaks on a gasp. "I'm gonna come."

I tighten my grip, not slowing down. "You'll mess up the sheets," I tease.

"Fuck! I don't care!" Ian's voice comes out as a hoarse groan. "I need to bust. Please don't stop."

Alright, then.

He throbs in my hand as I speed up, squeezing gently at the head before releasing on the downstroke. Ian sucks in a breath, convulsing, before letting it out in a gravelly moan.

And then he shoots. Oh boy, he *shoots*. All over my hands and onto the bed. His neck falls back, pressing his head into my chest while his body shudders.

"Oh my god, that was so good," he says, rolling toward me and onto his back.

I cock an eyebrow at him. "But I didn't even blow you."

"So? There's a lot to love about a good handjob—they fucking rule." Ian brings a hand to my cock and runs his fingers along it. "How about I give you one?" He tops that offer off with an effortless wink, removing my ability to speak properly.

I nod instead.

"Here, let's move to the other end of the bed," he suggests, eyeing his cum on the sheets. "That right there wasn't one of my best ideas."

I shrug, smirking. "I don't know. It was hot."

"I'll show you hot," he mutters. "Lie on your back and put your hands behind your head. Get *real* comfy."

I comply.

He proceeds to reach down and wrap around my shaft, thumbing the underside. "Lube or dry?"

"I...fuck, usually use lube." My reply is chopped up by spikes of bliss coursing through my body.

Ian stretches an arm over to the nightstand and pulls out a clear bottle, cracking it open and pouring a dollop of its contents into his right hand. He rubs the wetness around for a few seconds, the sound making my breath catch with anticipation.

After withdrawing his other hand, he fixes me with a sly little smile before leaning down to plant a kiss on my lips while slicking his wet palm along my engorged length, magnifying the delicious sensations in my groin tenfold.

I grunt out as he pulls back, and the noise tightens into a sharp exclamation when he brings his other hand into the mix, stimulating my entire dick all at once with perfect, gentle strokes.

Every single time Ian gets his hands on me, my brain turns to mush. It hasn't been long since we started getting physical, and he already has the keys to my body. He can have them.

And right when I think I'm already in the depths of this lubed-up massage from heaven, he starts twisting while still pumping me hard. Each hand moves in opposite directions, yanking a strangled, desperate cry out from my throat.

"Oh, you like that, don't you?" His teasing voice floats through the air, gentle and caring like he isn't dragging me through the first and best handjob of my life.

I nod furiously and moan, unable to get any real words out. He's right—handjobs fucking rule.

Ian says something that I'm too aroused to register, and as soon as the husky sound of his voice hits my eardrums, it's over for me. My body convulses under his touch, and I yell as my release sprays out onto my stomach. He tightens his grip, squeezing every last drop of my orgasm out before leaning down to kiss my tingling lips.

"You're so hot when you come," he murmurs, pulling back.

My eyes are still closed, but I feel him wiping me clean with something damp. Something unfamiliar washes over me, and I stick my arm out to wrap around Ian's shoulders, pulling him down onto my chest. He sighs, the quiet, content noise making both of us relax even more, and we exist like that in silence for a few minutes.

"So," he says, and I blink the static in my brain away. "Now that we can both think straight, I've been meaning to ask: do you have plans for spring break?"

"No. Do you?" I try to keep the nerves from showing on my face and making me look like a jerk. Deep down, I'd love to spend the week with Ian, but if he wants to see his parents, go south with friends, or whatever, who am I to stop him?

"Yeah, we should go to my family's cabin in Maine," he says. "They're working, so it'll just be us."

"You sure you don't want to go somewhere with your friends?"

Ian waves me off. "I'm sure. I want to chill with you."

My heart skips. Biting my tongue how I am right now isn't too healthy, but I have to stop myself from questioning him out of instinct. *Again*. It's new, someone actually wanting to spend time with me, and while I'm not used to it, I could be. I want to be.

"That sounds so fun," I say.

Ian flashes a cheeky smile at me, one that I couldn't misinterpret if I tried. "Oh, it will be." He reaches out to trail his fingers along my leg, the touch jolting me to full consciousness.

And then of course, my messy brain has to start overthinking.

I won't lie, I'm loving the physical stuff we're doing, but I want more. I could be getting ahead of myself. Still, Ian isn't playing games or hiding his feelings—he's giving me all the affection I never had and always craved, and there's no way to deny that.

We went out for the first time *yesterday*. Am I allowed to ask for more, *this* soon?

I don't know if that's possible.

But I don't want Ian to be the only one who initiates anything. He came out to me, he asked me out, and he takes the lead whenever it's something that matters.

I'll ask him at the cabin next week. I'll play it by ear until then. If it all goes badly, I can laugh it off or something, lean into bro banter, and say that I asked so I could keep all the blowjobs for myself.

That's ridiculous, like every other aspect of my social life. It's not like I have any better ideas.

CHAPTER TWENTY-ONE
IAN

Callum is broken.

Or at least his legs are. He's standing motionless, not even two steps into the entryway of the lake house.

"You said this is a *cabin*," he finally says, roving his head from one end of the place to the other.

I stretch, releasing the tension from the three-hour drive. "Only in the winter. I call it a lake house in the summer."

"This is...wow. Holy crap."

"It's wow, and it's all ours for the week. Let's unpack and enjoy it." I nudge my bags further into the house.

The first order of business is locking the wildlife gun away. While I'm properly trained, I don't exactly like carrying a gun around. Still, it's somewhat sensible, given where we are—the last thing I want is to hit a deer and leave it to die a slow death in the middle of the road.

Callum doesn't move from the entryway, as if he isn't allowed to come in, so I bring an arm down and nudge him forward. Do I shove him from the ass on purpose? Yes, yes, I do. It's a real fucking nice ass, and I'm not above wanting my hands on it. His face lights up whenever I do, too, so if it makes him happy, I'm game.

"Let me give you a tour," I say, sliding my hand up to the small of his back.

He nods, and we put our bags down in my bedroom before I show him the house. He takes a peek outside, but it's already dark, so there isn't much to see.

"So, is there anything you want to do first?" I ask.

He shrugs. "What are our options?"

"Let's go for a dip."

Not laughing at Callum's alarmed expression is an exercise in willpower.

"It's what, forty degrees out? No way," he says.

"Not in the lake, buddy. In the hot tub. I turned it on before we left our place, so it should be all toasty."

He parts his lips and stares at me. "You have a hot tub."

"Oh yeah. And it doubles as a pool in the summer. Let's go."

"Did you bring trunks? I don't have any."

"Neither do I," I reply, lifting my shirt off. "You could wear your straight dude boxers if you want—"

Callum snorts and rolls his eyes.

"—or we could go naked. We're alone, it's night, and the closest neighbors are a mile away." I step out of my jeans and hook my thumbs under the waistband of my underwear, relishing in his flustered blinking. "Care to join me?"

I turn around and discard my underwear before I hear rustling clothes and fabric hitting the floor behind me.

Hell yeah.

As much as the prospect of making out with a naked Callum in the hot tub is taking up most of my brain at this point, he's still the first person I've been able to bring to the cabin—that isn't lost on me.

And he's putting up with my clingy ass, too. I couldn't ask for more.

I swivel my head around to steal a blatant, appreciative look at Callum. Biting my tongue and smiling, I relish the way his dick stiffens as I rake my eyes over his body that I can't get enough of. I take a step closer, debating whether to save the hot tub for later in favor of christening my lake house bed with its first, and hopefully only, new guest *right fucking now*.

It's always a brutal dilemma. I'm constantly torn between wanting to get all cozy and soft with Callum and having him pin me against the wall so I can ravish his mouth and some other parts.

Nope. We can be feral idiots at home.

Not wanting to wait any more, I saunter to the door and press the button to open the pool cover before nipping out.

Ouch. Fricking *fuckballs*, it's cold.

With all the desperation of a guy freezing his nuts off, I sink into the warm water and let out an exaggerated sigh. Callum follows soon afterward, not making nearly as much of a scene as I did.

Such a showoff, this one. His ego is tiny, and the rest of him—

I can be polite. I can be polite. I can be polite.

"This place is sick," Callum says.

"It really is, but wait 'til you see this." I straddle his wonderful thick thighs in an unnecessary, gratuitous move, and reach behind him to open the outdoor refrigerator. "I'm grabbing us drinks. Beer or seltzer?"

Pausing to wait for a reply, I stay firmly planted on his lap. His pupils are blown wide, and his plush lips are apart—he's the perfect combo of adorable and sexy, and making his mind go blank sends my affection and libido into the damn stratosphere.

"Sure," he says, and I bark out a laugh.

"That's not an answer, buddy." I tilt my head, teasing him. "Why aren't you paying attention?"

Yeah, I'm not above fishing for compliments. Sue me.

"You're turning me on like *hell*," he says, letting out a quiet groan. "How do you expect me to focus when you're pressed up against me like..." Callum motions between us.

I cock an eyebrow, moving my face closer to his and brushing our noses together. "How? Like this?" My hands travel down his sides as I grind into his hips, sliding our hard cocks together.

"Uh-huh—" he starts, and I cut him off by smashing my lips against his, extracting a surprised little yelp from his throat that makes my dick beg for more action. I don't need the beer in the fridge behind him to get drunk—his addictive kisses do all the work, minus the hangover.

Still, I don't know how to clean cum out of a hot tub, and I'm not trying to find out, so I force myself to pull back after a final, satisfying roam around his soft mouth. Besides, we *just* got in.

"Anyway, it's beer time and wholesome relaxation time." I hand a beer from the fridge to Callum and check my watch for dramatic effect. "Sorry, I don't make the rules."

"Okay," he mutters. "I'm so hard it hurts."

"Aww, you're horny. What else is new?" I tease, and he scoffs, pressing his cold bottle to the back of my neck and making me scream. I don't retaliate—I actually want to tone things down a little, so I settle beside him and stick a wet arm around his shoulder instead. "Man, we're gonna have so much fun this week."

The way Callum nestles his head into my neck has gotta be the cutest thing about him.

"Thanks for inviting me. I'm always so freaking happy when I'm with you."

Scratch that—Callum's sweet little mouth is the cutest thing about him. How is it that he always manages to say exactly what I want to hear?

"You're so precious," I murmur. "Such a sweet talker."

He tenses, and doubt skewers my chest. "It's because I like you, Ian. I like you a lot."

Oh. He was scared of getting emotional.

I try not to smile like a creep, choosing to kiss his forehead instead. "I do too, if I haven't made it clear."

"It's so clear," he says. "Can I ask you something?"

"Yeah, sure." I nod, not knowing what to expect.

"I know it hasn't been that long, but..." Callum runs a hand down his face, pulling away, but avoiding eye contact. "Yeah, so I'd want to, shit, be, like..." He trails off, motioning between us with his large hands.

Holy—does he want to make things official?

I'm out here taking it slow and trying not to scare him off, and he goes ahead and moves things along himself. My chest is so full, yet so apprehensive at the same time, because the last time a guy started a sentence with something along the lines of "it hasn't been that long," he ended it with asking if I was cool taking it raw.

Freshman year was ass.

"Want me to finish that sentence for you?" I ask, and Callum nods. "You want to be together."

The silence that follows lets a nugget of doubt weasel into my brain.

Please, please *let that be what you were trying to say.*

He picks at the label on his beer bottle and returns my nervous smile. "Yeah." He sucks in a breath, averting his gaze. "Do you want to be my boyfriend?"

Is there a stronger word than "yes"?

I stick a finger under his chin and lift, returning his gorgeous eyes to my line of sight. "Of course I want that. I've wanted to be with you for ages."

That smile! Oh my god. My boyfriend's smile is *electric*, and I can't hold back from kissing it. Him. Kissing him. My boyfriend. Kissing my *boyfriend*.

"Not that you weren't already great, but I know you're gonna be an amazing boyfriend," I murmur. "Our friends are gonna be thrilled."

Callum tenses up, so I trail my hands down and rub circles into his lats with my thumbs, making his solid body soften under my touch.

"I don't know if I want to tell anyone else just yet," he says. "Like, I'm really close to getting comfortable with coming out some more, but I'll need a little time."

"Doesn't matter. I'll wait for you." Sensing an imminent apology, I press my mouth against Callum's to cut him off. As much as I want to hard-launch my man on social media immediately and tell the world that we're dating, I want him to be happy even more.

"Isn't it supposed to be wholesome time now?" he mumbles through his busy lips.

"Fuck that." I kiss Callum harder. "You're the best, and now you're my boyfriend."

We pull back to breathe, pressing our foreheads together.

"Ooh, right," he says. "We should consummate our bond later."

I lose it. Callum has to hold me up by my underarms because I can't help but keel over, laughing my head off, and that's one of the last things you want to do when you're chest-deep in water.

"Oh yes, my dearest," I choke out between my borderline cackling. "Shall we make our union whole in the sacred water of this hot tub?"

"Yup. We gotta seal the deal." He reaches for my cock, and I swat his hand away, even though the temptation to let him take me apart right here is threatening to overpower my few remaining scraps of common sense.

"You," I say, jabbing Callum in the chest, "are the biggest menace I've ever met. But I can't blame you."

He raises an eyebrow at me, so I continue.

"Because, you know, sex feels ten times better when you're in a relationship."

His face lights up. "Really?"

Holding back another round of laughter is a struggle, and I splash water at him as a distraction. "Not *ten* times better, but you should see your face!" I say, splashing Callum again for good measure. "I've created a monster."

"Oh yeah? I'll show you a monster."

That's when I get a fucking tsunami to my face.

"Hey, not fair!" I sputter through more torrential bursts of chlorinated water. He's having fun now, hurling wave after debilitating wave at me. I try to push back, but Callum has the size advantage.

So if I can't win by sheer force, I'll have to be strategic.

I reach out of the tub to flick the lights off, and I submerge myself, making Callum look around for me in the darkness.

When he turns away, I breach the surface and lunge, grabbing his wrists and holding them tight behind his back. He yells and wriggles around, trying to free himself, but he's stuck.

"Not so strong now, are you?" I tease, biting at his defined back muscles because I'm shameless and can't help myself.

And Callum...gasps?

I peek around his body. He's hard. *Very, very fucking hard.*

Oh. Oh my god.

"Say the word, and I'll let you go," I say, keeping my tone light-hearted.

His reply is anything but light. "Okay, this is gonna sound so weird, but I don't want you to let go."

Alright, he likes being restrained.

Arousal floods me. Callum is a gift that keeps on giving—if he wants to be tied up, I have a pair of cuffs at home that I've been itching to use on someone for *ages*.

Still gripping his wrists with my right hand, I move around to face him, trailing a single finger along his thigh, up his stomach, over his chest, and onto his throat, savoring the gulp he takes.

"Oh, man," I say through a grin. "We're gonna have a *lot* of fun with this."

"Huh." That's all he says before he bites his tongue, sticking it between his teeth. Hot damn, I never thought I'd find nerves to be cute as heck, but here I am.

I release his wrists, and we sit back down. "Did we, like, naturally discover your freaky side?"

"I kind of sensed a pattern," he says quietly. "I get super turned on when you hold my arms down as a joke."

Holy Jesus motherfuck, he's got it bad.

I walk my fingers up his thigh, and he sighs through a smile.

"Hmm, kinky Callum has a ring to it," I say, sliding into the warm divide between his thigh and his groin. For added measure, I brush my fingertips along the length of his hard cock. He stays silent, his eyes tracking my movements, and before he can say anything, I sling a leg over his lap to straddle him again, putting my weight on him as I press up against his eager mouth for a kiss, how he says he likes it.

The heavy, satisfied moan he makes into my mouth only gets

me to deepen the kiss and press harder into his body. If this is what he wants, I'm gonna indulge him.

"Uh-huh, this definitely turns me on," he says after pulling back for air.

I just smirk back at him. "You know I'm still being gentle, right?"

"You can be less gentle than you think you need to be. I like the idea of you being in complete control."

Jesus fuck. We need to get out of the hot tub and into the bedroom, stat.

"I'm gonna get off of you now so we can have some fun." I do just that. "Don't splash me again, or else I'll tie you to the bed."

Guess what—he splashes me again.

When I finish sputtering, I get right up in Callum's smirking face. "Oh, you're asking for it now, aren't you?"

His response is to brush his raging hard-on against mine, and whatever the horny equivalent of seeing red is, I see it.

"Alright, you kinky fucker," I say, hauling myself out of the pool. "It's shower time and then sex time. Don't keep me waiting."

With that, I run the outdoor shower, waiting and shivering until it's warm enough to step in. Beckoning Callum to join me, I give myself a quick wash, and I'm all done by the time he steps under the jets.

"Here, let me get my hands on you," I say.

He nods, and I trace all over his expansive back, along his front, and down into his crotch.

"Mm, yeah, I *really* don't want to suck on chlorine," I say, sliding my hand to his shaft. "I have to make sure you taste good."

"I think I'm—fuck," Callum grunts through his teeth, "clean enough down thereeee." He drags out that last syllable as I give him a solid jerk.

I stop, chuckling. "Okay, I'll take your word for how clean you are."

I shut the water off and toss a towel to Callum, drying myself quickly and darting inside to my bedroom.

He'll follow in a few seconds, and I have to be creative since I didn't bring any proper gear with me. If only I'd known about Callum's secret kinky side while packing, I would have thrown the handcuffs into my backpack along with some fun toys.

Ooh, I should work him over with a stroker sleeve sometime. I bet he'd lose his mind.

Focus, Ian. I have ten seconds to improvise some bondage that won't give him gangrene.

While I don't have any handcuffs, I do have a pull-up bar for him to grab. That'll have to do.

Callum walks in as I'm latching it to my open bedroom door, and I motion for him to hold on.

He does. I don't even have to say anything.

"Good boy," I coo.

He scoffs, but he doesn't let go.

"Here's how it's gonna go down," I start. "I'll make you feel good on my terms, and you won't let go. How does that sound?"

Callum gulps, a small, excited smile curling at the edges of his lips. "Perfect. Like, don't hurt me or anything, but don't hold back too much."

Kissing his shoulder, I savor the soft warmth of his skin. "I'd never hurt you, babe. If it gets too intense, say, uh, moose, and I'll stop."

"Moose?"

I snicker. "Yeah, because we're in Maine and whatever. The more random a safe word is, the better."

He nods, and I sink to my knees, giving that firm dick a strong tug. Callum inhales sharply, still holding onto the bar and letting out a whispered cuss.

That whisper turns into a rumbling grunt the second I wrap my lips around his cock, sucking hard. With how delightfully sensitive Callum is, I know I could get him off in under two minutes, but I don't, choosing instead to pull away when he says he's about to bust.

"Ian, fuck!" he hisses, arching his back and thrusting his helpless dick into thin air. "I was—why'd you stop? I was about to come!"

The sight of him all desperate goes right to my balls, and I smirk up at his betrayed face. "I stopped *because* you were about to come." My tongue stretches out to make the slightest teasing contact with Callum's tip, making him hold his breath. "It's called edging, and you're only gonna nut when I say you can."

"That sounds so painful and so hot."

Awesome. "Do you trust me?"

He nods hard. "I'd trust you with anything."

I dip my head and start sucking his perfect cock again, hiding the blush that I feel in my cheeks. Going all fuzzy over Callum handing his trust over isn't high on the list of dommy activities.

Being a little shit and edging his fucking brains out is.

When he begins to shake again, I slow down and smile around his length. As much as I miss the feeling of his fingers in my hair, hearing his little gasps and moans more than makes up for that.

"You okay?" I ask, pulling back.

"Yeah. God, this feels so good." Callum's eyes are rolled back, and his mouth is slack, so I might not have needed to ask in the first place. "I really want to touch you."

I tut at him. "Hey. I won't let you come if you stop holding on. Be good."

"I will. Fuck."

He swears some more when I go back down on him, and I drink in the sweet sound of Callum's needy, labored breaths.

"I want to come already," he groans when I yank myself away again.

"Shut up and stop being greedy." Yeah, that's a little mean, but it's all part of the act.

He lets out a frustrated noise. I flick my eyes up, and the sight of his flushed face silently pleading me to keep going makes me think I'm gonna come hands-free.

I wet my mouth and suck him as deep as I can, making him

throb hard as my lips stretch to their limit, tears pricking the corners of my eyes.

"Please," he mutters.

"Hmm?" I twist my fist as I bob my mouth back and forth, a little slower than how he likes it.

"Make me come, *please*—" Callum cuts himself off with a grunt when I clench around his head, and when he pulses against my lips, I don't stop.

Then, when I flick my tongue along that hyper-sensitive ring below his cockhead, he whimpers.

A helpless, full-throated, from-the-stomach whimper.

I've never... Shit, I've never made a guy *whimper* before, and Jesus, I have to hear that again so I can burn the sound into my brain for posterity.

I run my tongue over the same area. Same fucking result, a little quieter this time, but no less intoxicating. Callum shakes too, and I smile around him, savoring the sound of his heavy breaths and the feeling of his cock *begging* me to continue.

I've only brought him to the edge five times, and he's already like this. The possibilities, if he's down for more, are endless.

Humming, I slowly resume my previously scheduled program-ming and make firm drags along Callum's length with my lips. He bucks his hips forward within seconds, and I swallow around his climax as he yells and pours his load into me. It's warm and thick and everything I need.

I savor the way his softening dick still quivers after his orgasm crests, and I bring my right hand down to jerk myself off, keeping Callum in my mouth. My groin burns with need, and it takes under a minute for me to come hard.

Breathless, I pull off and lie on the cool floor, staring up at his flushed torso.

"Can I let go now?" he asks.

"Oh my god, of course," I reply. "Sorry, I should have—"

"It's fine. I liked that you had control."

I scramble to my feet, shrugging. "Yeah, I could kind of tell with your wild moaning."

"Shut up." He tries to cover his face with his hands, but I hug him and trap his arms instead, resting my face in his chest. "I really lose it when I'm with you, don't I?"

"And I'd say that's a good thing," I reply. "Once this week is over, your version of losing it is gonna be totally normal."

Scoffing, he brings his hands to my back and squeezes. "That's ambitious."

"Mmm. Maybe I'll pin your wrists to the bed and ride your big, needy cock until you run out of cum."

Shit, I haven't bottomed in over a year. I shouldn't bite off more than I can chew.

"Okay, that *sounds* hot," he says quietly. "But I don't know if I want to be on either end of that. Like, I'm good with experimenting down there and stuff, just not, uh, full anal?"

That's fine by me. I can just suck him dry instead.

"Whatever you're comfortable with," I reply, pressing a kiss to his cheek. "We don't have to figure anything out now. We can play it by ear—"

Callum's stomach rumbles, and I snicker.

"Someone's hungry," I say, smirking at him and rising to my feet. "Sit tight. I'm gonna make us some dinner."

CHAPTER TWENTY-TWO
CALLUM

"Did we *have* to come back?" Ian asks, dumping his duffel bag on the floor and jumping onto the couch.

We have class tomorrow, so yeah, we did have to come back, but I feel where he's coming from. That lake house is paradise on earth.

"I wish we didn't have to," I say, sitting down next to Ian. "This week was so fun."

"It sure was." Ian waggles his eyebrows. "Are you well rested and well fucked?"

I scoff and don't argue—we definitely did a lot of resting and... the second thing. While we didn't get as adventurous as the first night, we definitely took advantage of the lack of neighbors.

I shudder with recollection and anticipation, and it takes Ian waving his hand in front of my eyes for me to snap out of my daze.

"Callum," he says, dragging my name out, "you're making bedroom eyes again."

"Guilty," I reply. "Do I have a problem?"

Ian smirking at me and kissing my forehead tells me all I need to know. "Never change, man." He heads to the kitchen to cook lunch. I lean back into the couch cushion and pull my laptop out to waste some time, but a notification pops up that makes me squint in confusion.

Inbox: West Wisconsin Community College
From: Weber, Abigail

Who is *she*?

I had exactly one group project in community college, and my parents explicitly barred me from partnering up with any women, lest any of them lead me into temptation or whatever. Intrigued, I click on the email.

Hi Callum,
We don't know each other, but I wanted to give you a heads up in case it's useful. I'm in the Exercise Science program here, and some people claiming to be your parents showed up to a lecture this morning.

My stomach drops as soon as I read the word "parents." Will those two ever give up and let me go? It's been months, for Christ's sake.

They went around before it started and asked a bunch of people if they know where you are because they said you disappeared. I don't think anyone gave your parents (if they are your parents) an answer, probably because the whole thing was creepy as hell, but I searched up your email in the system and thought I'd let you know. Your parents seem worried, but if you don't want to be found, just be aware that your parents are looking, if you're still at WWCC.
Stay safe,
Abby Webber

My breath catches on a lump in my throat as I force the initial wave of panic down.

They're looking for me, but my parents don't know where I am. The only person back home who has any idea about my transfer is a nameless staff member who sent my transcript to WMU.

They won't find me.

But still, I don't know if I fully believe myself.

"What the actual fuck?" I mutter, more annoyed than scared.

Ian sticks his head out of the kitchen and raises an eyebrow before walking over. "What's up?"

"My parents crashed a lecture at my old community college and asked if anyone knows where I am." I swallow that lump in my throat.

"Shit. Are you okay?" Ian plops down next to me, and I drop my head to his shoulder.

"Yeah, I'm fine. They don't know where I am—it's just annoying that they aren't giving up."

"That's good." He slings an arm around my shoulder, pulling me closer. "But crashing a lecture? Your parents are kinda obsessed, not gonna lie."

"Maybe you'll be as obsessed with me one day," I joke, trying to lighten the mood.

He chuckles and tightens his grip around me. "I'm already obsessed with you."

God, his constant affirmations never fail to make my heart flip. For the first time ever, I feel like I *matter* to someone. Hell, this is more than that—Ian managed to turn a bunch of my insecurities around by *liking* them. My clothes, appearance, nerves, shyness, sex drive; things I tried to hide and change are what he tries to pull out of me.

"I'm kind of obsessed with you, too," I say back. "Even if I've only said that to *you*."

He shrugs. "Again, I don't mind. It's still super early for you, so I'll wait as long as you need to tell other people."

Sighing into his hair, I stay silent. The thought of coming out still sends an initial jolt of panic down my spine, but realistically, what's gonna happen if I go further?

Sabrina and Laura exist as they are. I've seen other gay couples doing PDA all across campus.

I'll be fine, at least here.

"I think I could come out some more," I say.

He tilts his head up, meeting my gaze. "Like to our friends?"

"No." I pause to suck in a grounding breath. "I was thinking more, uh, public."

"Really?"

"Yeah. I don't want to hide you away."

Ian smirks up at me, moving my hands down to his ass. "Ooh, I like possessive Callum. Sexy."

I squeeze the firm muscle under my fingers. "You're *mine,*" I growl.

It's meant to be funny, but Ian sucks in a sharp breath.

"Fuck," he hisses. "I like this way too much."

Hmm. Noted.

He keeps talking, and it's clear he's on a roll. "Ooh, I'll put your initials in my social media profile if you do, too."

"I don't have that," I say immediately. "But you're free to do whatever."

"Oh, right. I mean, you could make one. Especially if you keep your profile private." Ian shakes his head. "You don't have to, though. It's honestly not important—"

"I can make one," I insist. "After all, I *am* trying to be as normal as possible."

"There's no such thing as normal. You already are."

For a second, my heart stutters as doubt creeps into my brain. He's almost being *too* chill about everything, and it's giving me whatever the slow-motion, months-long version of whiplash is— I'm not used to being accepted, not at all.

Then I remind myself that Ian is my boyfriend. In theory, he has one of the widest dating pools out of anyone, but he's dating me. He wants me. I asked him to be official, and he not only said yes, but he also got all enthusiastic.

I let out a breath and tell myself that I'm fine.

"Right," I say, breaking the silence. "Let me do this social media thing."

Ian's face lights up as I navigate to the app store on my phone, and he pulls his profile up on his phone to show me while I wait for the download to finish.

Holy hell, all the baseball pictures and the couple of shirtless lakeside shots make me regret not signing up for this earlier.

I fumble through the sign-up screen on the app and immediately follow Ian's account. He accepts my request right away, and I peek at his profile again to copy his bio, taking a sneaky scroll through some of his shirtless pictures from last summer.

He catches me with a sly little smirk, and my cheeks heat. Hopefully, I'll work my way up to posting one of my own to get back at him. His eyes *do* go all glassy whenever I show any skin at all, and he's always pawing at the hem of my shirt whenever we're alone together.

Yup, he likes me back. And to think I doubted he ever could, even after he came out to me.

Shoot, I should focus on making my account. I flip back to Ian's bio—it's a string of the states he's from, our university, and his graduation year. I tap my own version into my account.

WI/NH
WMU

I pause. While I'm hoping to graduate in four years, including my year and a half of community college, all that is still up in the air. I'll leave it at *WMU*.

And I'll delete the *NH*. I don't need the world to know *exactly* where I am.

"So can I post a nauseating couple photo and tag you?" Ian asks. "That would be cute. Mostly because of you."

I think for a second. While that *would* get the job done, I think I owe it to my other friends to fill them in more directly. Especially Laura. Looking back, she all but told me that Ian liked me, too.

"Can I actually tell people face to face?" I say. "I want to do it myself."

The way Ian smiles makes me wonder if he's going to maul me with another hug.

He doesn't. "The Barrel is finally open again, and my team's heading there tonight. Do you think we should host a pre at our place and you could tell our friends then?"

"That sounds good." I smile back, and we go to the group chat to make the plan.

———

"They're gonna guess, right?" I ponder out loud, scanning the cleaned-up living room. "Like, none of my stuff is lying around."

"Nah." Ian waves me off. "And what if they do? We're gonna tell them anyway."

Right. Yeah.

There's a knock at the door, and Ian yells that it's open. Given that Nick is always late, my instincts tell me that it's Laura and Sabrina.

This is it. I'm coming out to Sabrina and announcing that Ian and I are boyfriends. My heart races, even though I know I'll be fine.

As soon as the door opens, I grab Ian's hand. He tilts his head to face me, smiling wide and pinching his lips together, and he gives me a squeeze.

Oh, it's Nick. For once, he's on time.

I squeeze tighter.

"Hey, am I the first to show up?" Nick says, kicking his boots off. "I never thought—" He stops in his tracks once he sees us, flicking his eyes between our hands and our faces.

Then he nods. "Fuck yeah." Nick deposits his backpack on the floor, causing the bottles inside to jangle loudly, before rushing over to give us a group hug. "Scotty's finally found someone who isn't an asshole."

"I'll, uh, try not to be one," I offer, not knowing what else to say in response.

Nick pulls back and slaps my shoulder. "Nah, you're a good guy. Celebration shots, anyone?"

Ian and I both nod in approval, and our night gets started. We don't go too wild, since Laura and Sabrina aren't even here yet, but before long, the front door opens again, and they stride in.

Right as Ian and I are mid-kiss.

Chuckling, I pull back and straighten up. "I didn't time this, I swear."

"Are you two..." Laura breaks into a wide grin, pointing at me and Ian.

I nod. "Yup, Ian is my boyfriend."

Woah. It's my first time saying that out loud, and it couldn't feel any better.

Sabrina makes a whooping sound. "That's so fucking cute, oh my god."

"Finally." Laura procures a bottle of prosecco from her bag. "I thought you guys would keep dancing around each other, but when you both went to Ian's lake house?" She pops the cork and thrusts the cold bottle into Ian's hands. "That's when I knew something good was going on."

Sabrina smiles. "This is too cute. I'm so happy for you two."

Ian hands me a glass, and I take a sip.

"Yeah, I think Ian's happy to have his living room back, too," I joke. "Hopefully I won't roast him alive once the weather warms up."

"You aren't going back once your dorm's fixed?" Nick asks, crossing his arms and flopping onto the couch.

"I hope not," Ian mumbles after he sees me tentatively shaking my head.

Wait, is that... Okay, we just agreed to move in with each other permanently. That's so fast, and also *amazing* for my budget. I'm gonna have to start paying rent. I'll have to insist.

Sabrina narrows her eyes, cutting her sip of wine short. "Wait, so you guys are all moved in with each other, like, for real."

Ian and I both nod.

"And you did that *before* getting together. You beat me and Laura," she continues.

Laura snickers. "Yeah, you guys stole our stereotype."

Staying silent, Ian simply smirks back as he takes a sip of prosecco.

———

Hoo boy, I'm *sloshed*. As is Ian. And Nick. And Laura and Sabrina. The room is spinning a little—I'm okay, and I still have my wits about me. This is fun.

"Guys," Ian says, "let's head out. I just have to take a leak first, and then we can go."

"We called dibs first!" Sabrina yells, dragging Laura to the bathroom.

Ian shrugs and sits cross-legged at the dining table, waiting for the two of them to finish up.

"Yo, Callum," Nick says to me, and I turn to him. "Wanna wait outside?"

I'm not sure why he'd want to do that when it's cold, but I don't question him.

Nick lets out a large breath once the front door shuts behind us. "At risk of being the toxic best friend, I need to give a little speech or whatever, guy to guy."

"Uh, sure?" I don't know what to expect.

"Okay. To preface everything, I like you. I think you're good for Ian, so if you're worried about what I'm gonna say, don't be."

Man, I love it when people make themselves clear. Such a relief.

"Still, I've been friends with Ian for as long as he's been in college, and I've seen some of the shit he's been through. I have to do my due diligence and whatnot."

I nod.

Nick purses his lips. "I'm not gonna reveal the full extent of what went down since it isn't my place, but he's..." He runs a hand along his face. "He's a great guy. He feels *a lot*, and it shows. Some assholes, mostly guys, have given him so much grief for that."

"Yeah, he mentioned it to me. They said he was too affectionate or whatever."

"They all did a number on him." Nick shoves his hands in his pockets and looks up at the ceiling. "It was so bad that he swore off *everyone*, at least until he met you. Basically, not that you aren't already, I'm asking you to keep that in mind with Ian. Show him that he's not too much, because my god, he really, really isn't."

"I know, and that affection? That's what I like about him. It's what gave me the courage to ask him if we could be official." Even if I got tongue-tied and Ian had to finish the question for me, I still started the conversation. That would have been unimaginable only two months ago.

"*You* asked *him*." Nick's eyes widen, and he smiles. "I had a good feeling about you. Ian has so much love to give, and other guys have been overwhelmed by that in the past." Nick lets out a sigh. "I'm so happy for him. He found someone good."

I chuckle as my heart clenches. "This isn't a toxic bestie conversation."

"Oh, right, I forgot," Nick says, laughing. His face firms up, and he frowns at me. "Don't hurt him. Or *else*." He jabs a finger into my chest before his smile breaks through again. "Just a formality. I'm sure you won't."

"I won't," I confirm, and Ian chooses that moment to come outside.

"Callummmmmm." He slides up to me and wraps an arm around my waist, pulling me toward him and making my heart flip. "I kind of had a lot to drink."

I snort. "Huh. I couldn't tell."

"I'm handsy and affectionate when I'm drunk."

"Good. Then I won't have to tell everyone at the bar that you're mine."

That makes Ian tighten his grip on me, and Nick snorts.

"God, you're so fucking cute. Have I ever told you that?" Ian asks.

"A few times, I'm sure."

"A few? Not enough. I've gotta step up my game."

"Hey, let's take a picture together. You look hot in that... You look hot." Before I can ask what Ian tried to say, he pulls his phone out and snaps a couple of selfies. I have no idea how to pose, so I make a smile that I hope isn't too weird.

"Damn, Cal, way to outshine me, holy fuck." Ian grins at me, leaning on my chest and zooming into the pictures. "You'll level up my feed, that's for sure."

I tense out of instinct before pausing—he might post a picture of us.

Who would even see? Ian's friends. Nobody else I know.

It...wouldn't matter if he did.

"I won't post you, don't worry," he adds quickly.

I swallow the lump in my throat. Ian shouldn't have to hide me, even from his short list of people on social media. Nobody here knows my family, I'm sure, and there's no way a random post from someone they don't know would get back to them.

"You can post me," I tell him. "I don't mind, and my account is private anyway. Nobody can find me."

"Oh." he smiles, raising his eyebrows. "Want me to tag you, too? Heads up, everyone I know would follow you because you're hot."

I slide an arm around Ian's waist, pulling his solid, warm frame into me. "We can work up to that. Let's just hang out tonight."

CHAPTER TWENTY-THREE
IAN

"Hey, hey, look at me," I tell Callum. "Come onnnn, babe, stop hiding from me."

All I hear is a muffled protest from underneath the couch cushion that he's holding over his face. I yank it away to reveal his sheepish, blushing cheeks.

As always, I melt at the sight. Fuckin' adorable, this guy.

"I am *not* making my social media username 'CockyCallum69,'" he insists.

"Okay, well, what about—"

"No shirtless profile picture, either!"

Wow, tough sell. "How else is the world gonna know how hot my boyfriend is?"

"They won't." He shrugs. "You're the only one who gets to see me like that because you're mine."

Okay, way to derail the joke train and send it into a head-on collision course with the Boner Express. For a guy who moans when I push him against the wall mid-makeout, he sure likes to flip the script and get territorial in the best way possible.

"Say that again, babe," I say.

"What?"

"Whose am I?"

He snickers, reaching up and pulling me onto him by the arm. "Mine."

"Attaboy." I give his hair a gentle fluff, restoring that heart-stopping bedhead I'm so drawn to.

I'm a week away from my first away-game road trip of the

season, and while I've spent a few nights on the road here and there over the past while, seven whole days apart from my boyfriend doesn't sound appealing in the slightest.

At least it's warming up, so the hotel beds won't feel *too* cold, but I'm a guy with needs. Emotional *and* physical. While distance might make the heart grow fonder, it also keeps my mouth empty and my dick deprived.

And my heart fucking *aches* as it grows fonder. Not nice.

I can't wait for June—I'll have a long summer of doing nothing more than relaxing with Callum at the lake house.

Unless he has a job or something.

Shoot, I didn't even clock the idea of him needing to work during the summer. I know he has a scholarship, but his work-study could require a summer component.

My jaw firms up as I kick myself for being inconsiderate. Way to be a good boyfriend. Not.

"So, do you have any plans for the summer?" I ask, trying to be casual.

Callum's head perks up. "Nah."

Oh, thank fuck. Visions of swimming and fishing and chilling with Callum re-enter my mind and make my chest expand with blissful anticipation.

"I'm not going home, that's for sure," he continues.

"Yeah, no, I wasn't thinking you would." I nod in agreement. "I'm gonna chill at the house in Maine. Gonna be *super* quiet if I'm all alone," I add, hoping he gets the hint.

He doesn't. "Oh, okay."

I groan, shaking his shoulder. "You should spend the summer with me at the lake house."

Callum's lips curve up into a little smile that makes my stomach simmer. "Yeah?"

I let myself flop down onto his chest, and he snakes a hand up my shirt, planting a firm hand on my back. "Yes, really," I manage to say. "I'm gonna have to start forcing you to impose on me."

My eyes roam to the plate of cookies I put on the coffee table, and I get a great idea. I grab a cookie and hold it in front of Callum, and like always, he stretches his neck forward to take a bite.

In a total asshole move, I yank it away at the last second.

Fuck. His sad, betrayed expression is almost enough to make me give in. Almost.

"Nuh-uh," I say. "You aren't getting a cookie until you tell me *one* impolite thing you're gonna do at the lake house this summer."

He rolls his eyes and reaches for the plate himself, and I drop onto his arm to trap it against the couch.

He scoffs. "Uh, I'm gonna... I don't know, make you do all of my laundry?"

"Nice try, but there won't *be* any laundry because we're gonna be buck-ass naked with our dicks out for four months straight. Try harder."

"I'll be lazy and sit on my ass all day."

Satisfied, I hand Callum the cookie. "Good boy."

"Fuck off," he replies through his mouthful of chocolate.

Since when were the words "fuck off" so endearing? I swear that guy can say *anything* and I'll eat it up. I wrap my arms around his waist, resting my head on his chest and listening to him chew.

"You okay there?" he asks between bites.

"Oh yeah. You're so warm, and I'm looking forward to watching you sit on your ass all day at the lake house."

Callum's face hardens a little after he scarfs down the last bite of his cookie. "Are your parents gonna be okay with me going there?"

"Totally. Besides, I already took you."

"It'll be for four whole months. That's a little different."

I chuckle. "Trust me, once I tell them you're my boyfriend, they'll be too excited to care about anything else."

He shifts around, almost making me fall off of him, and he sticks an arm out to save me while pinching his eyebrows together. "That would be nice. Are you *sure* they'd be fine?"

"Of course," I say. "They've been asking if I've found anyone for ages now. I've only held off because of your history with parents and stuff."

Callum puts his arms on my back and gives me a soul-melting scratch between my shoulder blades. "That makes sense. Thanks for considering that, but they're *your* parents. I'm sure they're great like you are."

"Should I tell them?"

"Go right ahead."

Grinning to myself, I pull my phone out to text the family chat.

Hey guys

DAD

sup

MOM

Hi Ian!

Flying to Zurich soon but I can talk now

What are you up to?

Nothing much, just finished breakfast with the bf

"And now we wait—"

INCOMING CALL FROM MOM IN THE GROUP
"FAMILY CHAOS"
DAD HAS JOINED THE GROUP CALL IN "FAMILY
CHAOS"

"That was fast," I say, picking up. "Hey, guys, what's up?"

I keep the camera in front of me so Callum doesn't appear in the frame.

"What's *up*?" Mom asks, sitting down in an airport lounge conference room. "You *know* why we're calling."

Dad is in his home office back in New York. "Boyfriend. Details. Now."

I can always count on him to get straight to the point.

"His name is Callum, we met in class, and he's awesome." Out of the corner of my eye, I catch Callum smiling when I mention him, and I squeeze his knee. "He's here right now."

He waves at the phone, even though the camera isn't fixed on him. "Hi."

"Ooh, he's got a nice voice!" Mom says, and Callum hides his growing smile. He sure does have a nice voice. It's hot, even if I don't say it out loud.

"Can we meet him?" Dad asks.

I glance over at Callum, stalling for time, and that typical tentative smile tugs at his lips. My god, it's as adorable as ever. I don't think I'll ever get tired of seeing it.

He sticks his hand out, and my heart races.

"Yeah," I say. "Here he is."

I hand the phone over, and he gives a small wave to my parents.

"Nice to meet you. I'm Callum."

I rest my head on his chest, listening to his heart thump and his conversation with my parents. They're both excited, asking him how we met and if I'm behaving myself, and I take the phone back after a few minutes so I don't overwhelm Callum from the start. My parents are smiling back at me, Mom mouths "he's cute," which makes my face heat up, and we sign off.

"Your parents are so nice," Callum tells me.

"They are. They weren't around that much after I turned sixteen, but they're awesome."

Tilting his head, he parts his lips. "What do you mean by that?"

"I was mature enough to take care of myself alone, I guess. Doesn't every sixteen-year-old dream of running amok without parental supervision?"

"And did you?"

"Not enough to get noticed." I shoot Callum a little wink that makes him blush, and my heart squeezes at the sight. "You can say we had really different childhoods."

My phone lights up with more messages in the group chat before I can elaborate, and I take a look.

MOM

Turning my phone off soon, about to take off

All good. You should swing by and visit our place the next time you're in Boston

Hold on a second

OUR place?

Do you guys live together already???

Oops.

:)

I WILL pay for the overpriced WiFi to know what you say

Okok yes I invited Callum to move in w me bc a tree fell on his dorm

That was before we were together and then… yeah

Ok that's actually cute

Just be safe and whatnot

Have a safe flight

Thanks Ian. Love you

My warm heart sinks when Dad sends three messages in quick succession.

> **DAD**
>
> Callum seems like a good guy
>
> How much does he charge to put up with you
>
> He can invoice us directly

I scoff. Like, I know it's a joke, but it still stings.

> Ouch?

> **MOM**
>
> Jake, stop being an ass
>
> **DAD**
>
> Sorry
>
> I'm just happy you finally found someone nice

I brace for the words "I never thought it'd happen" to show up on my screen, and they don't. Sighing, I put my phone down, and Callum scrunches his eyebrows together, clearly concerned.

"Are you okay?" he asks.

"Yeah." I let the word out on a huff. "My dad made a joke about paying you to put up with me. It's nothing."

Callum opens his arms, and I fall onto his chest, relishing the warmth of his body heat. "It's not nothing, Ian," he says firmly. "That was a mean comment, especially since you've gotten shit for supposedly being too much before."

"Like, I haven't told my parents much about my guy problems," I counter. "No parent wants to hear that their son is a loser who catches feelings for everyone he makes out with."

"If that's true, I'm glad I kiss you so often to keep you interested."

That manages to get a sad chuckle out of me. "You're different. I caught feelings for you *long* before we shared spit."

Callum cups my ass and gives it a teasing squeeze. "Aww, I feel so special."

He really is special to me, but before I can fire back with a joke of my own, his phone beeps.

"Uh, I think your parents requested to follow me on social media," he says. "Jake Scott and Elanor Greene?"

"Yup, that's them," I confirm. "You should post one of the cute selfies from the lake house to restore their confidence in me."

Callum snickers and smacks my leg. "Absolutely not."

"Fine, *I'll* post one." I pull my phone out for effect, and he grabs my knees to drag me across the couch, proceeding to lie down and trap me under him.

Yeah, I'm definitely going to threaten that more often. I'll do anything to get the weighted blanket treatment.

CHAPTER TWENTY-FOUR
CALLUM

"Can you join the baseball team so I don't have to leave you for so long?" Ian asks, giving me a wistful stare.

"Do you guys need some unwieldy, uncoordinated comic relief? I can do that."

"Nah, we could use a few more hitters, and you already have the body for it." He doesn't take my silence as an answer, choosing to punch my shoulder instead. "Jesus, you in a tight uniform would end me, I swear."

I scoff. "Me in a baseball uniform? I don't see it."

"Nah, you've totally got the buns and guns to rock it." He waves me off and bats his eyelashes. "Come on, flex for me, babe. Give me one last look at my sexy, sexy boyfriend before I leave."

My cheeks heat up, predictably, at the compliment, and I oblige. Rolling my eyes, I lift my arms and squeeze. Ian releases an exaggerated whistle, bringing his hands over and digging them into my biceps.

"We'll make a baseball player out of you yet," he says, chuckling and releasing me after another round of fondling. "We can practice over the summer."

He can't be serious—he's a varsity player, and the only bat and balls I've ever touched are his metaphorical set, and my own. Still, I'll agree to some summer practices at his lake house if he goes shirtless while we do so.

He leaves to grab his bag from the bedroom, and his absence already bites a little. Fuck, how am I gonna make it through the next *week*?

At least I can scroll longingly through his social media whenever I miss him. Even though I already know his pictures off by heart, I still pull out his profile to take another scan. This is like a modern-day locket, with higher definition and more content. I won't complain.

Huh, I have a message request from someone who doesn't follow me.

I open it, and my blood runs cold.

REGINA CROSS

Where are you.

Come home NOW.

Or else I'll find you and drag you here myself.

Shit. Shit, shit, shit.

For a second, everything stops, and I stand in the middle of the living room, phone in hand, motionless, and holding my breath.

Then, everything hits me all at once. My stomach slams down at the same time my heart jolts, the combination sending me stepping backward and tripping onto the couch, landing ass-first. The phone slips in my shaking, sweat-slicked hands, and I grip it tighter, my eyes still glued to the messages.

They found me. My parents found me.

I try to swipe out of the message, but my finger is too slippery —I waste a precious second to wipe my right hand on the couch before succeeding.

I go to delete the thread from my inbox. There's a block option, and I hit that instead. The message disappears, but the damage is done. There's no undoing anything.

I clear my profile. Not that it matters, since they've already seen it.

Then I go to the menu and hit the first red button I see. Maybe it logs me out, I don't know. And for good measure, I delete the whole app.

I thought I was doing so well.

I thought I was finally free, and now this.

Tension builds in my core, threatening to rise in my throat and spill out. I toss my phone across the couch and bury my face in my hands, trying to get my breathing under control.

In. Hold. Out. In. Hold. Out. And repeat.

It doesn't work. All that does is help me see somewhat clearly again, and the first thing that hits my eyeballs is a blurry Ian entering the living room.

"Callum, babe, what's wrong?" He rushes over and slings an arm around my shoulders, concern darkening his expression. He's changed into my old hoodie, which is far too big on him, and the fabric bunches up around his elbows.

The cozy sight fails to provide its usual comfort.

"It's my parents," I say. Short, simple, and still painful. "They found my profile and messaged me."

"How bad is it?"

"My mom asked me where I am and told me to come home." I leave out the part where she laced her typical malice through the texts—I don't even know how I'd explain it to him.

He lets out a slow breath and tightens his grip around me, and I lean my head onto his. "How shaken are you?"

"I deleted everything."

"Okay, let's talk through it," Ian starts, and I groan, resting my face in my palms.

"You have a bus to catch," I say. If I make him late because of my personal issues, I don't think I could forgive myself.

"So what? We don't have a game today, and Nick's gonna be late, too." He pulls out his phone and sends a text. "There. I told them something came up. Now I can focus on you." With my eyes covered, I can only feel Ian placing a gentle hand on my shoulder.

I lift my head and give him a weak, appreciative smile. "Thanks."

"Your mom asked where you were, your profile was private, and all you had in your bio was the abbreviation for Wisconsin, and 'WMU.'"

"Right."

"There's gotta be at least fifty WMUs in the country. Think of all the states that start with M and have a western part. Western Michigan, Montana, Maine, Missouri, whatever. They might even think the W stands for Wisconsin. You're gonna be okay."

I press harder into Ian, and he trails off, leaning back so my head falls into his lap.

"That makes sense. It's, like, I'm fine," I say, trying and failing to convince myself.

The chances of my parents knowing where I am are slim, and even if they did know, there isn't much, or anything, they could do. Even so, it's like the thin veneer of safety that I had is now punctured, leaving me vulnerable in a way I can't put my finger on.

No matter how minuscule the chance is of me seeing my parents again, the fact that it isn't *zero* is nothing short of unsettling.

To top that off, Ian's leaving for a week, and he stands for a lot about my new life: freedom, growth, happiness, you name it. Now that my old life is creeping back, I don't want to be apart from him.

A little voice in the back of my head asks me if I'm becoming codependent.

The feeling of gentle fingers through my hair shuts that voice up. Being a *little* codependent can't hurt too much, right?

"Are you sure you're okay?" he asks.

No.

"Yeah. I'm a little unsettled, but I'll be fine," I reply.

He crosses his arms, looking me up and down. It's like Ian's taking in everything about me—my expression, posture, and everything I'm not saying but desperately trying to hide.

"I don't buy it," he says after a while. "You can tell me anything, Cal."

"This isn't a great time for me to be alone." I inhale a sharp breath and let it out along with my words. "But you have your away games, so don't worry about me. I'll figure something out."

His eyebrows bunch, and his lips part tentatively, like he's finding the right words. Then he sighs, reaching out to pull me closer by the waist.

"Nah. You're coming with me. We'll stay at my parents' place in New York, and we'll figure things out from there. I'm not leaving you behind like this."

My eyes fly open. Does he have a solution to *everything*? I tilt my head up so he won't see my shock, and when he leans over to plant a kiss on my head, that shock morphs into guilt. It's not that he has a solution for everything.

He *has* to, for my sake.

"I always make you take care of me," I murmur. "It isn't fair."

Ian shakes his head, frowning at me. "That's not true, and even if it was, I wouldn't mind."

Sure, he doesn't mind *now*, but what about in a month? Or after that, if he doesn't get sick and tired of getting nothing back for everything he gives?

"I don't want you to resent me for being useless. I'll take care of myself," I insist.

Christ, I'm even parroting my parents. They really squirmed back into my life with nothing more than a two-line DM.

"What the—" Ian cuts himself off and regroups. "Callum. If you need something, I'll help. That's what people do in a relationship."

"Yeah, and there's supposed to be balance," I reply. There aren't too many ways he can spin the facts—anyone can see that it's him who's doing all the heavy lifting between us, and I'm just lying around, taking endlessly.

"I'm not with you for what you can do for me." Ian's voice is firm and measured, more than I would have expected. "Me helping isn't out of grudging obligation; it's because I care about the guy I —" He pauses, leaving me hanging as he lets out a huff. "I like you *so much*, Cal. This is just a part of that."

"I don't like feeling useless," I counter.

"Callum..." Ian tenses. "Look, I'm not usually blunt, but I'm gonna be for a bit." He sucks in air and shuts his eyes. "Shut the fuck up about being useless."

Jesus, what'll it take for me to get through to him? Unfamiliar, unwelcome exasperation bubbles up, and even though I try to push it down, I'm not successful.

His arm is still on my waist, and I push it away, making him blink as his mouth falls open.

"I still *feel* useless." My voice is shaky, and I hardly recognize it. "I need to do stuff on my own, too. I can't sit on my ass and rely on you to save me whenever my screwed-up past messes with me."

Ian stays silent. For a second, his eyes go soft, giving him a hurt, wounded expression, but he hardens as soon as my gaze connects with his.

My heart sinks. I never, ever want to see him resigned and quiet like this again, but I can't take back words that already left my stupid mouth. Whatever guilt was sinking in my gut before is amplified by a magnitude of a hundred.

It's crushing, and I don't see a way out of it. I already messed up.

"Okay," he finally says. "If you want to go through this alone, I'm not going to stop you." He takes my hoodie off, getting ready to leave, and smooths his T-shirt down. "But if you need *anything*, call me. I'm here for you."

"I know. Thank you." I shut my eyes and exhale a shaky breath. "I just need to learn how to take care of myself."

"And I need to let you do that." Ian, the saint he always is, comes closer and hugs me from above. A tiny, tiny morsel of tension leaves my body as soon as he touches me, but the tangle in my core is still heavy. "I'm gonna miss you this week."

I tighten my grip around him "Same. Gonna miss you lots."

Ian's phone beeps, he checks it, and then he's off with a final wave. With the quiet click of the front door closing, I'm left with nothing more than my darkening thoughts.

Damn it, now that I'm completely alone, the weight of what happened sinks in even more.

I essentially told Ian that he was doing too much and then *pushed him away* because of it. Not just in a figurative sense—I pushed him off me, too.

Without even thinking, I stuck a knife into one of his biggest insecurities and twisted over and over again.

Is it too late to run after Ian and tell him I'm an idiot?

Yeah, it is.

Sinking down further into the couch, I bury my face in my hands and let out a loud, gritty groan. I could have been next to my kind, caring boyfriend right now, comfortable and safe with everything he *offered* me, but I decided to be an asshole, and now I'm alone in *his* apartment.

I'm not even in a better position than I was ten minutes ago. My parents still found me.

And I'm *alone.*

A chill runs through my body, fear compounding the guilt that's still growing.

Fuck, I learned techniques for this. Grabbing a pillow, I scan the room.

Right, what can I see? Coffee table, carpet, TV, uh, my reflection in the TV? Nope. Lamp. That's better. Alright, one more: textbook.

I'm touching the pillow, my hands, the couch under my ass, and uh, my socks. Those are feelings.

I can hear a clock, my pulse in my ears, and cars outside.

Ian's smell is in the pillow and the room spray is wafting through the air.

My dehydrated mouth is something I can taste—dry and metallic. Not the most pleasant, but it's identifiable.

Okay. I take a breath, hold it, and let it out.

I'm...a little better. Calmer, even. I squeeze the pillow tighter in my arms and curl into it, listening to my heartbeat slow down.

I'll be fine. I'm alone, and Ian's gone for a week, but nobody's coming for me.

Besides, what would I have done if I'd gone with Ian? He'll have his games, and I'd be skipping a week of classes and exams.

And if my parents actually wanted to track me down, they'd have a list of ten WMUs to search through. I doubt they even care that much.

To be honest, I'm probably dead to them now. That thought gives me some kind of sickening, relieving peace.

Still, I could use a hug, and Ian isn't here to give me any. Even if he was, I threw his affection back in his face, so he'd probably be hesitant to touch me at risk of making me mad.

I get a text notification, and my heart jolts, my hands shaking again as I pick up my phone to read it. Did my parents manage to find my number, too?

IAN SCOTT

Fuck, I already miss you

Gonna be thinking about you lots

God, I miss him too.
This is gonna be a long week.

————

"Why do baseball players have so many away games?" I ask, picking at a blade of grass.

Laura shrugs, glancing up from her laptop. "Dude, it's his *first* extended road trip. You'll get used to it." She remains silent for a few seconds, sizing me up before smiling. "Oh, you *miss him*, miss him. Got it."

I groan. "I do."

"You aren't gonna deny it?"

"Why should I?"

"Good answer. Still, he'll be back in two days. Be patient."

"I've *been* patient," I mutter. A leaf blows onto my laptop screen, and I flick it away. "Sheesh, and I was a dick to him before he left, too."

I did tell Laura and Sabrina about the spat Ian and I had, and they said I was overthinking the whole situation, even if I was a bit of an idiot.

"Everyone's a dick sometimes," Laura reassures me. "Besides, if staying was what you wanted, Ian's the kind of person to respect that."

"I thought I wanted to be independent or whatever, but I got all lonely the second he left and then I regretted everything."

A text pops up, and I snatch my phone to read it.

IAN SCOTT

Hey! Whatcha up to?

I smile as my chest goes fuzzy. I tried sending an apology text to Ian, but he predicted it as soon as I sent the first message, and preemptively forbade me from apologizing over "nothing." Still, I don't think I've fully shaken my residual guilt, not yet.

Nothing much, studying with Laura rn

How are your games going?

I don't need to ask—I've been following his games online, and they haven't been going well at all.

Ian's typing indicator appears and stays for an excruciating few minutes.

They're going okay ig, we're doing what we can
but the team has a ton of injuries

Doesn't help that a bunch of our strong players
got drafted last summer and dipped

Lowkey stressed about making regionals

Make that highkey lmao

"How's Ian?" Laura asks, and I tuck my phone away.

"Stressed."

She winces. "Yeah, I took a peek at the stats for the men's team. Yikes. How stressed is he?"

I check my phone again.

> Like I'm not trying to go pro but man it'd suck if we got knocked out
>
> Maybe TMI but I wanna puke

I grimace. "Very."

"Oh, shit. I'm sorry to hear that."

"Yeah, I wanna cheer him up," I say. "But that's kind of hard to do from all the way over here."

Laura nods.

"I could visit him?" I speculate out loud.

What?

Hello, intrusive thoughts.

Laura doesn't seem to think so—she's smiling. "Now *that's* a good idea. You should do it."

"Wouldn't that be clingy?"

"Clingy?" Laura scoffs. "Are you kidding me? Have you met Ian? If the roles were flipped and *you* were nervous, he would, I don't know, come home and feed you a seven-course meal he cooked himself."

I snicker. That *does* sound like something he would do. "You're right."

Today is Friday. There's a game against Boston University College tomorrow, and then the team is coming back on Sunday.

I don't have another exam until Wednesday.

My bank account is padded from my library job and the rent I'm not paying.

I can swing it.

"You know what, I think I'll go to him," I say.

"Ooh, make it a surprise," Laura suggests. "He's gonna love that. See if you can coordinate with Nick."

Grinning, I grab my phone to do just that.

Grinning, I grab my phone to do just that.

> Hey Nick, hope the road trip is going well. I was thinking of visiting Ian before the game against Boston tomorrow
>
> Was hoping I could plan a surprise and get your help

NICK RUSSELL

yo

that's a great idea

Ian's a lil stressed ngl so it'd actually be helpful if you visited

> Yeah he was telling me

I'll gets deets from coach but I'll keep this a secret, hang tight

He texts back a few minutes later.

our coach gave you the all-clear

we're staying at the university heights hotel near BUC and greenwall park

you have to use the code BUCPREF5 when booking or else you're gonna get fleeced

> Awesome, I'll book something

alright, we're about to get ready for our game but keep me posted

"I'm doing it," I confirm to Laura, and then I fix my attention on my laptop to book a room. My initial whiplash from seeing the price dissolves as soon as I enter the discount code, and after paying, I check the bus schedule from campus to Boston, snagging a departure that's in two hours.

"Are you ready?" Laura asks.

"I have a hotel and a bus, and I have to pack," I blurt out, stuffing my books into my backpack. "Sorry to leave so abruptly, but—"

Laura waves me off. "Don't worry about it. Go to your man."

I'm on it.

At home, I empty my backpack and run into the bedroom, packing two random changes of clothes. At the bed, I unplug my charger and pack that, too, and my focus creeps back to the nightstand.

One of the drawers is ajar.

It's Ian's sex drawer.

He says it's *our* sex drawer now, but I haven't gone digging around in it or anything. Ian tried to show me a few weeks ago, but that was before we went to the cabin, when I was squeamish about anything more than a simple blowjob. He stopped as soon as I tensed up, which wasn't my proudest moment.

Still, I pause after opening the drawer, wondering if I need to bring lube on a two-day trip and whether now is a good time to rummage through what lies behind the bottle.

Screw it. I get on my knees to take a look.

Rifling through everything, I don't know what I was so intimidated by—there's a box of condoms, more lube, and a couple of other things that he says he wants to use with me.

Oh, and a bag full of sturdy fabric straps. Knowing what I do now, it's clear what they're for, and I get boned-up as I grab it, gears turning in my head.

We'll have our own room in Boston. Win or lose, he's going to want to burn off some energy. He always does after a game.

Alright, it's settled. I'm taking the restraints with me. The game tomorrow is scheduled to end early in the afternoon, and we'll have *hours* before he has to go to any kind of dinner thing, if there's even one planned.

Smiling to myself, I stuff the bag into the bottom of my backpack. It's wild how far I've come in barely over three months. I'm still quieter, that's for sure, but I went from being a clammed-up, repression-laden shell of a person to someone with a boyfriend and everything that we've decided will go with that label.

While there's still more growing and learning and hard stuff left ahead for me, it's a process. I'm stepping up, and I'm going to keep at it.

Mentally cursing myself for not booking an earlier departure, I pace around the apartment, nervous anticipation building with every little step I take, and when I've had enough, I run out the door and get to the bus station half an hour before I'm supposed to. At least the bus is already there, so I board and settle into my seat at the back.

It's only then I realize it's the same seat as all the ones I booked for the trip when I first moved here. That's where the similarities end—this time, I'm traveling for fun.

CHAPTER TWENTY-FIVE
IAN

After what, thirteen years of baseball, I should be used to everything that comes with the game, right?

For the most part, I think I am, but getting a lungful of dust while sliding home isn't something I ever want to get used to.

Sure, we beat Providence U, just at the expense of putting me on all fours, hacking like I hit a cigarette for the first time. It's all for the love of the game, I guess.

I finally stop coughing and accept the bottle of water that Nick thrusts into my face, and I take a massive swig. Then, since I'm now freshly recovered, my teammates swarm me, slapping my back and pulling me in a bunch of different directions for a shot at a side hug.

This long-ass stretch of away games is finally coming to an end, having brought us from New York to what feels like every single college in New England with a baseball team. At least we have a two-week stretch of home games before our next overnight, and the prospect of sleeping on my own cushy mattress with Callum curled up next to me has my brain spinning in anticipation.

These hotel mattresses have a whole lot of lumps and a painful absence of Callum. *My* mattress has a whole lot of Callum and a wonderful absence of lumps.

I'm freshly twenty, and I'm already picky about sleeping conditions. Does that make me a diva? Maybe.

Okay, yes, it definitely does, and I don't want to change that.

The post-game debrief is over in a flash; Coach Ramirez probably wants to get some rest as much as the rest of us, so we scramble for the limited showers as soon as he's done, and I'm lucky enough to snag one first.

I'm efficient, and I sneak past Nick, who claims my stall the second I unlatch the door. Honestly, the team should set up a sprinkler on the field or something so we could get this over with faster, without having to fight our own team for a stream of cold water.

After getting dressed, I reach for my phone, and I break into a wide, lip-splitting smile as soon as I see the message from him.

CALLUM CROSS

How'd the game go?

My face is visible to the whole team, but they can call me whipped, sentimental, soppy, or whatever. I don't care. Callum's mine, I'm his, I'm head over heels for him, and that's the way things are.

Good! We won

Thanks to me lmao I scored the winning run

That's awesome!

Can't wait for you to get back

Oof. I'm fine. I'm fine, I'm fine, I'm fine. It's just that my chest tightens and sends dull pangs of longing through my whole body.

I miss him so bad all of a sudden. Like, I've *been* missing him, but not in an achy, urgent way all the time—it's more that his adorable quirks are notably absent from my life, like the way he mumbles nonsense as he's falling asleep, how he twitches when he's about to wake up, and how he randomly hugs me from behind.

Yeah, oh boy, I'm so gone. Callum lets me be my whole, over-the-top, affectionate self without pushing me away.

"You're thinking about Callum, aren't you?" Jeremy nudges me and grins, which makes my face heat up.

"I am. He's texting me." There isn't a situation I can think of where I'd ever want to deny it.

Jeremy scoffs. "Oh, man, you're so fucked in the best way. You're stone-cold sober, yet you're smiling like you're crossed on a fifth of liquor and, like, a hundred edibles. "

That's quite the visual, and I crack up. "Love is one hell of a drug, man—"

Whatever the modern equivalent of a record scratch is, that happens.

Holy shit. I said it out loud. Not to Callum, but I said it. It's the first time I've *ever* said it in that way, and my god, it feels so right.

"Are you... Is that..." Jeremy tilts his head.

"Yup, I love him." That rolls off the tongue so easily.

"What's going on here?" Nick asks, toweling his hair and joining us.

Jeremy replies before I can. "Scotty's in loooove."

Nick looks to me for confirmation, and I give it to him.

"That's fast," he says.

"Yeah, we're almost two months in," I reply. "And I don't have anything to compare it to, but I just know."

"Like how?" Nick squints at me.

"I'd take a bullet for him."

Jeremy jerks his head up. "Woah, easy there, bro. That's intense."

I smile back. "It's only a figure of speech. You know what I mean."

Nick raises an eyebrow. "Are you gonna tell him?"

I nod. "Uh-huh. I will in a bit. Like, I know it's still early, so I'm gonna sit on it for a while. But it'll slip out soon."

"What if he says it to you first?" Nick asks.

"Yeah, he might steal your thunder," Jeremy adds.

Scoffing, I pretend to tie my shoelaces so I don't have to look either of them in the eyes with a blush on my face. "He wouldn't steal my thunder. That'd only make me fall for him even more."

When I straighten back up, Nick is rolling his eyes while laughing, and Jeremy makes a short, mocking gagging noise.

"Dude, you're gonna give me a hundred cavities. Stop it." Jeremy tries to punch my shoulder, and I dodge, making him slam his fist into the wall instead. "For real, though, I'm glad you two found each other. You seem way happier now."

"That's 'cause he is," Nick says for me.

And it's true.

———

Surprising nobody, the hour-long ride up to Boston turns into two, thanks to traffic. Callum has an afternoon class, so I don't text him, and I spend the bus ride reviewing the incoming freshmen who've already decided to join our team next year.

Hunter from Michigan and Oscar from Taiwan. They both seem solid, and Hunter went to the same high school as Jeremy did, so it'll be good for him to have a friend on the team right from the start.

The five minutes it takes me to review their stats passes in a blink, and then I'm back to staring out the window. At least it's kind of pretty outside, or as pretty as I-95 can get in Southern Mass.

Callum's face is prettier than some dumb trees.

Fuck, I miss him. He tried to say sorry for getting "mad" at me before I left, which I had to shut down in a hurry. He wasn't mad, and he wasn't being unreasonable at all. He's *allowed* to do what he wants and to stand his ground, and that's what he did. The last thing I want is for Callum to go along with everything I suggest and bottle up what he actually thinks. That'd be plain unhealthy.

At least I'll be back home in two days so we can return to our normal life of classes, games, and waking up next to each other.

Grr. I need my strong-armed morning hugs like nothing else.

We pull up to our hotel in Back Bay, which is way swankier than the dingy suburban pit-stops we've holed up in so far. Playing against Boston University College does have its perks, especially with their neighborhood connections.

As usual, the team hangs around in the lobby while the team admin staff hand out our keycards. I stick next to Nick since we're rooming together, and the rest of the team filters up to their rooms, leaving us behind.

Finally, Coach Ramirez gets to the last card, and flicks his eyes to Nick. "Russell, you're in 405. That's it."

That's it? What am I gonna do, sleep on someone's balcony? I shoot a confused look at Nick, and he shrugs, a weird half-suppressed smile on his face. I'm about to ask him what the hell he's thinking when he sends a nod to someone behind me, before heading for the elevators.

Then there's a tap on my shoulder, and I turn around.

And I almost trip backward over my own feet.

It's Callum.

Callum's here.

"Holy shit, it's you," I blurt out.

Jesus, I could *not* have come up with a worse welcome line. He came all the way here for me, all adorable, kind-eyed, and smoking hot in that blue Henley, and I greet him with *disbelief*.

"It is," he says, stepping closer. He pulls me into a tight hug, not giving me a chance to save myself, and kisses the top of my head. "I missed you."

"So did I, oh my god." I grip him tighter and spin him around. "What's going on?"

"I heard you were a little nervous, so I got us a room for tonight and tomorrow."

"Just like that?" I ask, and he nods, smiling wide. "This means so much to me. Thank you for coming."

Manners? Found at last.

"Come on, let's go," he says, reaching out to relieve me of my gear bag.

We make our way up to our room, and yeah, I'm *so* gloating

about this to the team—Callum snagged a Deluxe room with a king-sized bed.

As soon as he puts my bag down, he hugs me from behind and shuts my brain off, flooding it with pure affection.

"Have I ever told you that you're the best?" I murmur into Callum's bicep. "I'm so freaking lucky to have you."

He hugs me tighter, resting his head on my shoulder. "You have. But don't say it again because you're activating my praise kink."

Okay, he wants to stay wholesome for now. I bite back the temptation to shower him in compliments—I'm strong enough to hold out. I've done that for days, so what's a few more hours? Or minutes? Hopefully minutes.

I'm a mess.

The tight grip he has on me, coupled with how good he smells, is decimating my resolve. I slide out of his arms and sit on the bed, facing him. "Are you feeling better now? It's been a week since, uh, that DM."

He nods once, resting against the wall and crossing his arms. I force my eyes away from his burly forearms and up to his face, which doesn't change how attracted I am to him.

"I sure am," he says. "Once I realized that my parents can't realistically do much, or anything at all, I got over myself super quickly."

"Still, that must have been scary," I reply.

"It was." Callum uncrosses his arms and joins me on the bed, reaching out for my hand. I accept it, placing my fingers over his and sliding them through the gaps, and he squeezes once. "If I want to live my life the way I want to, I have to, you know, actually do that. If I have to do a little faking it 'till I make it, I'm gonna do that."

"That's really brave of you," I say. He sure is one tough cookie. If I was in his shoes, it'd take me ages to get to where he's at, and I don't even know the fullest extent of what went down when he was growing up. Hell, he could be holding back on giving me the dirty, gritty details about his parents, not that I'd blame him, but fuck. "You've gotta be the strongest person I know."

Callum sighs. "I still have so far to go, though. Like, I still get nervous and stuff. That anxiety isn't gone, but I'm trying to push through it when it's not based on anything realistic."

"That's already so good." I give him a squeeze back, and he slides our hands down my leg, resting them in my inner thigh. "I'm so proud of you."

He presses his palm into my thigh, taking my brain where it doesn't need to go right now.

Then he does it again. Harder.

Fucker. Does he know what he's doing to me? I will not let my pent-up horny energy ruin this emotional moment. No way—

He brings his other hand over to cup my semi, chuckling. "Aww, is all this mental health talk turning you on?"

"I haven't come in four days," I grumble. "*And* you showed up wearing my favorite outfit, baring your tempting forearms." I instinctively press up into Callum's touch. "We were having a moment. I can wait."

"Four days?" He digs in again, and my vision goes blurry. "That's not okay."

"Yeah, well, I've had exactly zero privacy. Kinda hard to rub one out with Nick in the room and a glass wall looking into the bathroom." I have to force my words out past the sheer urgency enveloping my crotch, which is made way worse by those teasing fingers.

Yeah, he's not helping my situation, not at all, especially when —oh fuck, when he slips under the waistband of my shorts and massages me through my underwear.

"Good thing we're alone, then." Callum guides me onto my back and gets on his knees. "I've wanted this for ages."

Alright, this is happening; I'm finally getting relief. He keeps rubbing me, humming contentedly, and I'm already at risk of busting.

"I'm kind of short on clean clothes," I warn, "so you're gonna have to—"

Callum finishes my sentence by yanking my shorts and underwear down, freeing me. He strokes a couple of times, firm and electrifying, and my breath catches.

"Better?" he asks.

"Much. I'm—"

Callum opens his mouth and envelops my dick.

Holy flying fucking shit. Callum is sucking my cock. Nope, not just that—he's sucking my cock with pure, enthusiastic devotion, and it feels so good, I think my mind shatters into tiny fragments. He's being slow and so deliberate, pausing for brief, torturous moments to listen whenever I so much as take a labored breath. My entire core is encased in addictive, delicious pleasure, only for it to be ripped away when he pulls back for air.

"Am I doing okay?" he asks. "Tell me what you like."

I meet his gaze, and I can only whine. "Yeah. Don't stop. Don't you dare." My thoughts are cut off when he gives me a couple of strokes, and I have to power through the clouds of arousal in my brain to keep talking. "Be gentle with the tip and don't pull too hard, but *please* keep going."

He chuckles, his warm breath landing on the head of my dick, and even that is enough to make it pulse. "Gotcha."

Then he takes me back into his mouth, jerking my shaft while making warm, delightful swipes at the tip. The pressure in my nuts was already killing me in the background before Callum showed up, and now it's built up to something stratospheric.

I tap him on the shoulder. "Gonna come," I get out, biting back a moan. "Jerk me."

He slides off, tightening his fist around me while stroking hard and smiling up, and the sight of his bright eyes and expectant grin tips me over. I shoot with a desperate yell, letting my head fall back while my toes spasm.

Am I gonna need to use any muscles tomorrow? I sure hope not—I think they're all out of commission.

Yup, Callum wrested my entire soul out of my body through my cock, leaving me limp and spent.

His voice breaks through my foggy brain. "God, that was so hot."

I let out a weak grunt, glancing down to get an eyeful of Callum wiping off his cum-streaked face with a tissue. Sex with him has been spectacular from the start, but right then, he leveled it up to something I don't think I can give up.

That was the *first* blowjob he ever gave, and it sent my eyes rolling into the back of my head. Holy hell, I'm definitely the luckiest guy on earth.

"How did you do that?" I ask. "Don't tell me you secretly sucked a bunch of dicks and got a ton of practice while I was gone."

"Nah. Let's just say I read some stuff online and borrowed a carrot from the fridge."

"Well, I'd like to give my thanks to the internet and the produce aisle." I blow out a tired breath, hauling myself off the bed. "Want me to take care of you now?" I check my watch and silently curse the passing of time.

He waves me off. "Nah. You can try owing *me* for once."

"Not having it." I power through my orgasm-weakened muscles to lunge at Callum, tackling him onto the bed with my shorts still around my ankles. My mouth is on his a second later, and I fumble with his belt, whipping it out of the loops and discarding it onto the floor next to me. "Still gonna turn down a blowjob?"

He shakes his head, unbuttoning his jeans and shoving them off.

I sink to my knees and whip his hard dick out of his boxers, wetting my hungry mouth before diving in and giving him what we both need. It doesn't take long for him to tense up and come down my throat, his body weakening under my touch and falling back into the mattress.

"We really needed that," he breathes out, and I lie down next to him, nestling my head into the crook of his neck.

"Oh yeah." My hand traces his right pec, skimming through the light fuzz and moving with his breathing. "I never want to take another road trip again."

He tilts his head down to look me in the eye. "Even if I visit you?"

"That might get me to reconsider." I sigh, knowing that it'd be entirely impractical for Callum to join me for every away game. The hotel bills would rack up fast, and the rest of the guys would start badgering their partners to come along, too.

But Callum's here now. Right when I was missing the heck out of having him around, he showed up out of nowhere. If the roles were reversed, visiting him would be something I'd overthink for *ages*, wondering if it'd be over the top, or if he'd be weirded out.

And he came here for me.

I'm *not* too much.

Together, Callum and I make sense. We fill each other's cups and laugh at how much we overflow, instead of holding back and pretending we're too cool for affection.

Man, I love him.

———

The next day, at some inhumane hour, my blissful, Callum-warmed slumber is rudely interrupted by my piercing, shrieking alarm.

Fine, it's eight in the morning and my phone alarm is set to vibrate. Still, I shut it off to avoid disturbing Callum, who has a hand on my leg that's drawing sleepy circles in my inner thigh. Light stubble appeared on his face overnight, and I run my fingers along his jaw, savoring the scratchy texture and contemplating a brazen theft of his razors. He always goes clean-shaven, even when he'd kill it with a little facial hair.

Callum can rock whatever look he wants to and still be hot as hell, and I'm the lucky guy who gets to enjoy him.

"Morning," he mumbles, brushing my roaming fingers away and nuzzling into my neck.

Waking up with him always puts a silly smile on my face, even on days when he sprawls like a starfish and jolts me awake with an accidental backhand to the face. Him being next to me is what matters, and I'll never get tired of him being the first thing I see when I open my eyes.

My alarm goes off again, beeping this time, and I stretch out to silence it. Groaning, I heave my heavy, tired body off of the plush mattress to get changed for today's pre-game practice.

And because I'm me, I make a little show out of it for Callum. His soul-piercing gaze stays fixed on me, and he lets out a disappointed sigh when I slip a sweater on.

"Are you heading out already?" he asks, and I nod.

"I have to be downstairs at eight-thirty. We're getting breakfast before practice, so I won't see you until after the game."

He stretches out his arms. "Alright then. Gimme a hug before you go."

This man is gonna be the end of me, I swear. I oblige, sinking into the comfort of his body, letting him tighten around me.

"I still can't believe you surprised me here," I say, pulling back. "This is exactly what I needed."

Callum shrugs, beaming at me with that adorable grin plastered over his defined face. "What can I say? I missed you."

He said that before, but this time, it hits me harder. Warmth diffuses through my body, under every square inch of my skin. I sit next to him on the bed, holding his hand, and when he squeezes, I can't take any more.

Sucking in a breath, I lock eyes with him.

"I love you, Callum."

He blinks, his pretty lips parted in what looks like disbelief. His eyebrows are raised, his head is tilted, and he's...

Coming in for a kiss.

Yes, please.

I accept his mouth hungrily, flicking my tongue past his teeth and letting him return the favor.

"I love you too, Ian," he murmurs. "My god, I love you so *much*." Callum dives back in, claiming my mouth again and drawing a heated moan from the depths of my throat. "You're the first person who's ever said that to me."

Oh. My heart splinters, and I rest my forehead against his, holding back tears. "I'll have to make up for lost time, then."

In the back of my mind, I *knew*, but for me to be the first person ever to love him? That's downright *criminal*. He's *twenty*, for crying out loud. I had to hold myself back from saying it to him too soon, yet *nobody's* loved the easiest person on earth to love?

I wrap my arms around him and pull him close. "I know I'm a lot, but you're gonna have to deal with that. I love you so fucking much, and I'm *going* to love you even more with every single day we spend together. I'm gonna make you *sick* of hearing those words with how often I'll say it, but—" I bury my face in Callum's chest and savor his addictive, masculine scent. "I love you, and I'm never. Going. To. Stop." I jab a finger into his chest after each of those words.

He tightens his grip on me. "I'm never going to get sick of it."

"Good." My phone beeps again. "Now I'm gonna go to practice, and later today, I'm gonna score some runs for you, babe. Cheer me on."

CHAPTER TWENTY-SIX

CALLUM

Someone loves me.

Ian.

Ian loves me.

My eyes remain glued to a certain batter at the top of every inning, and to a certain third baseman at the bottom. Even from a distance, Ian is sexy as heck, and he's all mine.

And he loves me, exactly how I love him.

That plays through my mind on repeat throughout the whole game. The internet says you're supposed to complete yourself instead of relying on someone else to do so, but I don't think anyone is *ever* complete. I'm still working on myself—that's never going to stop—and I'm not getting Ian to bridge any gaps.

I'd be okay on my own, but he adds to my life in a way I couldn't do myself. Like how black coffee does the job to wake me up, and I like it alright, but milk helps it go down smoother. My life would be fine if I was lactose intolerant, but his cream makes it so much better—

Oh, god. That analogy took a filthy turn, even if it's true.

I would have thought blunting my sexual hang-ups would also blunt my intrusive bedroom thoughts, but it's done the opposite.

I have to take my mind out of the sewer and focus on the game.

Ooh, action! Awesome. Ian pulled WMU ahead by one at the top of the ninth, and BUC just got a second strikeout with a runner still on second.

WMU's place in the playoffs is hinging on Jeremy. Man, the poor guy looks like he's shitting king-sized bricks with how he's white-knuckling the ball on the mound. He fires off a...fastball, I think, and it sails toward BUC's batter.

Fuck, it connects. The hit sounds crisp and looks even better, and the ball sails far into the outfield.

Please don't be a home run.

Nick answers my prayers. He's running toward the back of the ballpark, eyes fixed on the falling ball, tracking it, homing in, stretching out, jumping...

Catching it.

Dropping his body to the ground. With his glove still around the ball.

BUC is out.

WMU won. Holy shit, they *won*.

Groans of disappointment surround me as I pump my fist in celebration, heading down so I can get closer to the dugout. Ian's going to do a debrief like he always does, but I want to congratulate him beforehand, if I can. The few people heading for the exits let me pass as I go in the opposite direction to them, and I lean over the railing above the visitor's dugout, waving at Ian, who's looking out onto the field.

I'm about to call his name when one of the WMU coaches, Ramirez, based on the name at the back of his coaching sweater, spots me and grins, motioning for me to climb over.

Jeremy spins Ian around and shoves him closer. I jump the low railing into the dugout, and Ian catches me as I stumble on the landing.

"Hey." He's all smiles, his face flushed and shimmering with hard-earned sweat. "Did you enjoy the game?"

My god, that smile. It's blinding, perfect, and all mine.

"Yeah, I did." My voice is flat, my mind distracted by the amazing sight of a win-fueled, elated Ian in front of me. I reach down and turn his hat backward. Red dust clings to the stray sweat-dampened strands of hair sticking out from under the brim and on his sun-kissed skin.

He looks too good to be real. This man is completely, utterly breathtaking, he's mine, and *he loves me.*

"You good, Cal?" he asks, his mouth crooking up to one side.

"More than good," I want to say back, but the words don't come. The emotions, the everything, it's overwhelming, and at the same time, it's not nearly enough.

I grin and run my thumb along his jaw. He jerks once, a shiver echoing across his face, but that beautiful expression of his doesn't break.

We're in public. There are hundreds of people around us. I'm sure nobody is watching, but still. This is so intimate, anyone who catches so much as a glimpse of me and Ian would assume we're more than friends, and they'd be right.

But do I even care? The whole team knows. What's a few more people who I might never see again?

Ian opens his mouth, probably to ask me why I'm clamming up, but if he says anything, it doesn't register. My pulse is deafening, unrelenting, and somehow, it's also clarifying.

I *don't* care.

Those parted lips, soft, tempting, and *there*, might as well be an open invitation.

Maybe it is. I don't know, and only two words ricochet around in my head.

Fuck it.

Without another thought, I close the distance between us and crash my mouth onto his.

The buzz around us fades into nothing. Ian loves me back. He loves me and my awkward, messed-up self, and I want to show how much I appreciate having him in my life.

He doesn't doubt me. He doesn't stop, question, pull back, or stiffen. He gives me the lead, and I deepen the kiss, smiling through every satisfied breath he takes.

Yeah, we're still in public, but I don't stop myself from sneaking in a little tongue here and there. He tastes like the gum he was chewing on the field, mixed with salty ballpark, and it's pure *him*. My head spins, and I know I need to take a breath soon, but I don't want to. When Ian makes the decision for us, I have to hold myself back from grabbing onto his tongue to make sure he doesn't go too far.

His lids droop over molten eyes, his pupils wide. "Callum, holy shit. That was amazing."

"Was it?" I smirk at him, making those defined cheeks pinken. "But you cut us off."

"Excuse me for breathing," he mumbles, and he hauls me back down for more.

In the fog of the world around us, I register a few noises of acknowledgement from Ian's teammates, and that only emboldens me to keep going. I'm living. *We're* living, free and unencumbered. Before, I told myself that I don't care, and I was wrong. I actually *do* care about what we're doing—I care and know that this isn't something I'm ever going to give up. There's no going back for me. This life, open, happy, and so right, is mine.

"Jesus, babe, save some of that heat for later," Ian says, pulling back again and giving his teammates a cursory glance.

I do the same, and Nick sends us a friendly nod before taking another swig from his bottle, like seeing his best friend making out with another guy is the most normal thing in the world.

Outside of the bubble I grew up in, it could very well be the case.

I kiss Ian again, gentler this time, holding back on the tongue and not on the pressure. After a few blissful seconds, I release him and stare down into those beautiful hazel eyes, tracing the small, happy creases at the outer corners.

"I love you so much," I murmur.

"Love you, too. God, saying that feels so *right*," he replies.

We both take a step away from each other, and when we do, I spot someone, probably a student, wearing a lanyard and regarding us...tentatively.

She catches my gaze and clears her throat. "Hi, I'm Lana

Cheung, sports reporter for the BUC newspaper." She extends her hand to us. "First off, congrats on the win, and I wanted to get your go-ahead for a social media post that includes a candid picture of you two."

"Okay," I say automatically. "What's the post about?"

"It's part of a series focusing on the game today," Lana replies. "One of our photographers got a picture of you guys celebrating. Here, you can see."

She turns her phone around to show us the photo, and as soon as I see it, my heart melts. It's immaculate. We're gazing longingly at each other, Ian looks spectacular with his backward hat and his game-winning smile, and I look like I belong. I'm caressing his jaw. He's got a hand gripping behind my neck.

The love is so obvious, no one could miss it if they tried.

"This would be posted?" Ian asks, and Lana nods.

I take another look at the picture. It's so good.

"I'm okay if you are," I say to Ian.

"Babe," he starts. "That'll be public."

"I know, and I don't care."

Is my confidence a little false? It sure is. Still, deep down, I know this is the right thing to do. Nobody is coming for me. The only people who know me and would give a shit are my parents, and what are they gonna do? If they see it, and that's a massive if, all they can do is get pissed, try to DM me again, and wallow in their own displeasure.

"Then go right ahead," Ian says, and he slings an arm around my waist.

"Want a tag?" Lana asks, handing Ian her phone.

"I'm good with that." Ian puts his account tag in, and once he's done, I take the phone out of his hands to do the same for myself.

"Awesome. Thanks so much!" Lana says when I give her phone back. "I'll add a nice caption, and it'll go up in a few minutes."

She walks away, and it sinks in.

It's out there.

A picture of me so obviously in love with my amazing boyfriend. Not hidden, not posted to a private account, nothing like that—it's on the BUC newspaper's social media and maybe their website, too. WMU's paper might repost it.

"Are you doing okay?" Ian asks. "You seem a little tense."

I tell the truth. "I'm good, but I'm overthinking the photo a little, but I don't regret it. I needed to take that step."

"That's amazing," he says. "I'm glad you're feeling good about it, and I'm here for you if the nerves stick around."

Right as I'm about to speak, one of the WMU coaches calls the team over.

Ian gives me an apologetic smile. "I'm gonna have to debrief and then shower here. You can head back to the hotel to wait."

"No rush," I say as nonchalantly as I can manage, and I remember my sexy little plan for after the game. Lowering my voice and brushing my lips against his ear, I add. "I might be tied up myself."

He blinks, widening his eyes more with each time he opens them. "What do you mean by that?"

I swat his ass. "I said what I said, Scotty. I might have done some digging in our sex drawer, so don't keep me waiting."

As I straighten, Ian's face is flushed. Seriously flushed. His mouth hangs open, and he shakes his head, still standing motionless.

The coach calls for Ian.

"I'll be back as fast as I can. Trust me." With that, Ian spins around and sprints over to where the rest of the team is gathered, not like that'll make his coach speak any faster.

Smiling to myself, I saunter out of the ballpark and back to our hotel, trying to keep myself from getting inappropriately hard in my jeans while letting my mind wander.

I'm getting what I want today—I came out to a bunch of people and nothing bad happened, and soon, I'm gonna get laid out and ravaged by my sex god of a boyfriend.

As soon as I'm in the room, I strip and head for the shower, getting myself nice and clean in preparation for getting downright filthy. Ian texts me as I'm toweling off, telling me he's already on his way back, so I speed up.

I fish the handcuffs out of my backpack and fix the straps to the bedposts, leaving them draped on top of the sheets. He's gonna be here any second now, so I flop onto the bed and cover my hard, impatient cock with a clean sock.

The lock clicks open as soon as I put my hands behind my head.

"Hey," I say. "You kept me waiting."

He stands frozen, his mouth open, eyes sweeping over my almost-naked body. He's changed, and his hair is still damp from the ballpark shower, and he tears his gaze off me, darting to the black fabric above my shoulders.

He lets out a huff of laughter. "You weren't kidding, were you?"

I reply with a shrug. "I wasn't. Now are you gonna get your ass over here and do what you want with me?

Ian hisses in a breath, closing his eyes and smiling. "Man, I love you."

Dropping his gear bag to the floor, he stumbles over, discarding his clothes in the process. He's still in his boxer briefs by the time he reaches the bed, and I stick my arm out and yank them off, exposing his erection so I can give him a few firm strokes.

"Hands off," he instructs. "I didn't say you could touch me."

"Yes, sir," I tease.

He flicks me on the forehead. "Shut up. I'm not fucking *sir*."

"Yeah, I got it backward. Sir's fucking me."

"Stop it and put your hands up."

I pause. Since I'm mere seconds away from getting restrained, I want to get one last feel of his body, so I pull Ian down for a kiss. Tangling my tongue with his, I let my hands roam across his skin, feeling the dick-stiffening curve of his ass under my fingertips and the hard ridges of his torso pressed against me.

He moans softly before pulling back, hooded lids covering smoldering eyes. "That's enough of that," he says, reluctance in his tone. "Do what I told you."

I comply, sticking my four limbs out, one toward each corner of the mattress.

Ian lets out a whispered curse of disbelief. "Jesus, you're perfect like this."

He runs his hands along my chest and up my arms, feeling them up and making my cock harden even more. Those strong fingers are nowhere close to my groin, yet I'm so turned on I'm already leaking.

"Same word as before. Moose," he continues, pulling the first nylon strips toward my wrist.

"Got it."

One by one, Ian loops the restraints around my wrists, fastening them tightly. Arousal surges through my body, and as he moves away to secure my feet, I bend my arms to test the cuffs, and I'm still able to move a fair distance.

I don't have full movement, but I know for a fact that I could be a lot less mobile.

"I left a little give up there so you'd be comfortable," he says. He's finished tying my ankles to the legs of the bed, and same as with the wrists, there's room for me to shuffle around. "Is that okay?"

"Sure," I start, "but it might be a little too much."

"Oh, you want me to untie your legs—"

"No. Tie them tighter. My arms, too."

Ian's mouth hangs open, maybe from surprise, or maybe from the fact that I cut him off mid-sentence. "Hold up." He presses his lips together and smirks. "Tell me *exactly* what you want."

My heart jolts with excitement, and I clear my throat. "Tie me up tighter. Make me completely fucking helpless."

"Completely fucking helpless..." He trails off, still smiling.

"Yeah. I've wanted that for weeks. I just didn't think to ask until now."

I may or may not be stealing lines from the internet again.

"Holy shit, Cal, you're so…"

"Freaky?" I supply. And suddenly, that word gets a whole new, better meaning.

"Oh yeah," he says, chuckling. He winches the wrist cuffs tighter so they're right against the edges of the mattress, and then adjusts the ones around my feet to leave me, as promised, completely helpless.

I don't think I've been hornier. Ever. Not even when I made myself hold back from jerking off. Because now, I want this with unfathomable intensity.

I twitch as Ian trails his fingers over my stomach, and he flattens his palms so they lie flat on my skin.

"Look at you," he purrs, planting his hands on my chest and dragging them down to my thighs. "All this fucking muscle, and you're still so *vulnerable*."

He's taunting me, too?

If those words weren't enough, Ian gives my knees a quick squeeze, making me try to bend my legs out of instinct, only to be stopped by the amazing tightness around my ankles. All that does is remind me of how defenseless I am, in spite of my now-useless muscles.

Shit, I don't know if I can take being *this* aroused.

Ian leans lower and places gentle, dry kisses down my stomach and around my groin, deliberately avoiding my aching erection. I try to make it jump so it nudges him, in case he forgot about it, but all he does is give the underside a quick, unsatisfying lick before continuing to tease the daylights out of me.

"I'm kind of desperate here," I complain.

"Good. Now shush. I'm in control, like you asked."

Jesus.

He keeps at the teasing for who knows how long, making my dick throb and my breaths raspy with need. When he sticks his tongue out and drags it under my cockhead, I pull at the restraints and let out a weak whine. That tiny bit of contact feels outsized, drawing a heavy bead of precum from my slit. It falls onto my core, and Ian proceeds to move up and lick it clean, making sure to brush my dickhead with his tongue while he's at it.

"Needy?" he asks when I release a pleasured yelp. "Just how I like you."

I don't have time to register that—he darts down and takes me into his mouth without warning, plunging my entire body into ecstatic bliss and making my balls contract with arousal.

Ian's blowjobs are downright ferocious. It's impossible for me to clock how he achieves that electrifying balance of aggression and care that sends me into overdrive. Before long, I'm twisting around and flexing my thighs, ready to burst.

"Gonna come," I grunt, and he pulls off.

My cock jumps in protest, and I thrust up to chase his mouth, but it's too far away.

"Okay, you're edging me again," I say, hoping I'm right.

"You bet. Try to fight it. I bet you can't."

"Challenge accepted."

Ian doesn't reply, and he reaches into my bag and fishes out the bottle of lube. Instead of coating my shaft, he slicks a finger and nudges at my hole.

"Are you okay if I play with your ass a little?" he asks.

I nod, and he sticks his finger in. The sensation is unusual, and I scrunch my eyes closed for a second until it feels better. He curves up, which also feels weird, but not unpleasant at all.

"Is this okay?" he asks.

"Yup. I'm still turned-on as hell."

Ian starts sucking me again, bringing me back to the brink in seconds, and instead of letting him know like I always do, I keep my mouth closed and my body still.

Oh yeah, I'm close. I'm almost there. I'm gonna come so hard and he's gonna be so freaking mad—

He pulls off with milliseconds to spare.

"Shit!" I yell. How the... I yank at the restraints and buck my hips up into thin air, my cock all but begging for attention it isn't getting.

Ian lets out a curt laugh. "You thought you could sneak past me, didn't you? Unfortunately, your body doesn't lie."

I stay quiet.

"So basically, a bunch of muscles clench when a guy's about to come," he continues, and I crook my neck to look at him. "With a finger up your ass, I can feel that happening, which lets me know I have to stop. You can try to stay quiet all you want, but your body's gonna tell on you every single time."

Ian simply smiles. It's colder than usual, which sends a shiver down my back and makes me pulse. If there's a fun, horny version of dread, that's what's crawling through my veins right now.

I handed control over to some kind of erotic supervillain.

"I think I'll call it the asshole technique," he muses. "Because, well, you have to be a certain kind of asshole to use it."

Arousal clouds my judgment and opens my mouth. "Show me how much of an asshole you can be, Ian."

He smirks up at me, parting his lips and darting his tongue out to lick them. "Be careful what you wish for."

With that, he bends down, his finger still in my ass, and sucks me into his mouth. The sheer warmth pushes me back to the edge, and the slow drags of his soft tongue along the underside tips me so I'm leaning over it.

I don't know how many times he denies me after that. It could be five. Or ten. Or a hundred. I lose count after three. My dick begs for release, my entire groin is blanketed in desperate static, and my jaw hangs open, halfway between delirium and pure, conscious arousal.

"Hey, hey, stay with me," he says, shuffling up and cupping my chin. "Sheesh, your face is red as hell."

Words are hard to come by, but I manage, "Need to come."

He squeezes my cheeks, sending more heat surging through my body. "Nah."

I let out a wail of protest.

"It sounds like you're having too much fun," Ian continues.

"You aren't wrong."

He tuts, running a gentle thumb under my dickhead that almost makes me shoot. "Tell me how much you like being helpless, Cal."

I suck in a sharp, needy breath. "Holy shit, I'm in heaven right now."

"Why's that?"

"I like that I don't have control."

"Almost there," he teases.

Jesus. I hold back on giving myself up, but only for a second. Ian is Ian. He's safe, and I trust him.

"I love the way you own me."

He goes back down, his breath tickling the head of my cock, which makes my brain spiral with need. "That's what I like to hear."

Shutting my eyes, I thrust my head back into the mattress, letting out a weak moan. I'm bordering on overstimulated; I'm so pent-up, and there's nowhere for any of it to go.

At least until Ian surprises me by enveloping my shaft with his molten fucking mouth, blanking my mind with sheer pleasure.

If he pulls back again, I'm gonna lose it. I'm saying moose if he does.

"Please," I grit out.

"Hmm?" he hums, putting me in danger of shooting off.

"Please let me come," I moan. "Please, I can't take any more."

He hums again, the vibrations bringing me even closer to coming. Powerless, I erupt after two little swipes of tongue against my cockhead. All four of my limbs spasm, each trying to pull me in a different direction, but I still can't move as the white-hot orgasm sears outward, down into my feet and coiling hard in my core. Every single swear word in my vocabulary flies through my brain and out of my mouth, my voice catching in my throat as I begin the slow, euphoric descent back to reality.

I love the way you own me.

I said that, and I meant every single word. Outside of sex, Ian never would, and I wouldn't let him, but when we're in bed? Yeah, I'm handing him everything. He can have all of me and then some more.

The tightness around my wrists loosens, and I blink my eyes open. Ian undoes the restraints around my ankles, and again, I'm lost in the view of his round ass.

Then he turns back to me, showing off his front. I don't know which side of him I prefer.

"Not to get all clinical, but what do you need from me right now?" he asks.

I don't even have to think. "Hold me. Please. Can you do that?"

His arms are around me not a second later, and my muscles dissolve even more. "Of course I can," he says, pressing his lips to the top of my head. "I'm gonna take care of you."

Duality of man, manifested in Ian being downright evil one second and a total sweetheart the next. I wouldn't have it any other way.

With Ian still gripping me, I rest on his chest and sigh. It's like my body melts, totally taken by this amazing, amazing man. I still don't think I deserve him, but he says I do, so I indulge that opinion of his. He ruffles my hair and then plants a kiss in it—that's a signature move at this point, and I don't foresee ever growing tired of it.

I open my eyes, still blissed-out and boneless, and I focus on what's in front of me.

Ian's swollen, leaking dick.

He hasn't come yet, and even though I'm totally spent, I can't leave him hanging like a jerk.

I shuffle down and lick up his shaft, finishing at the tip where I know he's sensitive.

He moans. "You don't have to."

I take the head in and give a firm suck, making him squirm.

"But I want to taste you," I say, pulling back. "And it sounds like you need to come."

"Yeah, I do. Real fucking bad," he concedes. "Shit. I'm so close already."

This is no time to get any kind of sexy revenge on Ian for edging me out of my mind, so I take him to the back of my throat, clenching and sucking the way I did yesterday, over and over again. When his balls tighten underneath my touch and his cock pulses in my mouth, I don't stop, not even when he taps my head desperately and tells me that he's gonna bust.

I relish in his gritty yell as he comes, and I swallow every rope of his salty release. It's a little bitter, too, but I don't care. It's Ian's.

It takes a few seconds for him to finish, and I slide off to take a swig of water.

"Holy fuck, Callum, that was amazing," he wheezes. "Did you have fun being helpless?"

I snort. "Did you miss me whimpering like a total idiot, or what? I might as well change my major to astronomy because I saw every star in the damn galaxy."

"I'll take that as a yes, then."

"Oh, yeah. That's hands down the hottest thing we've done together."

"Yet."

My eyes fly open. "Yet?"

Ian stretches back on the bed, resting his head on his hands. "Oh, yeah. Trust me, we only scratched the surface. There's a lot more the two of us can try."

He shoots me a wink, and while that'd normally make me hard, I'm far too spent for any of that. I drag myself off the bed and into the shower again to scrub the sweat off, and when I return to the bedroom in sweats and a sweater, Ian's on his phone.

And he's squinting.

"Uh, Cal?" He clicks his phone off. "You know that picture the BUC paper posted of us?"

I nod, keeping my eyes fixed on his pretty face.

"It's going viral."

My heart jumps, and then it settles.

I don't care like I would have even a month ago.

Letting out a chuckle, I walk over to the bed and join him. "Awesome. Let me see."

CHAPTER TWENTY-SEVEN
IAN

Ten thousand.

Publicity is never something I've chased. I like my circle loud and fun, but small. Having ten thousand people liking a post with me in it was never on my bucket list.

Either way, I won't complain about a sports blog reposting the picture of me and Callum. We look fucking great. Mostly Callum, if I'm being real. He's a dream, and that picture is visual proof. Hell, if "picture-perfect" wasn't already a phrase, this shot would jumpstart it.

But a gossip magazine reposting it and dubbing us "Dugout Daddies" is something I *will* complain about. We're both twenty, for god's sake—that's closer to infancy than Daddy age, seriously.

Home Plate Hotties, Ballpark Boyfriends—those are all viable, better, alternatives.

Switch Pitching Sweethearts, too, although I'm the only one who's bi, and I'm not about to switch my affection away from Callum.

Ha, Tent Pitchers would work.

I snicker at my own creativity, and Sabrina smacks my leg. "Oh, are you too famous to talk to us now? I see how it is."

Grabbing my glass of water, I grip it gently with my fingertips, pretending it's a fragile crystal vessel. "Oh yes," I croon. "You are most decidedly correct. I, for one, am far superior to you common vagrants now that I am of elevated repute."

Not two seconds later, I get an ice cube to the face, courtesy of Nick. Then Callum picks it up, dropping it down the back of my shirt, making me yell. He's such a douche, but I love him anyway. Or because of it.

I am so, so gone for this man.

"How are you still making horny eyes at Callum with an ice cube in your asscrack?" Nick asks.

"Because it gives me sexy flashbacks to what we did last night," I shoot back, knowing full well that Callum and I gorged on lasagna and passed out at ten. Nothing happened.

"Ugh, gross," Sabrina says, screwing her face up. "Get a room."

"Uh, excuse me, but this is *our* house." I give Callum a wet, exaggerated kiss on the lips for effect, and he gags along with Nick and Sabrina.

Nick shakes his head and stands up. "Alright, I think it's time for us to get ready. I'm removing you."

Before I have time to read into that, Nick hauls me up by the arm and gives me a playful shove toward the door. I glance back at Callum for support, hoping his possessive side comes out in my defense, but all he does is laugh.

And then he pushes me. On the ass.

He's a damn traitor, but he's my traitor.

————

"Bro, I don't think that's your size," Nick says, squeezing my shoulders.

"It isn't meant to be." Our pre-game briefing ended a lot faster than I expected, and now I'm standing over the vinyl transfer machine in the athletic center, prepping a spare team hoodie.

"Wait a second..." Nick trails off as the machine beeps, and he peers over my shoulder as I lift the heating element. "That shit's cute, not gonna lie."

I smile, surveying my handiwork. I've customized the hoodie with my last name like all the others I have. The only difference is that this one isn't meant for me; it's for Callum. Call me egotistical, but I dig the idea of him walking around and coming to games in my hoodie—leaving my mark on him this way is a lot more wholesome than marring his neck with a bunch of hickeys, that's for sure.

He sure has a good neck for that, though. So soft and supple. Grr.

"Do you think he'll like it?" I ask, snapping out of my Callum-induced daydream.

"Buddy, have you seen the way Callum looks at you when you aren't paying attention?" It takes a while for Nick to catch himself. "Right. Anyway, that guy is *obsessed* with you. He'll love it."

I pull out my phone to text Callum.

> You here yet?

CALLUM CROSS

> Yeah, waiting outside

> Hold tight I'm omw. Meet me at the third gate

Hoodie in hand, I dash outside and scan the crowd for Callum, homing in on his imposing, recognizable figure and making a beeline for him.

"Hey, Ian. What's up?" he asks as I approach, bending down to give me a kiss.

I resist the urge to make out with him in public, limiting myself to a quick, chaste peck on the lips. "Nothing much, I wanted to give you some merch for the game."

I hand the hoodie to Callum, who unfolds it and inspects the front.

"It looks nice, thank you." He goes for a hug, and I stick an arm out to stop him, chuckling as I connect with his pec and give it a gratuitous, unnecessary squeeze.

"Cal, you should see the back," I say, using my free hand to flip the hoodie around.

His eyes widen, a smile tugging at his lips and at my heart-strings. He runs a hand over my name on the back before slipping the sweater on, and my chest blooms with warmth when his head pokes out of the top.

"I love it," he says, running a hand through his hair to mess it up again.

I shrug. "You don't get to be the only possessive guy in this relationship."

Callum grins. "Now everyone is gonna know I'm all yours."

My god, I like the sound of that. "I'll make it so clear. Maybe I'll play better if I know there's a kiss waiting for me at the end of a game."

"Hmm, I think I'll have to keep climbing into the dugout to make out with you."

As appealing as that sounds, it might raise some eyebrows. "That's one way to make the news. You'd be all over the internet *again*."

He leans into me, nudging his head onto mine and almost making me fall over. "That happened once. What's one more time?"

"You wouldn't be nervous or anything?" Shit. I shouldn't stoke that, so I course-correct. "Not that you *should* be or anything, but—"

Callum chuckles and bumps his shoulder against mine. "Ian, you don't have to worry about me like this." He wraps me in a hug, and I get a sudden, predictable urge to skip today's game and climb my boyfriend like a sexy jungle gym instead. "I *want* people to know we're together. Everyone, even people from my hometown. Man, I wish I still had friends from there who could update me."

"And that'd get back to your parents," I remind him.

He gives me a casual, unbothered tilt of the head. "I'm not scared of them anymore. I can't live my life concerned with what they'd think about me, not when I chose to slip out at midnight and leave them behind."

"I'm so proud of you." I beckon Callum down for another

kiss, and he obliges, brushing his lips across mine so gently, I grab the back of his neck and pull him in out of instinct.

Scoffing, he jerks away and swats my ass. "Enough of that, lover boy. Go play baseball."

CHAPTER TWENTY-EIGHT
CALLUM

Ian disappears back into the ballpark, leaving me with the remnants of our scorching kiss on my lips. It was a little peck. A chaste, PG-rated moment that still left me craving more and undressing his departing figure with my mind.

Sometimes, I still can't believe that I'm all his.

I grin to myself, grounding myself in the moment and keeping calm. While I don't have eyes on the back of my head, I can still tell that people are at least noticing the name I'm wearing. While I'm not sure how well student athletes are known on campus, we're at a baseball game—most of the crowd is gonna know who Ian is, and we're precisely where an athlete's hoodie is gonna stand out. They don't sell them, and the team colors are distinctive—dark blue with gold lettering and subtle green accents.

I smile, knowing that I'm Ian's, and that it shows. The semester is wrapping up in a few weeks, and if I went back in time and told January Callum that I'd not only have a boyfriend, but that I'd be wearing clothes that basically say "Property of Ian Scott" on it, I think I'd send my past self into a spiral.

Oh, I think someone's calling my name? They're pretty far away, but—

"Callum."

My first instinct to hearing my name is that it's Sabrina or Laura, but their voices aren't as—

"Callum! Look at me."

My blood runs cold, all the warmth leaving my body in a single, shocked breath.

I recognize that voice.

It's Mom.

My parents found me for real.

I ball one hand up into a fist and put the other in my pocket, palming my phone as I steel myself to face them. If I need to call campus security on them, I will. I have half a mind to make a break for it right now and do that.

But what would I even say?

Fighting every instinct in my body, I force my feet to turn my body around, and I swallow my nerves.

Both of them are no more than ten feet away from me.

The crowd of students falls silent and steps back, forming a kind of oval around my parents. While I *could* walk with them and try disappearing into the crowd, my parents are already here. They've already seen me.

It'll be better if I deal with them now and try to make them leave, if that's even possible.

I stay still, and now, the three of us are surrounded like a clearing in the woods.

Every last one of my instincts tells me to shrink down and hide. My mom is fixing me with a withering, disgusted stare, one that I got well acquainted with when I was a kid, and I have to take a breath to keep myself stable. Well, a couple of breaths. One isn't nearly enough.

"Okay, you found me." I keep my voice level. "What do you want?"

Mom's nostrils flare, her face reddening. "How *dare* you speak to me like that?"

I wince. Nobody's raised their voice at me since I left, and before I have a chance to respond, she lunges at me, forcing me to take a large step back. She doesn't stop approaching, and I keep walking backward.

"Are you going to keep chasing me in a circle?" I ask, raising my hands in a questioning gesture.

Oh, thank god, she stops.

Mom stays still, huffing breaths in and out, before she purses her lips. "What on *earth* were you thinking?"

I shrug like the bad son I already am. "What on earth are you referring to?"

For the first time since I saw him today, Dad speaks up. "Everything. Callum, you absconded in the night and left your family, just to run amok and commit every sin under the sun."

And I was having a great time doing so, at least until you guys showed up.

"It's what I needed to do," I reply, and I hold back from apologizing. "I couldn't live the life you wanted for me, so I had to leave."

"The life we wanted for you was respectable, Callum!" Mom yells. "How could you treat your family like this? Why did you have to throw everything away?"

A small, familiar tendril of guilt snakes into my throat, and I swallow it down. "Because it wasn't respectable to *me!*" Never before have I raised my voice around my parents, but fucking hell, it was a long time coming. I take a much-needed breath to calm down. "Not that either of you cared, but I was *miserable*. What did you expect me to do, suck it up and hate my life?"

"You don't seem to have a problem sucking something else, do you? You were my perfect, pure boy! Why did you have to go run around and corrupt yourself like it's *normal?*"

I almost laugh. Almost. Now that I've finally gotten away from my parents, seeing the way they're acting...

How did I ever think their behavior was normal?

The fact that I was ever used to their thinking makes my stomach churn.

Feeling more frustrated than anything else, I rub my temples, resolving to end this. It isn't worth my time or energy to keep engaging with my parents, and in the long run, the three of us will be way happier if we part ways now.

"Do you even have a plan beyond driving for twenty hours to shout at me on the street?" I wave my hands, realizing a little too late that I'm doing so exactly how my mom does, and I stick them into my pockets. "What now? Are you going to kidnap me and shove me into a car in front of hundreds of people?"

I gesture at the crowd around us. Some people are filming. Good for them. They'll capture my delusional, dumbfounded parents.

Dad crosses his arms. "Your behavior has been nothing short of disobedient and reckless." He pauses, and I use the last remaining bits of my tact to avoid rolling my eyes in the silence. "You've gone against *everything* we taught you."

"Like what? That *existing* in public was basically a shortcut to hell? That no woman would ever be good enough for Mom's *special little boy*, to the point where I was forbidden from even thinking about girls?" *Or having any kind of sexual thoughts, lest I act on them.* I scoff out a dry, humorless laugh. "Well, you specified a woman, but I found a *man*, and he's *too* good for me, so I don't know why you're so mad."

Am I poking the proverbial bear? Absolutely. I know Mom's problem is with me dating and having sex, no matter who it's with. Add that to her hatred of gay people, and that's a recipe for pure rage.

Mom points at me, her lips curled into a sneer. "Look, he's wearing that degenerate fruitcake's sweater."

She called Ian a *what?* How unhinged *is* she? Is that how she's going to deflect—

"Grant, our son really is a fucking f—"

Are you fucking kidding me?

What surprises me is that I'm more insulted by my mom referring to my boyfriend as a degenerate fruitcake than her calling me an *actual slur*.

"You aren't wrong," I say, ignoring her insult and keeping to a monotone. "I'm gay."

I expect my parents to do a dramatic recoil, but their faces screw up in disgust instead, not that I care.

"And I've known since I was fourteen," I continue. "That was *before* I learned about it in school. Oh, and guess what—pulling me *out* of school did nothing to change that because they didn't even teach us what being gay *was* by then." I let out a frustrated chuckle. "Sorry, but there's nothing that could have changed me. You failed."

I have enough restraint left in me to not tack on "as parents" to the end of that sentence.

"You have some nerve, don't you!" Mom raises her hand and jabs a finger in my direction. "Do you even care about how this looks on us?"

"No, Mom, I don't," I deadpan.

"Was four months all it took for you to forget everything we taught you?"

Again, no, but it was enough for me to stop caring as much.

"Are you going to say something?"

"Why should I?" I shrug my hands, making both of my parents blink in surprise. "I have nothing to say to anyone who wants to make me hate myself. We're done here."

"No, we aren't!" Mom spits out.

"Yes, *we are.*" I point my thumbs to the entrance of the ballpark. "Yeah, I'm gonna...like, head out now."

Wishful thinking on my part, because I don't make more than two steps back before Mom reaches to her rear and—

My veins turn to ice.

She unholsters a gun.

Fuck, I didn't think to check for one on her, I thought she got her license revoked—

None of that matters. She has a pistol in her hands, and she's pointing it straight at me.

I flick my eyes between her and Dad, blocking out the panicked, scattering students in my peripheral vision. Dad looks as shocked as I am.

Mom's hands shake. "We're taking you home, no matter what. You need to be saved."

My brain must not be fully online, because it's apparently still in fight, not flight mode. "You're trying to save me by...pointing a gun at my head?"

Shut up, Callum. You're gonna get yourself killed.

The expression on Mom's face makes me believe I just signed off on my own death sentence.

CHAPTER TWENTY-NINE
IAN

"Yo, Ian, hold up a second," Nick calls out. "I made something for you."

I swallow my water abruptly, almost choking. "Yeah? What is it?"

Jeremy plants his hands on my shoulders and shakes me hard. He slammed two energy drinks ten minutes ago, and they're clearly hitting. "You'll see. Oh my god, I can't wait to see your face!"

"It'll be easier to see my face if you aren't shaking me like protein," I say, wresting out of Jeremy's grip and stabilizing myself against a pillar.

Nick chuckles, handing me a balled-up sweater, and I unfold it.

It's a team hoodie, and when I flip it around, it has Callum's name on it. His *first* name.

And it's in my size.

Nick peers over my shoulder. "Yeah, I used his first name so people wouldn't confuse Callum with Johnny C."

John Cross was a first baseman who graduated last year. He wouldn't want to date me, and the reverse was, and still is, very true.

"I hope that's—"

I cut Nick off with a hug. "This is great. Holy crap. I fucking love you guys."

"Aww, do you?" Jeremy coos. "Come give me a kiss." He puckers his lips and turns his right cheek toward me, and I reach over to flick it.

"Fuck off, dude," I say, snorting.

"Yeah, he's practically married," Nick adds. "If you were better-looking, I'd warn you not to tempt Ian astray, but man, you're so chopped—"

Jeremy swings for Nick's nuts before calling the attack off, probably remembering that Nick's wearing a cup. Usually, I'd laugh at them, but the doors haven't opened for the game yet—Callum's still outside.

"I have to show this to Callum," I say, putting the hoodie on. "I'll be right back."

Not wanting to waste time, I dart out of the building and weave my way to the front of the thick crowd. I almost give up, since finding him is bound to be impossible with everyone gathered like this, but I push past a line of students into emptiness, stumbling forward a few steps.

What the hell is going on? Why is everyone leaving the center of the plaza empty?

Hold up.

That's *Callum,* standing in the middle of the plaza, and he's being confronted by two people? What in the—

"Motherfuck," I say.

Those are his parents. I can't make out what they're saying from this far away, and I'm about to give them a piece of my mind when Callum turns to walk in my direction.

The second I step forward to join him, his mom reaches behind her and—

Fuck.

She retrieves a pistol.

Then she points it straight at him.

My blood runs cold. They exchange words, and it's even harder to hear what they're saying with the commotion of dispersing students surrounding me.

My feet stay frozen. I've been through at least one drill a year about this since I was five—shooter means take cover. Get the hell away if you can, and don't draw their attention.

But none of those drills involved what to do if someone is pointing a gun at your boyfriend.

Everyone else is gone, and still, I don't move.

Where the fuck is campus police? Maybe they're waiting for someone *armed*, and that doesn't help.

That's when Callum's mom notices me, standing alone, and exposed.

Her face darkens even more as she takes me in, and I'm expecting her to turn the gun on me.

Callum follows his mom's gaze. His eyes land on mine, and his expression crumples.

Jesus, I hate seeing him like that.

"You." His mom spits that one word out, grating, low, and loud, and it sends a chill down my back. "Get over here so I can deal with you."

That sounds like the last thing I should do—get *closer* to the unstable, gun-wielding zealot.

But she wants that, and I want her to stop pointing a gun at my boyfriend.

"Lower the gun. Then I'll go!" I yell back.

"You don't tell me what to do!" His mom waves her hands around, her finger *on the fucking trigger*. Who on earth gave her a gun?

"Do you want me to come over?"

She grits her teeth. "Do you want me to shoot Callum? What's stopping me?"

The fact that I'll kill you myself if you do.

My resolve breaks. "Just...please lower it. Or at least aim away from him."

She turns the barrel to me, and my heart races. I dig my fingernails into my thumb—the sharp, biting pain registers, but it doesn't begin to compete with the nerves in my stomach.

I send a pointed look at Callum, silently trying to tell him to make a run for it, but he stays motionless.

"Okay," I say. "I'm walking now."

Putting one foot in front of the other, I make slow work of the walk over to where the three of them are gathered. Anything to stall for time.

I stop a few yards away from the two of them, keeping Callum in my field of vision. His mom sneers at me like I'm smeared excrement on the bottom of her shoe, and if I wasn't staring into the muzzle of a pistol, I'd give that contempt back ten times worse.

"Damn infidel," she mutters.

Huh. Her morals *and* her vocabulary are stuck in biblical times.

I don't reply.

She sizes me up, fixing her steely eyes on me. I know who Callum got his from, and it's uncanny. I don't break my stare, and she blinks first, thankfully lowering the gun. I let out a quiet breath, not knowing what's coming next.

Then she passes the gun to Callum's dad. "This is yours anyway. You do it."

She pulled a gun that's not even her own—

"Why did you bring—"

Callum's dad receives a smack to the shoulder. He accepts the pistol, gingerly palming the grip, and furrows his brows.

"*Dispatch him*," his mom says, nodding at me like I'm wounded livestock.

"Regina, that's not—"

"Grant. Just *do it*. He's the one who took Callum away from us. Make things right."

I flick my gaze to meet Callum's, and it's painful. His eyes are clouded, and I only break contact when I register movement in my peripheral vision.

Grant raises his arms, not to aim but to get a closer look at something on the top of the barrel.

And Callum—

Holy shit.

He takes the chance and lunges, slamming his six-five frame clean into his dad.

The gun drops to the ground with a wimpy clatter, sliding away from the tussling pair of bodies.

Regina rushes toward the weapon, and I make a dive for it at the same time, grabbing the piece of metal before she can reach it.

Then I straighten up, moving into a ready stance. Regina doesn't stop rushing over.

"Don't come closer," I blurt out. She flinches, considering, before continuing, and I step back, giving myself space and keeping my index finger pressed across the guard, how you're *supposed* to handle a weapon. "I said stop!"

This time, she listens.

The silence that follows sinks deep into my guts, wrenching me right from the core.

What is going on? In the space of five minutes, I went from laughing at Callum's name on a hoodie to pointing a fucking gun at his parents. Or rather, his mom.

I don't dare look away from Regina in case she tries to come for me again, but when I step back a few more steps, Callum and Grant come into view.

Callum is still lying on top of his dad, who isn't putting up much of a fight.

Nobody moves. Callum stares at me, his mouth parted. I can't see more of his expression. My body shakes, and I tense my muscles, forcing myself to stop.

And that's when I inspect the top of the barrel. The chamber indicator is down.

The gun isn't loaded.

My stomach gets lighter, even though the weight that's lifted is infinitesimal—Callum's parents are still here, still out of their minds, and they might have more weapons on them.

I need to keep Callum safe. That comes first.

Grant, who's still splayed underneath Callum, is less likely to try something stupid, even if I don't have much to back that assessment up.

Callum needs to make a break for it and get far, far away.

"Callum, get out of here," I say, jerking my head in his direction. The words come out way harsher than I intended, which makes sense, given the tension in every muscle of my body. "Don't worry about me. I'll handle this."

He stays silent, his eyes not leaving mine. I give him another nod, firmer this time, and he scrambles to his feet, bolting toward the ballpark entrance.

Grant sits up, still not saying a word, and I can only describe his expression as exasperated and *done*.

He might not be the one instigating right now, but he still isn't getting any credit. He had nineteen years to treat Callum better, countless chances to talk Regina down, and he didn't. These two are operating as one fucked-up unit.

I return my attention to Regina, who's scowling at me.

"You think you've won, haven't you?" she spits out. "I'm pressing charges for kidnapping my son."

She's fucking delusional, and in the interest of my own safety, I don't respond. There's no telling what she'd do. There's two of them, one of me, and still no sign of the police.

Regina flails an arm at me. "Hello? I'm talking to you, f—"

Ouch. Well, getting called that was bound to happen someday, I guess. I just got lucky avoiding it so far.

"What, are you too much of a pussy to shoot, or what?"

Is she being for real right now?

I don't say anything, at least until Callum is far enough away. He hangs back, standing on the steps leading up to the ballpark, watching us.

"I can't shoot something that isn't loaded!" I yell, loud enough for Callum to hear. He deserves to know that the gun *his own mother pointed at him* wasn't lethal.

I release the empty magazine and slide it out, pocketing it and gripping the gun by the barrel. I simply shrug back at Regina, not knowing what else to do.

It's like she's frozen, save for the subtle twitch in her right eye. Grant's face has hardened into something unreadable.

The tension in the air doesn't dissipate.

"It's over," I say. "You pulled a gun on a college campus around hundreds of students and security cameras. You've lost it."

If I need to, I'll run from them, but it's better to keep them in one place to avoid a frantic campus-wide search.

Regina glowers at me. "He's our son. We can do what we see fit."

"He's *twenty*," I grit out. "He ran away from you for a *reason*."

"Oh, so it *was* you who corrupted him." She waves her hands, gesticulating at nobody in particular. "You're going to rot in hell for what you are."

If I do, I'll see her there.

I don't respond, and her face twists up even more as she turns to Callum. "How much are you getting to take it up the ass like a poof? Is it worth it? Is it worth giving up salvation?" Regina scoffs and takes a step toward him. "I need to fucking talk to him—"

"Don't come here!" Callum yells. "Leave me alone."

She turns her attention to me, some kind of unplaceable rage behind her eyes. "Look what you've done. You turned our own son against us."

"I only know Callum because he *ran away from you*," I retort. "He left because of you, Regina. Nobody flees at midnight without a word for no reason."

Her face reddens, and she turns to her husband. "Grant, do something!"

"Like what?" Grant says. "What do you want me to do?"

"Something! Fix this."

How they plan on doing so is beyond me, and I sure don't want to find out.

Thankfully, I don't have to, because a sharp voice rings out behind me, making me jump.

"Drop your weapon!"

Finally.

I jerk my head to the voice, and I'm met with a view of four campus police officers in full tactical gear, fixing their guns on me.

With my hand fisting the barrel and fighting the urge to drop the gun like a piece of red-hot iron, I bend down, placing it to my right. I step away, and an officer rushes toward me, grabbing my wrists and slipping them into handcuffs. Against my better judgment, I glance over at Grant and Regina, who are watching me with dirty, smug expressions.

At least until they're handcuffed, too.

That's when all hell breaks loose.

Regina screams. She kicks. She tries to wrench herself away from the officer who handcuffed her, and somehow, she's successful, at least for a few seconds. She makes a run for it, managing no more than five steps before she's tackled to the ground by another two officers.

Even if I wanted to look away, I don't think I could.

Grant, to his credit, has the smarts to stay silent.

What a *shitshow*.

"Come on," the officer behind me says, nudging me to the left by the wrists. "Let's go."

"Am I under arrest?" I ask.

"No, you're being detained. I want to ask you some questions."

"I'm not saying anything further without legal representation."

"Fine."

"You're a fucking whore, you dirty f—!" Regina yells at me, making me and the officer yank our heads up in surprise. "You'd better sleep with one eye open tonight, because *nobody* gets to come between a mother and her son!"

That has to be one of the worst things she could have chosen to say, but I don't tell her. If she wants to incriminate herself, she can be my guest.

"How do those handcuffs feel? I'll bet—"

Callum appears and cuts her off. "I'll bet they're a lot less comfortable than the ones we use during our long, *ungodly* sex marathons. Now *shut up*."

Regina screams and calls Callum a Satan-worshipping slut. The officer behind me chokes on a surprised cough, and Callum sighs.

I shouldn't laugh right now.

But Callum said what he said. I don't know how he managed that. This is not the time for humor.

Still, I can't help but let out a restrained snicker.

I'm handcuffed, detained, and shivering. Laughing is the only thing I can do.

CHAPTER THIRTY
CALLUM

I curl my fingers around the crinkly plastic emergency blanket the police handed to me. It's the most uncomfortable thing I've ever worn, but it's all I've got. My body shudders, not from any cold, but from shock.

What in the fuck just happened?

What in the fuck *could have* happened if Ian hadn't shown up?

There's a chance everything would have been fine. Campus police would have still shown up when they did, but my mom would have been a lot harder to disarm than Ian and that unloaded gun.

I shiver again. This blanket reflects warmth with a distinctly artificial quality—it's too intense and insufficient at the same time. The real warmth I need right now can only come from Ian, who's currently handcuffed and bent over a fence like the criminal he isn't. My parents, on the other hand, are causing the biggest scene I've ever seen them start. That's saying something, especially given the hell they raised when the school handed out sex ed pamphlets.

Yeah, the incident that sparked my isolated homeschooling purgatory pales in comparison to watching my parents try to escape arrest.

Well, it's my mom. She's swinging her cuffed arms around and kicking at anyone who tries to get close to her, while my dad, as usual, is silent. He's sitting in the back of a cop car, not saying a word.

A sick, intrusive chuckle rises from my throat and surfaces in a strangled bark. This is ridiculous.

Oh, good, my mom is being bundled into a cop car. Finally.

It only took three burly officers to contain her. It's clear who the criminals are, and it's not Ian.

"Again, he's the one who got me out," I say, to the police officer who's holding Ian's wrists down. "He didn't do anything wrong."

"Callum, don't say any more. Wait for my lawyer." Ian's breathing quickly and shaking—no, shivering, probably because he's still in thin baseball pants and the temperature is plunging like the sun behind the horizon.

He's always cold, and I don't want him to be. I unhook the metallic blanket from my shoulders and gesture it toward him. The officer gives me a tired grunt before lifting Ian's arms, letting me stick the blanket over Ian's back and around his chest.

"You're gonna freeze," Ian says.

"I'm wearing jeans, flannel, and a sweater. You need this."

The officer's face firms up, but he doesn't say anything, at least not for a few seconds. He shuts his eyes, sighing. "What the hell," he mutters. "Okay, the elder Crosses have already volunteered enough information for us to determine that they're the immediate priority for containment." He bends down and unlocks the cuffs. "Do *not* leave the scene, but you can wait inside for further instructions."

"Thank you," Ian says gruffly. He shakes himself off and straightens up, and it takes all of my willpower to not wrap around him like a tropical snake.

We're escorted into the empty ballpark, and we slump down onto a bench, basking in the heating and silence. The game got canceled, obviously, and we're the only two people here.

"Are you okay?" I ask, and Ian turns to me.

"Are *you?*" He runs a hand through his hair before latching onto me. "Fuck, you're still shaking."

"I gave you the blanket."

My joke only puts a quivering smile at one corner of his mouth, and he silently drapes half of the plastic sheet over me. I curl into it and suck in a breath. It now smells like him. Like home.

I just want to go home.

The two of us fall further into silence. Come to think of it, this is the first bout of silence I can remember where it's anything less than comfortable. With Ian, it's always mutual and right, not because we don't know what to say. That's what's happening now, but I can't bring myself to change that.

Ian does. "Callum, how are you not a total *wreck* right now?"

"Because you showed up," I say plainly. "I can't put into words how grateful I am that you stood up for me. I just closed off and didn't say anything until the end after you showed up."

Scoffing, he plants a gentle hand on my thigh. "Yeah, until you scarred your mom by telling her about our kinky bedroom escapades."

A blush surges up from my chest, through my neck, and into my face. I still can't believe I said all that, but it sure drove the point home that I'm too far gone for her and Dad to "save."

"Right, but you're the one who said everything I always wanted to," I murmur.

Ian shrugs. "Hey, someone had to. Thanks for giving me the honor."

"And you did it at gunpoint," I add. "That was kind of badass."

Shuddering, he tenses up. "I never want to do that ever again. God. Callum, your mom swiped your dad's gun and tried to shoot you. I just jumped at the chance to take it away."

"Look, I don't want to speculate about whether my mom would have tried to shoot me for real," I say, swallowing hard, which doesn't help to dissolve the tense lump in my throat. "The gun was unloaded, I know that, and I'll unpack the rest in therapy. All that matters now is that they're gone."

Ian gives me a weak smile. "You're free."

"I am."

Thanks to him. Again, he's the one who stepped in to stand up for me, and guilt creeps through my body.

"Fuck, I'm so sorry you got caught up in this," I say. "None of this should have happened."

Ian swivels his head at me, his eyes wide. "You're right that this shouldn't have happened, but it was on your parents to not act like idiots." He pauses, placing his hand on mine. "I did what I had to in the moment to keep you safe."

"It wasn't your responsibility—"

"Stop, Callum." Gripping my hand tighter and sending sparks flying up my arm and into my stomach, he chuckles. "I've never been in a relationship before you, but helping you is what I signed up for. It's what I do. That means I get to love you, and my god, I love you to fucking bits."

"Stop it, you're gonna make me cry," I say, chuckling to try distracting myself from the tears pricking my eyes.

"My shoulder's free if you need it, because I'm not done. I'll never be done loving you, Callum. You make that impossible. I said it last week to my team, and I'll say it to you now—I'd take a bullet for you."

That does it for me. I shut my eyes, letting tears spill out of the sides and run down my face. I haven't cried like this in years, not since I confirmed to myself that I was gay in the dark hours of the morning when I was fourteen. Back then, I was resigned and terrified, not knowing what was laid out for me.

Back then, I was already petrified of anything sexual, with lust being the ultimate sin in my family. I thought I'd automatically catch some horrible illness if I so much as touched someone else with any kind of intention. Add being gay on top of that, I couldn't see a difference between life and death, because to me, both looked like hell.

How wrong I was—crying still yanks at my heart, tightening my chest and making me choke on every other breath I take, but now, I'm going through that with a smile.

Ian isn't the one who pulled me out of my dark spiral and onto a better path—that was me, and the constant decision to get better is still on me to make. If anything, he's grounding. He's stable.

He's a walking, talking, living personification of kindness, and he makes it so clear that I deserve that.

He tells me constantly, and I'm starting to believe it—I deserve what he gives me.

"I love you so much," I croak out, wiping my face with the front of my hand. "You're the best."

He wraps around me, holding tight. "I'm only trying to be good for you."

"You're...you're more than the guy I imagined when I was younger. I was stretching my reality at the seams just to think about being with *someone*, and I didn't know anyone as good as you even existed in real life."

"Okay, you're going to make me cry now, so fuck you," he says, snickering. "We're ridiculous, aren't we?"

I nod, returning his choked-up laughter.

Adrenaline is a wild thing. Case in point: it has us making tearful, emotional confessions under the harsh fluorescent lighting of a deserted college athletic facility, huddled together beneath a police blanket.

Love exists and persists, no matter the environment.

Our tender moment is breached abruptly with the arrival of a different police officer, who's carrying a stack of papers. She slows her pace as she gets closer—I guess seeing two guys crying gives her some pause.

"Sorry to interrupt, but I have an update..." she says, stopping a few steps away from us.

"That's fine. We were just waiting for one," Ian replies.

"Okay," she continues. "It's getting late, and the students we spoke to all informed us that the elder Crosses instigated this afternoon's events."

Ian and I nod.

"You'll both need to send us written statements within five days." She hands two thin stacks of paper to us. "This contains details on where to send your statements, as well as how to proceed. I'm here if you have any questions, but otherwise, you're free to go."

"Thank you," Ian says. He turns to me, eyes soft, and I purse my lips.

"I don't have any questions," I supply.

"Of course." The officer clasps her hands. "There's contact information in the dossier if that changes." Giving us a quick, polite nod, she backs away and leaves the building.

Ian stands up and extends an arm. "Home?"

"Please. I want to go home."

Hand in hand, we do just that.

CHAPTER THIRTY-ONE

IAN

"I'm just saying, you could have milked the whole situation for some leeway," I tell Callum, who's hunched over his laptop. "Like, one of your profs had to *force* you to accept an extension."

We're at the tail-end of finals season, barely two weeks after Callum's parents showed up and did what's now being investigated as possible domestic terrorism. It seems like some of the students overheard Regina's rambling, and then reported ideological motivations to the police, so now the fucking FBI are involved.

As I said before, and as I'm still saying, what a *shitshow*. At least we've only had to send written statements through my lawyer at this point, given the extent to which Regina and Grant incriminated themselves. The actual trial is gonna come later. Much later.

Callum looks up at me, his eyes tired but no less pretty than they always are. "I didn't come to college to get out of assignments. If anything, I want to prove a point."

I can't argue with that. I could try, but Callum is gonna do what he wants to do. His therapist Anita called him into an urgent check-in, given that news of what went down spread to every corner of the WMU community within hours, but he insists he's fine and working through things with her. He hasn't been acting any differently, at least from what I can tell, and believe me, I'm keeping my eyes peeled for any signs of distress.

The fact that his parents are in prison helps for sure. My family's lawyer says the chances of Callum ever seeing Regina and Grant again are slim to none. There's an emergency restraining order in place, with a permanent one all but guaranteed, and the elder Crosses are facing years for reckless conduct alone.

Still, Callum could have at *least* asked for an extension on his final papers. Seeing him stressed and typing frantically, in between studying for exams and taking them, consumes me with a need to take care of him more than usual. It isn't like I can magic all of his finals away, and I have my own to worry about, so I've had to settle for ordering takeout for the two of us and giving him a ton of motivational back massages.

He slams his finger down on the trackpad and shuts his laptop, the sound echoing through the dining room and jolting my attention back to him. "Fucking finally," he says triumphantly. "Now all I have is a French test in an hour, and then we're free."

"*You're* free," I correct. "I've been waiting for you to be done for ages."

Taking a lighter course load in spring semester usually works out well for the playoffs, but handling a firearm on campus got me a quiet suspension from the team for the rest of the season. As much as I love playing baseball, I don't regret giving it up in favor of disarming my boyfriend's delusional parents, especially since I'll be back on the team next fall. At least I'm not trying to go pro.

Callum rises to his feet, stretching his arms up, which lifts the hem of his T-shirt. He steps over to wrap his arms around me, and even though it's pushing an unusual eighty degrees outside, I still relish the warmth. "I'll try to finish my exam as fast as I can."

I huff out a sigh. "Didn't you just say that you aren't trying to get out of doing work?"

He squeezes me tighter. "Hey, I only need fifty percent to get an A-minus. I'm good."

"Oh, you actually did the math." I scoff. "Look who's learning the ways of college."

"Blame yourself. You're the bad influence I always needed."

And before I can agree, Callum cuts me off with a gentle, brain-melting kiss.

"Mm, I'd rather French kiss than take my French test," he says. "Say the word, and I'll skip the final."

I don't have a chance to say any words, much less talk some

sense into him, because the fucker shoves his tongue into my mouth and grabs the back of my neck, sending a delicious spiral of energy down south.

Jesus. He knows that drives me up the damn wall.

"Babe, you can't do that," I protest, breaking away.

"Why not?" A mischievous smile plays across his lips. "I know you want me to."

Callum almost, *almost*, gets me to agree by slipping his fingers under my shirt and giving my back a disarming squeeze, but he hasn't figured out how to dissolve all of my willpower, at least not yet.

"You're evil"—I pull away and give his ass a firm swat—"and you're a fucking menace. Go take your exam."

He just bats his luscious lashes at me and waves goodbye as he heads off.

———

Whoever made Callum's French final two hours long obviously wasn't thinking about their students' lonely, long-suffering significant others.

Checking my phone isn't going to make time pass any faster, so with great reluctance, I keep myself focused on packing our bags for the lake house. The two of us won't need much, and as much as I want to be a little shit and pack one T-shirt and a pair of swim trunks for Callum to wear, and *nothing* else, that'd be mean. I do what's honorable and place the rest of his clothes into a duffel bag.

Including the five-inch inseam swim trunks I got for him. What can I say? I know what I like—giving things to Callum, and checking him out.

My god, I want it to be tomorrow already. Putting me and Callum together in a secluded house for four months with no responsibilities is my idea of a good time, and I'm not known for being too patient.

From the bedroom, I hear the lock click, and my heart jumps into my throat.

Is he back already?

I dart into the living room, ready to launch myself at Callum, and barely stop myself from lunging when I realize that it's Nick.

"You thought I was Callum, didn't you?" he asks, and heat rises up my neck.

"How'd you guess?"

"Please." Nick scoffs. "You have a dreamy look in your eyes, and I'd be a little concerned if you were making it for me."

"Aww, it *could* be for you," I tease. "Callum and I might want a third." For effect, I drag my fingers along his exposed forearm, and he swats my hand away.

"Man, fuck off," he says with a grin. "There's no way you'd share, anyway."

"You aren't wrong." I rest my shoulder against the wall. "What's up?"

"Nothing much, just thought I'd stop by before warmups later." He slips his shoes off. "I'm not interrupting anything, am I?"

"Nah. I'm just packing for the lake house." Heading for the couch, I notice Nick isn't following me, and I turn back. "You okay?"

He jerks his head up, blinking as he walks over. "Yeah, yeah. I, uh, forgot you're leaving tomorrow."

I sink into the couch and motion for Nick to sit next to me, and he lets out a huge sigh as he does, his tall body creating an indent in the center and almost making me lose my balance.

"It sounds like *someone* is gonna miss me." I shake him by the shoulder, and he chuckles weakly.

"I kind of already do. Games aren't the same, and... Damn, it feels like I haven't seen you in ages."

Oh, shit. I snap to attention and let sincerity take over. Nick isn't wrong—it's been weeks since the two of us properly hung out, and I don't want to be that friend who disappears after getting into a relationship.

"Yeah, I'm sorry, bro. I—"

"It's not you. Don't think that." His eyes widen. "You and Callum are dealing with the legal shit, and I'm sure finals are kicking all of our asses. I'll be fine."

He'll *be* fine? I tilt my head, prompting him to continue.

"I'm kinda lonely," he blurts out. "But that's *not* your problem—"

The fuck it isn't. "You're my buddy. It kind of is." I give Nick a hug, one of the too-strong, bro-y kinds, and he chuckles into my chest. "You still have an open invite to my family's lake house, just saying."

"I'd be intruding on you and Callum, no?"

I punch his arm gently. "Dude, no. Never. You're always welcome."

He shrugs. "It's whatever. I'm gonna be here for most of the summer coaching high schoolers at baseball camp anyway."

It seems the guys I'm close to have some kind of aversion to "imposing" on me or whatever. At least I don't mind being the one to break through that.

"That camp won't last for the whole summer, and I'll want to see you. Callum and I both will," I insist. "Please come over some-time. I'll drive back here and pick you up if I have to."

He presses his lips into a soft, lopsided smile. "You're the best, man. I mean it." Nick bumps his shoulder against mine, and I'm about to reply with some sappy line of my own when he smacks his hands on his knees. "Right, that's enough moping for me. Let's do something else."

Okay, casual Nick is back. I point my thumb at the TV and reach down to turn my console on. "For sure. Do you want to beat each other up on a screen?"

He nods, I toss him a controller, and then I proceed to pound a virtual version of Nick into a pixelated pulp, over and over again.

Callum comes back right as I deliver a devastating blow to end our latest game, and I leap up.

"How're you feeling?" I ask, running to the door and slinging my arms around his waist.

"Relieved more than anything." He releases a breathy laugh, walking me backward through the entryway and pressing his forehead to mine. "And not to be vulgar or anything, but I could really, *really* use a b...rewski?" His voice goes up an octave as soon as he spots Nick on the couch.

"Did you join a frat on the way back or something?" I ask as Nick and Callum give each other a wave. "Since when do you say *brewski*?"

Callum frowns at me, his face red, and drops his lips to my ear. "Since a second ago, when I was about to fucking ask you for a blowjob right in front of Nick."

"Am I interrupting your private time?" Nick calls out.

"No," Callum says.

I rest my head on his shoulder. "Yeah, he's a good, patient boy."

That earns me an elbow to the ribs. "Fuck off," mutters the good, patient boy.

We both laugh and pad over to the couch, and I deposit Callum next to Nick.

"Let me get you that beer," I offer, handing my controller to my still-blushing boyfriend. "Chill for a bit."

"Have you played this before?" Nick asks, and he pumps his fist, ready to win, when Callum shakes his head.

I stick around and watch Nick get absolutely smoked. Again. He smacks a hand to his forehead, groaning when the final score pops up on the screen, sealing his latest loss.

"Am I, like, totally inept or something?" he muses.

"Maybe. Or I'm just awesome," Callum says absentmindedly, not taking his eyes off of the TV.

"No way. We gotta swap controllers," Nick sputters. "Ian definitely gave me a janky one."

Snickering, I leave my best friend to bicker with my boyfriend, and head for the kitchen to get the beer I promised Callum five minutes ago. Leaning against the counter, I take a peek back into the living room to see Nick and Callum gaming and shooting the shit. My heart warms, and satisfaction washes over me.

Summer's here, my responsibilities have all but vanished, and the next four months are gonna hit different.

CHAPTER THIRTY-TWO
CALLUM

Ian and I have traded places.

According to him, I'm always the sleepy one who he's more than happy to drive around and take care of, but right now, he's passed out in the passenger seat of his car as I drive us down Route 302 toward his family's lake house.

Staying up until three in the morning will do that to someone. Last night didn't start out wild, but the women's softball team got knocked out of playoffs, Sabrina invited us to the team's commiseration party, and we all ended up at The Barrel, which interestingly enough, still isn't ID-ing anyone. Fun times, even when your boyfriend tries to drunkenly lick your face off in front of a hundred other people. At least he stayed sober enough to walk unassisted, and we both crashed in bed as soon as we made it home. Nothing was waiting for us in the morning—no tests, assignments, nothing. Not even parents. Ian's are in New York, and they gave us free rein of the lake house.

Mine are still in prison, awaiting the trial that's in nine months.

The GPS beeps, telling me that we're only five minutes away from the lake house.

Five minutes away from a promised four months of nothing. I know I would have been fine if I had to sort my own life out, but being with Ian and letting my hair down is plain easy. It's amazing how much my life is better with him in it. He really does wear his heart on his sleeve, no holds barred. For someone like me who's always been prone to doubt spirals and overthinking, how directly and *obviously* he loves me is nothing short of perfect—Not a single day goes by where I'm not grateful for falling into Ian's life the way I did—

"Are we there yet?" Ian mumbles, waking up. He stretches his arms, and his left hand makes gratuitous contact with my shoulder. Yawning, and probably feigning ignorance, he proceeds to drag his fingers down my sides and onto my leg.

"Babe, we're four minutes away," I say. "I *dare* you to keep your horny hands to yourself."

He snickers, keeping his hand on my thigh. "Ugh, let me love you."

"You can love me from the passenger seat."

That's met with another quiet laugh, and Ian rests his head on the window, staring out.

Right on time, I swing off the main road onto the fire lane that leads to the lake house. He pumps his fist when I park, letting out a quiet cheer, and unbuckles himself, turning to face me.

"Are you excited?" he asks. "We've got four months of fishing, frolicking, and fu—"

I chuckle and clap my right hand over his mouth. "Enough. Don't make me throw you into the lake."

He wriggles out of my grip. "Okay, okay. Let's unpack."

Huh, funny—he thinks I'm not gonna give that energy back to him. "Awesome. Let's unpack your package first." I dart my hand down to the waist of his jeans, and he smacks my hand away.

"You," he says, smirking at me, "are never allowed to change."

"Wasn't planning on it, unless you were talking about my clothes."

"Feel free to change out of those."

I don't, since I'm already dressed appropriately—old T-shirt, new shorts, and a pair of boat shoes Ian bought for me "just because." We unload the car and put the groceries away before dumping our bags in our room, and I get the deck furniture set up while Ian preps dinner. He comes out carrying a tray of meat and two beers, handing me one as I fire the grill up.

This right here is the definition of peace. The sun is still low in the sky, casting a warm orange glow across the lake. Ian's eyes catch in the light, and it's almost as if they shimmer at me. My heart clenches, the way it always does when he looks at me, and I put my beer down to give him a hug. His body molds to mine, natural, practiced, and so right. I tighten my arms around him—he isn't going anywhere, but I can't possibly get close enough to him.

"You good, Cal?" he asks, tilting his head up.

"Uh-huh. I'm feeling cuddly."

He snickers, checking the temperature on the grill before refocusing on me. "What else is new?"

My response is to tighten around him even more. Not leaving my embrace, he rotates his body to put the food on the grill, swaying us both from side to side. We're silent, and it's comfortable—waves crash against the shore, the deck creaks, and wind rustles in the trees.

Ian's body relaxes under my arms. "I don't know if I say this enough, but..." He lets his head roll back onto my chest. "I love you, Callum."

Warmth spreads to every distant corner of my body. "You can never say that enough. I love you so, so much."

I couldn't ask for any more than what I have right now. We'll spend summer at the lake house, and as for what comes after? College, jobs, traveling, and the rest of our lives.

A lot can change in a matter of months. I went from hoping, to running, to finally breathing. Everything I wanted for myself lies within reach, and now, I get to share that journey with Ian.

I plant a gentle kiss on the back of his neck, gazing out at the sun setting over the lake. A warm, comfortable feeling floods my body, making me smile into Ian's hair and tighten around his shoulders, savoring every second of his presence. Wherever we go together, I belong. That much is clear to me.

I really traded in one home for another—darkness for the dream I'm living.

EPILOGUE
IAN

TWO YEARS LATER
APRIL

I slide the roll of tape across the final box, sealing the seams shut.

Graduation was a week ago, but this was months in the making. I smile, tossing the tape dispenser into our tote bag for random supplies, and I step back to survey the scene.

The furniture is padded and wrapped, boxes are stacked, and it's time to head out.

Three years of life at this trusty apartment are all packed up and ready to go.

Two and a half of those years have been spent with Callum, and that number is only going to go up.

"Are you finally done?" he asks, resting against the wall. His hands are shoved in the pockets of some new gray jeans, and he's wearing a T-shirt that he got in Greece when we visited last winter. He knows how much I like that outfit, especially how the rich blue fabric molds to his frame and brings out his eyes, and he makes a point to wear that shirt whenever we do something special.

New clothes on the same lovable man I fell for in sophomore year. My chest still squeezes whenever I see him, calmer than when we first met, but I haven't grown tired of gazing at his handsome face or his cute hair. I'm quite certain I never will.

"Yeah," I say. "That was the last of my stuff."

Callum walks over, smiling that familiar, heart-stopping smile of his, and he wraps his strong arms around me. "I can't believe we're leaving here," he mumbles into my hair. "I should have tried staying for my master's."

"Right, but you decided to be a traitor instead and accept BUC's offer." I reach down and squeeze his ass for fun, and he snorts, shaking me in retaliation. The two of us are completely insufferable around each other, and I wouldn't have it any other way.

"In my defense, BUC gave me a bigger scholarship," he says. "Besides, I didn't want to deprive the Boston Falcons' newest trainer of his much-needed morning hugs."

"And I'm forever grateful for your sacrifice."

All things considered, there's very little that either of us are sacrificing; Callum's off to BUC for a master's in physical therapy, and I got a sweet gig as a junior trainer for Boston's major league baseball team. Still, I'm never going to rock BUC merch, and Callum isn't allowed to wear any around me.

Maybe.

I might soften my stance—BUC gave the two of us a chance to share our dream in the same city, so credit is due where it's due. We're gonna live in my family's brownstone in Back Bay, where we'll be walking distance from school and work. Callum is getting his own private study, I'll get to use a sick-ass kitchen every day, and we're finally getting a king-sized bed.

Yeah. New beginnings, but my god, I'm gonna miss college.

"This was a great place," I say, scanning the box-filled room again.

Callum hugs me from behind and swings us both forward. "It sure was." He plants a kiss in my hair, sending a familiar, ever-welcome buzz of affection down to my toes. "Lots of good memories, that's for sure."

I spin around to face him, and I trace his lopsided grin with my thumb before pressing my lips to his. The movers are gonna be here any second now, and as open as we are, PDA isn't exactly something we've tried to do too often.

Nodding, I pull back. "Ready to make some more of those in Boston?"

"Oh yeah." His eyes crinkle at the corners, and I get predictably lost in that mesmerizing sea of blue. "I can't wait."

Stepping aside, I grab my suitcase and open the door, letting him pass me before I head out behind him. For the last time, I stick my key in this lock, twist it shut, and drop the key in a lockbox for the movers. A few steps ahead, Callum is waiting, facing me and smiling with a small box of his things.

Huh. That's the same plastic container he had when I first moved him into our place that first winter he was here. It's a lot fuller now, carrying a lot more clothes and not nearly as much turmoil.

Callum and I have grown a lot over the years. We might have changed, but one thing hasn't: we're still perfect for each other. That might be a huge-ass cliché, but when I slide my fingers through his after we climb into the car, I feel nothing but confirmation.

Not a day goes by where I don't adore the hell out of him, ever grateful for Callum falling into my life three Januaries ago. We don't hide our affection for each other, and that's a huge part of what makes us work—the two of us thrive when we know where we stand with each other.

I back us out of the parking lot and onto the street. Callum plays some music on the speakers, I hit the interstate, and we both sit back while cruise control takes over. College is over, and the rest of our lives stretch ahead.

Of course, nothing is a given. Life can go anywhere, but I know there's nobody I'd rather face that fact with than Callum.

Thank you for reading *Free Base*! I hope you enjoyed reading Ian and Callum's story as much as I did writing it. If you did, please consider leaving a review—every bit of feedback helps others discover the book.

———

How did Callum escape his hometown, and what was going through his head on his first day at WMU? To read a bonus prologue and Chapter 1 from his perspective, sign up for my newsletter where you'll also get access to more bonus content and early updates.

https://www.sjcrawfordauthor.ca/

Want to read more from S.J. Crawford? Check out *Switch Pitching* and *Cross Checking*, a series of New Adult MM Sports Romance novels.